I0673521

The Billionaire's Secret Love

Love and Money Book #4

Natalie Dunbar

Dana Lorayne Publishing

Copyright © 2024 Natalie Dunbar

ISBN-13: 978-0-9913908-6-1
ISBN-10:

Cover design by: Mae at Coverfresh Designs
Library of Congress Control Number:
Printed in the United States of America

This book is dedicated to to those who don't believe in love, to those who who think they are unlovable, and to those who have given up hope. There is someone out there for you!

CONTENTS

CHAPTER ONE

Spirits high at the prospect of a successful acquisition for her company, Lady Zayne, Nicole Zayne walked the path confidently with her purse, laptop, and a packet of plant biology information. Her first hint of trouble came when she reached the stone entrance to the meeting place. A burly giant of a man in clothes resembling the camouflage outfits soldiers wore stepped into her path. He frowned at Nicole and her bodyguards.

"No weapons and no guards allowed inside!" one of the lethal-looking men flanking him declared.

Inches away from the dangerous-looking man blocking their path, she stopped and turned to Liam Beck, the head of her security team. He shook his head. His dark eyes were expressionless, his big hand meaningfully close to his gun. She trusted Liam and knew he was frighteningly good at what he did. They'd talked about her meeting, and it had taken days to convince him that she'd be going, with or without her team. He'd only accompanied her today when she promised that no matter what, she would not agree to be separated from him.

Shoulders straight, her face arranged in what she hoped was her version of Badass, she swallowed. Getting the African Poule flower had been her goal for months. She didn't want to give up now.

"No guns and no bodyguard?" Liam repeated, his eyes on Nicole. "We need you to be safe. This is not a meeting for us."

Surprising everyone, including herself, Nicole turned in her black Louboutin booties. There were no others on the walkway as she took a few steps. Each invitee had been given a tight window for arrival to guarantee everyone's privacy. Her heart felt heavy, and a need to scream in frustration threatened. The compulsion to do something to redirect her rapidly disappearing opportunity ate at her, but what?

A new, cultured-sounding voice intruded on her frantic thoughts. "Ms. Zayne? I am Andre, the host for this event. Please don't walk away from this promising opportunity for your company and yourself. Perhaps we can find a solution to the current problem."

Halting on the stone pavement, she turned around. An urbane-looking man in an expensive black suit stood with the hired muscle. "Can we discuss it?" He smiled, soothing the rough edges of her nerves.

Nicole was certain Liam's jaw clenched tight enough to bite a brick as she headed back to the entrance with her security detail. She refused to look at her bodyguard. This was another chance to get the African Poule flowers, and she didn't plan to waste it.

They walked back to the entrance. The lethal-looking men backed off, the man in the business suit obviously in charge. "What did you have in mind?" Liam bit out.

Ignoring Liam, the man gave his attention to Nicole. "No guns, but perhaps we could allow you one bodyguard. Would that suit your needs?"

The suggestion made her think of having an attack dog for protection but removing his teeth so he couldn't bite anyone. Liam was among the best, but to go in with no gun... She darted a glance at him. She wanted this chance.

The jaw of her security team's leader looked like granite, but his expression was blank. Apparently coming to a decision, he nodded slightly. Yes! Suppressing the urge to break out in a happy dance, Nicole barely reined in the joy that washed over her.

She waited as Liam dismissed the team and told them he would attend the negotiations with her. He met each man's gaze, silently reminding them that they knew what to do. Then Liam surrendered his gun, and they followed Andre into the gray stone structure. Inside, things proceeded like an airport security checkpoint. They emptied their pockets and walked through an x-ray machine. A female guard did a pat down of Nicole while her partner performed a more thorough search of Liam.

Their belongings went down the conveyor belt into another x-ray machine. Andre shook his head and made a clicking sound with his teeth as the equipment identified two more weapons in Liam's backpack. He made a big show of placing Liam's guns and knives in a box to be returned when the auction was over.

Andre and his team led them deeper into the stone structure. She tried to ignore a growing sense of foreboding. Her bodyguard was severely outnumbered, and it looked like they'd taken all his weapons. So far, she still wore the tracking device, a bug, and a camera. Had she done right to push for this auction? The Poule flower was rare and very valuable, but so was she.

Finally, they arrived at a room furnished with a desk, two chairs, and an ice bucket containing several bottles of water. A stage could be seen through a dark tinted window, and the desk held a laptop that displayed the empty stage.

Andre stood in the doorway, two other men close behind him. "Please make yourselves comfortable. Keep the laptop on. That's how we will be communicating with you. The room is wired for sound. You can watch the demonstration in privacy from the window, but the closeups will be on the laptop screen."

As Nicole glanced around the room, Andre shut and locked the door.

"Hey!" Liam yelled, rushing to the door.

"Someone will let you out after the auction," Andre said from the other side of the door.

"I figured they would lock everyone in to maintain privacy and security, but I don't like it," Liam muttered. He stood at the door, thoroughly examining the lock.

Nicole brushed a strand of blond hair back from her ear, subtly reminding him that she still had a lock pick threaded through her earring. He nodded. She set her laptop on the desk next to theirs and turned it on. As the startup sequence began, she checked out the bottled water resting in the ice bucket. She examined the seal on one. It was intact.

"Don't drink their water," he said.

She held up the bottle for him to see. "It's sealed."

"Your fingers are wet," he said in a tone that sounded like he was speaking to a child. "Are they damp from the ice in the bucket, or has the integrity of the bottle been compromised?"

She dropped the bottle back into the bucket and wiped her hands on a tissue from her purse. What seemed like an abundance of caution on Liam's part amped up her growing sense of unease. Why would anyone want to drug her when she was here to verify the rare plant her company needed and negotiate for it?

"I've got a bottle of water. You can chill it on their ice." He reached into his backpack and put a sealed bottle of tepid water in her hand.

"Thanks." She placed it next to the other bottles on the ice. Then she watched silently as Liam walked around the room, examining every nook, cranny, and device with an excruciating attention to detail.

Andre's now familiar voice came through the sound system. Through the tinted window, they saw him onstage with a sandy-haired, older man in a baggy brown suit. "Good afternoon, most honored guests. Our auction is about to start.

Our Dr. Smith will go through the product verification process on stage, and you will be able to verify that what we have is indeed a healthy crop of the very rare Poule plant."

She took the chair behind the desk and Liam sat in the one on the other side. The laptop screen mirrored what they saw on the stage through the window.

Dr. Smith proceeded to open a cardboard box of carefully packaged plants. Extracting one of the potted plants, he displayed its leaves, blooms, stems, and roots for the cameras. Nicole compared what she saw on the screen to the pictures in her plant biology packet. Their sample looked like the Poule plant. With gloved hands, Dr. Smith snipped one of the stems and the expected white, milky substance flowed, turning slightly pink as it oxidized. That told her it was the treasured plant she'd come for.

There was a hard edge to Andre's smile. He could act urbane and charming, but beneath it all he was still a thug, ready to enforce his way. "Any questions? Any need for further proof? You may speak through your microphones or type your questions into the laptop on your desks, and I will have Dr. Smith address them."

Dr. Smith expounded on a few questions from the other potential buyers. Nicole felt that all had been answered with the demonstration, but she listened carefully. Before she knew it, Dr. Smith was exiting the stage, and two men were uncovering a large number display. Andre stood beside it. "Honored guests, the bidding starts now. Due to our administrative costs, the extraordinary value of our product, and the obvious market for it, our minimum bid has been increased to one million dollars. Can I get a bid for one-and-a-half million?"

Nicole didn't hesitate. She entered her bid through the laptop. Andre glanced at a panel to his left and nodded. "I have a bid for one-point-five million. Do I hear two?"

The bidding continued at a brisk pace until it reached ten

million dollars. She hesitated. She'd blown a fifth of the Lady Zayne Cosmetics research and development budget for the year. Were the plants worth it?

She thought about the millions she'd spent on an age-reversing formula with results comparable to expensive plastic surgery. The Poule flower was a key ingredient. Surely, she could get the company biologists to work on growing more of the rare plant, synthesizing its derivatives, and commercializing the formula. She entered another bid.

When the bidding reached twelve million dollars, she realized this was a battle she might not win. She had to live within Lady Zayne budget constraints. Obviously, someone with deep pockets was bidding against her. Who could it be? The plant was rumored to also have properties that could make inroads in cancer-fighting drugs, among other diseases. Could the billionaire behind Foreststone Pharmaceuticals, Jaxson Forest, have found out about the exclusive negotiations?

Holding her breath, Nicole submitted her last bid on a prayer and waited. It wasn't enough. She briefly considered adding some of her personal finances to the pile, but those funds gave her an independence she refused to give up.

She watched the bids rise another three million. The plants were rare and valuable, but the rising bids reminded her that she could fund her own expedition and search for more of the plants. Money always provided more opportunities and people willing to capitalize on the circumstances.

Liam gave her a sympathetic look. "With bids this high, you can count on there being another auction."

Already shutting down her laptop since she wouldn't be transferring funds, she nodded in agreement.

Liam spoke in a low rumble. "Things could get tricky from here on. Stay alert. Remember everything I've taught you."

"Okay." She shoved her laptop back into the case, then

snagged the freshly cooled bottle of water and took a long sip. It calmed her nerves a bit. Liam watched her, his look prompting her to offer him the rest of the bottle. He took it, gulping down the rest.

Twenty minutes later they heard approaching footsteps and a key in the lock. The door opened. Andre stood there with two heavyset men. "It was a pleasure to host you, Ms. Zayne. Perhaps we can do business together another time."

"If you get another crop of the Poule flower plants, I'm in." Nicole gathered the items she'd brought in and headed for the door with Liam a step ahead of her. Andre widened the opening. He smiled pleasantly.

Returning the smile, she could only hope it would be this easy to walk out of the stone fortress. But at the door one of the men grabbed Liam and suddenly they were fighting, and another man joined in, two on one. Nicole gasped. Her bodyguard was efficient and tough, but each of the two men seemed just as capable. What could she do to help?

Andre grabbed her arm and steered her away from the fighting men. "Let him do his job and you do yours."

She dropped her laptop and purse. Turning her body, she grabbed his arm and ground the heel of her bootie into his foot. As she prepared to execute the martial arts maneuver that had enabled her to throw Liam, she felt a needle prick her arm.

Nicole's vision blurred. A wave of dizziness assailed her. She heard the men still punching and kicking each other in the background. Breaking her fall, Andre made a clicking sound against his teeth as the ground rushed up to meet her. "Nice try, Ms. Zayne, but that was not your job."

***

CHAPTER TWO

Nicole awoke blindfolded. She guessed that she was in the dark because there was no indication of light coming from the edges of her blindfold. Her body ached as if she'd been in a hell of a fight and had the bruises to prove it. Vaguely, she remembered trying to give Andre a fight before someone jabbed her with a needle. Cold seeped up from the floor to kiss the side of her face that was smashed against it. It almost felt good. Marshaling her strength and commandeering her sore limbs, she tried to get up. Nothing happened. Abruptly she realized that her hands were securely tied behind her back. Her feet were tied, too. The dry cottony feel in her mouth and the inability to swallow properly were because someone had stuffed a hopefully clean rag in her mouth and finished it off with a blindfold over her eyes. Was she even alone? Too late to play dead.

She sank into herself with the deep, limp-bodied surrender she'd learned from years of yoga classes. Her ears strained in the darkness, her senses stretching out to what she couldn't see or touch. Gradually, she recognized the labored sound of breathing nearby. She wasn't alone. Was her bodyguard tied up close? They would have been rougher, more deadly, with him. Or was someone watching her in some sick sort of cat and mouse game? It didn't feel like she was being watched.

Several minutes went by and nothing happened. From all the things her bodyguard had told her in training sessions, she knew that time was of the essence. She needed to escape.

Body vibrating with the need to do something, she lay still for a few minutes more. Should she slide across the floor or roll her body until she encountered someone or something in the dark? She could just as easily roll off a ledge. The thought frightened her. So did the thought of waiting for the inevitable things that happened to helpless women under someone else's control.

Reaching a decision, she began a slow, full body roll. Once, twice, she rolled across the cold, hard floor and fortunately encountered no one and nothing. Her thoughts went back to the room she and her bodyguard had occupied. Was she there now? Two more rotations would take her halfway across that room before she banged into the desk or one of the chairs.

She tried to slow the last rotation, anticipating that she would bang into furniture. Instead, her body slammed into a warm, muscular body. *Oomph!* It knocked the wind out of her. She heard a muffled grunt in response. Her bodyguard?

Nicole's hopes bloomed, but her nose told her otherwise. The faint scent of a light but expensive men's fragrance filled her nostrils. It wasn't one of her family's brands. The woody, spicy scent reminded her of Dolce and Gabbana's The One for Men, but something had been added to make it more intriguing.

Where was Liam? No, she'd remember if he smelled this good. Was he elsewhere in the room, or had he been eliminated? Being here now, bruised and tied up like a Christmas turkey, was her fault. She held onto the hope that Liam was alive and working on her rescue. And what about the rest of his team that had been left outside the meeting fortress? Hopefully they were bringing the calvary.

Another deep muffled grunt brought her back to the present. Her face and her entire front were flush against a warm male body. Her face hovered next to what felt like an expensive silk shirt. This fellow captive was not her bodyguard. She tried to speak through the rag and gag over her mouth. It came out in a grunt not much different from the sounds he'd made. He had to realize that she'd been bound and gagged, too.

Taking a moment to regroup, she did her best to ignore the alluring illusion that the man's intriguing scent and the warm, muscular feel of his body conjured in her mind. In a moment of inspiration, Nicole rolled backward until she was on her side again, but with her back to him. Then she inched across the cold floor on her still-tender side. Her fingers touched the material of his suit jacket and slid to what felt like a metal belt buckle. She felt him recoil and roll away. Then she heard him sliding across the floor. His beefy form bumped hers in the dark.

Yes! Nicole felt his fingers touch, then grip hers. Already, his nimble fingers worked at whatever held her hands bound together. At least ten minutes went by. Then twenty. She bit her lips at the constant tugging on the rope and gouging against her soft skin. She felt moisture on her wrists that had to be blood.

Just when she began to think she would remain tied up, she heard a satisfied grunt. The bindings fell away from her wrists. Nicole used her newly freed but cramped fingers to push herself into a sitting position. Wrenching down the cover over her eyes and mouth, she withdrew the rag and swallowed painfully. "Thank you!" she whispered. She couldn't see the face of her Apple Watch and missed the little sounds it made. They must have taken it. Verifying with her fingers that her eyes weren't covered, she glanced around the dark room, noting a thin line of light beneath what had to be the door, but little else. Leaning forward, Nicole began to work at the bindings on her legs.

Grunting, her fellow captive bumped into her side impatiently. "Give me a minute! I'm working as fast as I can," she whispered back. She wanted to be completely free, so that if their captors returned before she completely freed the man in the dark, at least she could try to escape. *Am I being selfish?* It was something she'd been told many times in her life, most often by someone with something to gain. Untying her bonds first had been a necessary act. She decided that she could at least return the favor promptly.

Reaching for him in the darkness, she touched cloth-covered toned and fit male flesh, skidded past his muscular chest and slid her fingers up to his gag. Jerking it down, she drew the damp rag from his mouth and removed his blindfold.

"Thank you!" he sighed in relief. She heard him swallow.

Nicole froze momentarily. No, he wasn't her bodyguard, but she sensed something familiar in the sound of his low tone. He nudged her with his bound hands, shaking her out of her thoughts. Her mind on the need to hurry, she struggled with his bindings. Working in the dark, she ploughed through the knots. Apparently, all those sailing lessons and classes on knots, bends, and hitches had stayed with her. In much less time than it had taken him, the rope loosened and fell away from his wrist. He grunted in approval.

With that out of the way, Nicole bent over her bound legs once more. She felt the other captive's shoulder brush hers as he sat up beside her. The knots securing the bindings that all but cut off the circulation in her legs felt tight and intricate, but she quickly went through them, too. Finally free, she got to her knees, then settled back down to remove her impractical high-heeled boots. "Do you need help?" she whispered in the darkness.

"Almost there," he whispered back.

"I'm going to try the door." She stood in stockinged feet on the cold stone floor, her hands outstretched to feel her way in the dark.

"Careful; they could be waiting outside," he hissed back urgently.

She halted. She wanted nothing more than to escape this room and get back to her life. The door was probably locked anyway, but what if there was a guard outside? Alerting him would bring more trouble than they were prepared to deal with. "I'll wait for you at the door."

Shuffling across the frigid floor, she found solace in her

ability to move. Her fingers touched the solid door. Dropping to her knees, she bent down, intent on catching a glimpse of the corridor outside. No such luck. The slice of light beneath the door was much too thin. Pressing her ear to the door's smooth surface, she strained her ears. No sound, no vibration, nothing.

She glided her fingers upward until they closed on a metal ring in the recess of the door where one would normally expect a doorknob or latch. Yes! She heard faint footsteps and felt the vibrations from her fellow captive making his way to the door. She couldn't see him. Instinctively turning toward the sound, she felt a hand on her back, then her arm. "Knob or latch?" He removed his hand.

"There's a metal ring," Nicole whispered back. "I'm not sure if there's a lock on the other side."

Nicole ran her fingers along the edges of the door in the dark, trying to find a mechanism that could be used to open the door to what had become their cell. Her fingers clenched around a metal ring. "I found the way to pull the door open," she whispered.

His hand curled around her shoulder, as if to hold her in place. "Wait a minute," he whispered back, "It could be locked, but in case it's not, what's the plan if there's someone outside the door?"

Nicole froze. Did she know this man? She knew that he wasn't her bodyguard, who was much lighter on his feet, but there was something familiar in the cadence of his whisper. Did she know him? She opened her mouth to ask. Then she decided that it didn't matter. When the door opened to the lighted passageway, she would see his face soon enough.

He whispered insistently. "I fight off the guard and you run down the corridor, and I follow as soon as possible?"

"That sounds good to me," she said, glad that chivalry wasn't dead but still confident she could do more than run away like the wimpy women in the movies. "What if there's two of them? What if there's only one but he's taking you down? I know how to defend myself, and I might be able to help you."

She heard his surprised intake of breath. "Any help would be appreciated, but only with the understanding that it's not worth the risk of them recapturing both of us."

"Understood." She gathered herself, preparing to fight for her life. Her fingers grasped the metal ring and she tugged with all her strength. At first, nothing happened. Apparently, she did need help. Then she heard a much-too-loud grating, metal on metal sound as the door slowly dragged open. Heart in her throat, she gasped, committed to getting the door open, no matter what.

The other captive stepped around her, using his strength to push on the edge of the door as it cleared, making it easier to open. The widening strips of light around the door grew brighter. Nicole blinked in blinding light, suddenly aware that she and her co-captive were at a distinct disadvantage if there was someone in the corridor.

The door was open, but Nicole couldn't make out anything. She felt like a sitting duck. As she stood in the entrance of their prison, her eyes slowly adjusted to the overwhelming influx of light. The man in the cell with her rushed past and charged into the corridor.

She heard a grunt. Something metallic clattered to the stone floor. Someone cursed in Spanish. She heard the frightening sounds of a struggle. Hands on the door, Nicole shook with the urge to run, to get away. Pushing herself, she covered her eyes with one hand, extended the other to make sure she didn't run into anything, and hurried away from the fight.

Gradually, she saw that she was headed down a long corridor with doors on both sides. Did each room hold a prisoner? she wondered. The need to get as far away as she could from where she'd been imprisoned fueled her steps and kept her from trying one of the doors. Thank God, she didn't hear anything but her co-captive fighting with the guard.

Abruptly, silence fell. Shit! Had the guard knocked out the guy who'd been in her cell? She risked a quick backward glance and saw a tall, beefy black guy standing over an apparently unconscious camouflage-suited guard. As he bent down to retrieve the guard's gun, another wave of familiarity hit Nicole. Who was this guy?

The man stuffed the gun in the pocket of his expensive-looking slacks, and quickly used the guard's cotton shirt to tie his hands behind him. Then he dragged the guard into their cell and closed the door. As he turned to face her, the light clearly illuminated his handsome face. Nicole locked gazes with her nemesis, Jaxson Forest. His eyes widened, his dark brows drawing together in something that resembled a scowl. He mumbled something and his sensual lips formed a straight line. Could fate be this cruel? Hell, no!

She realized she'd said the words out loud when he started running toward her. Nicole ran, too. He easily caught up with her. "I'm just as pleased about this as you are," he muttered.

"I doubt that!" she snapped back, still running. She struggled to keep up with him.

He made a grinding sound in his throat. "We're going to have to put our petty differences aside until we escape from this place."

Nicole cut her eyes at him. She acknowledged his words with a brief jerk of her head and kept running. Obviously in better shape than she was, he was already ahead.

"We've got to get as far away from here as we can before they figure out that we've escaped!" he said breathlessly.

She pressed her lips together, trying to resist the need to hurl all the insults that had been building inside her since he arrived on the scene with his billion-dollar pharmaceutical company bent on repurposing many of the rare and innovative materials she discovered for Lady Zayne beauty treatments to formulate new cancer fighting drugs. She heard shouting in the distance. *No! It's too soon for them to discover we've escaped!* She nearly stumbled as he caught her arm.

"We've got to get out of this corridor!" he said. He began to push on the closest door. It didn't budge. She tried the next. Same result. The sounds of other voices and footsteps moving down the corridor grew louder.

Her nemesis tried another door. With a grinding noise, it gave way. They scrambled inside, leveraging their weight to slam it shut. The chamber was dark, but at least they were no longer in the corridor. Nicole listened for any sounds that would indicate they were not alone. If there were other captives in the dark room, tied up and gagged as she had been, they might not be able to make a sound.

CHAPTER THREE

Now that the adrenalin rush from having escaped their cell had eased, she felt the cold seeping up from the floor. With the sound of her own anxious breathing in her ears, Nicole forced herself to use the techniques she'd learned in her yoga classes. She stretched out her arms and carefully began to explore the room in the dark. A light came on. She turned to see that her nemesis was holding a flashlight.

"I took the guard's flashlight," he explained, bouncing the light around the room. Nicole's eyes took in the cold stone floor, roughhewn walls, and a lightbulb hanging from the ceiling. This was more basic than the room where she and Liam had watched the auction. With her nemesis' flashlight flitting around the room, she found the light switch and flicked it on. The harsh light from the bulb served to illuminate just how hopeless their situation was.

Her gaze strayed back to the pile of rocks, screens, and some old equipment at the rear of the room. In a pinch, at least they'd have somewhere to hide.

As if he heard her thought, her nemesis crossed the room toward the pile of rubble, old equipment, and trash. Then he began moving the rubble as if searching for something.

"We could throw these if we have to," she remarked, coming close and brushing aside rocks and stones as big as her hand.

"There's an opening back here," he announced.

Nicole froze. A quick way out? Could it be this easy? She

inched closer and watched him remove some loose stones from a narrow opening.

"Getting through this is going to be a challenge," he muttered.

Her gaze touched his big, buff body in the wrinkled and stained remains of his custom tropical suit. At any other time, with any other man, she would have paused to savor the poetic mix of his dark brown coloring, the thick curling hair, lush lashes and brows. And how could she ignore the square jaw and full, sensual lips. She forced her gaze away from the muscular body and stared at the gap in the stone wall. She didn't think he would make it. Somewhat curvy and definitely not skinny herself, Nicole didn't look forward to using the opening to escape. *We're screwed!*

"We should see if we can use this way to escape while they still think we're locked up."

His words made sense. Shifting closer, she tried to peer around him. "What if it's just an opening and goes nowhere?"

"It isn't." He used the flashlight to illuminate the opening. She saw a passage leading who knew where. Deeper into the surrounding mountain, or out into a valley below? Wherever it led, Nicole was certain there would be bats, rodents, and all sorts of creepy crawlies. She shivered.

"You can do this." At his words Nicole glanced up to find him watching her with his golden brown eyes. Had she spoken her fears aloud? She needed that encouragement, but coming from him? Her shoulders straightened. What was the worst that could happen? An image of a fat rat nibbling her ankle in the dark formed in her mind. She stifled a gasp.

"Here, take the flashlight. I'll go first."

Instead of taking the light, Nicole gritted her teeth and shook her head, coming to a decision. "No, I'll go first. I'm smaller, and it should be easier for me to squeeze through."

Something close to amusement flickered across his face. "You'd be surprised at what you can do with your body when you have the right motivation."

What? She stared at him blankly for a few beats, certain she was missing something, but determined not to ask. Propelling herself forward, she went around him and peered into the narrow chasm. He used the light to illuminate it.

Some areas appeared wider than others. None of the edges looked sharp. Beginning to view it as something of an obstacle course, she took a step forward.

"Hold tight while I turn the light off," he said, abruptly moving away. "We don't want them to know we were here in this room if this works."

Nicole closed her eyes and did her best to center herself and remain calm. All she had to do was stay alive until Liam or someone from his team arrived to rescue her.

The bulb in the center of the room went out. Jaxson quickly returned, lighting his way with the flashlight. "Ready?"

Lifting one leg, she inserted it into the opening. Then she twisted and shimmied against the hard surface until it seemed she could go no further. Where had she gone wrong? She'd known it wouldn't be easy, but it had seemed doable. Imprisoned in an immovable stone vise, she tried to twist her body. Nothing happened. Nicole stifled a frantic breath.

"Hold a minute." Jaxson shifted closer, shining the light above and below where she seemed to be stuck. "It might seem like you're stuck, but there's still a little room to maneuver." She felt a hand on her elbow. "Twist your arm this way." She obeyed slowly. He tapped her leg. "And turn this leg the other way." Again, she followed his instructions.

Despite the cool stone, a trickle of moisture ran down her neck. An earthy, dirt-like aroma reached her from the inside passage. Suddenly his warm hands clamped down where her waist dovetailed into her hips. Startled, an involuntary gasp escaped her throat, but she couldn't move.

"Sorry," he muttered. "You're almost free. Just wanted to show you how you can shift your hips and get out of this."

Rotating her stiff hips in the direction he urged, she found her arms and legs could now move as well. The urgent need to get free propelled her.

"Careful!" he warned.

But it was too late. Nicole suddenly found herself free-falling in the darkness on the other side. She tried to protect her head while keeping her arms and legs bent. It seemed to take forever to reach the ground. She managed to roll before she lay stunned on the harsh surface.

"Are you okay?" she heard him ask from the other side.

"Yes," she mumbled. She had to be.

***

Cold seeped up from the stone floor to chill the cheek resting on her hand. She wiggled the toes of her cold feet. Where was she? She opened her eyes. It was dark. Had she merely dreamed of escaping her prison with her nemesis? Her body felt stiff and bruised. A low moan escaped her as she struggled to a seated position, rejecting all thoughts of bugs, rats, and bats searching for her in the dark. She heard nothing.

Suddenly a light switched on and filtered through the stone opening beside her. "Welcome back."

She hugged herself. Was Jaxson Forest up there smirking? Just about anything was better than being alone and lost in the stone prison of this mountain fortress. "I was beginning to think I was alone."

His near whisper held a tinge of amusement. "No, I helped you get through and then you fell and stunned yourself. You've being lying there for about five minutes or so. I switched off the light to conserve the battery."

She surveyed what she could see of her side of the opening. "Do you still think you can get through this?"

"We have to get out of here, so I don't have much of a choice. On the plus side, I've always been something of an athlete and I'm double-jointed. On the minus…"

"You're a big guy," she finished for him. "Let me know when you're ready. If you pass the flashlight through first, I'll keep the light on you and help as much as I can."

The sound of metal hitting the stone reached her. She glanced up and saw the flashlight on an outcropping of the rock. "Thanks." Palming it, she moved the light and slowly re-examined the chasm. No way could he get through that. Her teeth hit her bottom lip.

More rustling sounds came from the other side. Interest piqued, she stood in her thin stockings on the cold floor. "Take this first," he said. "It'll only get caught on something."

She shifted on her feet and caught the dust- and dirt-soiled jacket he thrust through the opening. The suit jacket still held the warmth of his body. Needing the comfort of that warmth, she slipped it over her shoulders. It felt wonderful! He tossed the water bottle next. She caught it, staring at the contents with a throat that felt dry as chalk.

"Take a couple of sips, but remember, it's got to last us," he said from the other side.

Twisting off the cap, Nicole lifted the bottle and swallowed gratefully. Soothing, cool water slid down her parched throat. She stopped after two quick swallows and screwed the top back on. "Ready."

Stepping closer with the flashlight, she caught her breath in anticipation of seeing her nemesis ease his big body through the chasm that had challenged her much smaller frame. Nothing happened. Was he meditating or something? For several long moments she saw and heard nothing. Then long, thick fingers with well-manicured nails appeared, followed by a thick, shirt-covered arm that seemed to flow from the other side.

He turned, infinitesimally rotating his body, twisting, flattening, and contorting himself in ways that didn't seem possible.

A head of closely cropped black hair came next. Shifting smoothly, the angular planes of his deep brown face followed. Full, sensually shaped lips pulled back from his perfect-looking white teeth as he grimaced. Golden-brown eyes filled with frustration and something she couldn't name pinned her to the spot. Then she realized that he'd stopped moving.

"Problem?" she asked, trying not to sound too concerned. *You said you could do it*, she thought, and he'd been putting on a damned good show. The truth was that she didn't look forward to traveling through the dark corridor with what looked like varying ceiling heights and who knew what kinds of bugs, bats, rodents, and guys with guns. She didn't want to go alone.

He released his breath. His body seemed to fold in on itself, but she detected no more progress through the chasm. "You may have been right about me not fitting through this opening. I'm stuck."

Mouth opening slightly, she stepped closer, using the light to carefully examine just how much he'd achieved. His head, one arm, one leg, and a good part of his chest were on her side of the chasm. The rest of his body appeared to be one with the surrounding stone structure. "How can I help?"

"Grab my arm and try to drag me out of this hole."

Nicole frowned. "Some of the stone edges seem a little sharper than I thought. You might get cut."

Golden brown eyes pinned her once more as he rasped, "It beats the alternative."

It took a minute, but she found a way to prop the flashlight up against the wall so that it illuminated Jaxson. She grabbed his arm and tugged hard. She felt a fractional amount of movement. Nicole stopped when she heard Jaxson groan in pain. "Just do it!" he urged.

Studying what she could see of his body, she decided to try a different tack. She reached in and hooked one hand in the waistband of his pants and used the other to grab his leg. With a grunt, she tugged with all her might. She tried to pull his body upward, then straight out, then down. The struggle seemed to go on forever.

The muffled sounds of his groans and moans filled her ears. Negative taunts about her ability to get this done tortured her mind. Of all her dreams of hurting her nemesis, this reality was unbearable. She felt the warmth of tears on her face. She would do this!

Abruptly, he came free of the channel, and she felt herself falling backward with his weight. Oh, crap! She tucked her chin and tried to relax her body. Nicole hit the ground for the second time, and it knocked the breath from her body. Stunned, she lay there for several moments.

It felt as if she'd been hit by a truck. She prayed that no bones were broken, although she had to be bruised. At least she managed to fall without hitting her head. And her nemesis? Her leg and the tip of one finger touched his beefy form. He wasn't moving. Was he okay? Thank God he'd fallen clear of her.

Light from the flashlight still illuminated the tunnel ceiling. Grateful that it still worked, she inched toward it in the dark, blanking out all thoughts of what might be lurking in the dark part of the corridor. Finally, flashlight in hand, she shut it off and allowed herself to rest.

She awakened to the sound of sliding movements in the dark. "Is that you?" she whispered.

"Yes. Thanks for the help. I did what I could to land clear of you. You okay?" he whispered back.

"I've been better."

"You can say that again!" He slid closer. "We've got to get moving. If they come into the room and shine a flashlight back here, we're sitting ducks."

"Do you know how we're going to get out of here?"

"Not really, but I read that this place used to be an old monastery. There should be more than one way out. I'm hoping that heading downward will lead us to an opening to the outside or another room we can escape from."

Nicole switched on the flashlight. Jaxson stood just inches from her. She saw the ripped front of his shirt. There was even a little blood in a couple of spots. "Are you okay?"

He shrugged off the question. "I made to the other side."

Nicole narrowed her eyes at his dismissive tone and handed him his jacket. He put it on and extended a hand for the flashlight. She gave it to him and watched as he used it to illuminate the downward-sloping corridor. What if the corridors cycled endlessly and they got lost? What if the tunnel led them straight to their captors? What if they never got rescued? Determinedly, she shut off the negative thoughts before they could paralyze her.

"Let's go," he said in a gruff tone. When she got to her feet, he was already moving down the stone pathway. Since he was leading, she didn't argue about him hogging the flashlight. "Try to stay close," he said.

CHAPTER FOUR

Nicole ducked beneath another low ceiling of rock, and her legs gave out. They'd been walking for what seemed like hours. She'd done her best to keep from complaining. Her feet felt like numb blocks of ice. Why hadn't she worn sensible shoes? She was paying for that.

Her nemesis took a few more halting steps then came back to drop down beside her. "Good time for a break."

Something eased within her, but she didn't respond. Leaning forward, she massaged her feet, trying to nudge some feeling back into them. He shone the light on her feet, revealing a few cuts and a lot of swelling.

"Why didn't you bring your shoes?"

"The stylish things weren't worth the trouble, so I left them with the ropes and gags they used on us," she ruefully admitted. "I couldn't run in them, and the heels wouldn't have worked down here."

He surprised her by showing no signs of amusement at her foolishness. "Maybe we can come up with something to make you more comfortable," he said, setting the flashlight down so that it lit part of where they sat.

Nicole shrugged. She still wore her designer suit jacket, silk blouse, pants, and thin socks. What could she do with them?

"I'm not cold," he said, removing his jacket. Then he ripped off the sleeves. She didn't know what he was doing until he'd slipped one cold foot into the sleeve. Sudden warmth made her sigh with relief.

"We could tie the end and try to find something to keep the top from slipping," he suggested, already knotting the end of the other jacket sleeve.

Searching for something, anything she could use, Nicole ripped the inside facing from the neckline of her silk blouse. She ripped it in two pieces and each piece made good ties to keep the sleeves from falling down her legs. She felt infinitely better. Her stomach growled demandingly. Heat rushed to her face.

"I can't help you with that," Jaxson said with a definitive note of humor.

"We need water, too," she said, not taking the bait.

He retrieved the flashlight. "Hopefully both our teams are mounting a rescue."

"Hopefully they didn't kill my bodyguard," she murmured, just beneath her breath.

He placed a surprisingly gentle hand on her shoulder. "Right now, our biggest worry is getting out of here. We don't know what their plan is. They may just decide to kill us."

Nicole forced herself to stand. "Don't think that hasn't crossed my mind. We should get going."

Beside her, he crouched low and continued down the corridor, waving the flashlight. Nicole followed close on his heels. It was a grueling task. She wondered if anyone had used the often low-ceilinged corridors and tunnels on a regular basis. The jacket sleeves, while keeping her feet from making direct contact with the cool stone floor, did not provide the padding of a shoe. Still, she was grateful.

They walked for hours and hours, stopping for as long as they dared to rest against the walls. They even found small, angular, out-of-the-way areas on the path to use as makeshift bathrooms. Finally, they slept shoulder-to-shoulder, sitting up against the wall in the corridor.

Nicole awakened with her head against Jaxson's shoulder. The overwhelming feeling of fatigue was gone, but her stomach was aching for food. She straightened and felt a pain in her neck. How long had they slept? They'd both been exhausted.

Rubbing his forehead, Jaxson got to his feet. "We'd better get moving again. I'm thinking that this is another day."

Thirsty, she lifted the water bottle. Half the water was gone. "One small sip?"

Jaxson nodded, and they each drank from the bottle. Then they headed down the corridor.

When they could go no more, they stopped to catch their breath. That was when they heard the voices coming from somewhere on the other side of the wall. Jaxson shut off the flashlight.

"Did they find them yet?"

"No, but they've gone for Juan's *abuelo*, his grandfather. He knows this place like the back of his hand. It shouldn't take long for him to lead us to them. *La mujer*, the woman, left her shoes when they got out, so they won't get far."

"Their security teams have been stirring up the locals and trying to recruit people to mount a rescue. I hear they've got reinforcements coming, too. We're not going to let that happen. We've got less than twenty-four hours before the helicopter arrives to take us out. We need this settled, one way or another, by then."

"*Si, senor.*"

They heard a door grind open, then slam shut. Nicole shivered. Her teeth were chattering loudly, and she couldn't stop them. Jaxson's warm hand caught hers and squeezed it. That helped her stop her teeth from chattering. Still, her body trembled.

Jaxson pulled her close and simply held her. "We're all right," he whispered, his warm breath close to her ear, "We're going to get out of this."

Of their own volition, her arms circled his waist. Her face lay against the warm, masculine-scented cotton covering his chest. The heat of his body enveloped her, spreading a warmth and comfort through her body that she hadn't known she needed. She closed her eyes. She'd never imagined that she could or would draw comfort from the man who'd outmaneuvered and fought with her over several rare and precious plants and ingredients used for medical and cosmetic purposes.

"Ready?" he whispered, close to her ear.

Nicole realized that he'd taken her thoughts away from her fears and she appreciated it. She'd even stopped shivering. "Yes," she whispered back.

He switched on the flashlight and began moving again. Treading as quietly as she could, Nicole followed. The next time they stopped, he'd found an alcove with an elevated clearing of flat rock along the wall. He ushered her onto it and got on behind her. Surprisingly, the stone bed didn't seem too hard, and she was too exhausted to care that he was so close. There was enough room for them to lie close without touching. She fell asleep, wishing she was still wearing her Apple watch.

***

Sometime later, Nicole awakened, enveloped in the heat of a big body, a man's body. His inviting scent teased her nostrils. The bed could have been more comfortable, but this was a dream she liked! Stretching, she rotated her butt against the hard member pressed close to the fullness of her bottom. Big, hot hands grabbed her hips and halted their movement.

"Don't start something you can't finish," a low voice virtually growled in her ear.

She froze. Everything started coming back. Had she really

been ready to hump her nemesis? A bit embarrassed, and certain her face was flushed, Nicole was glad for the darkness. She searched for something to say. "I was...asleep," she managed with a little bit of attitude.

"I like the way you wake up," he said, amusement in his voice. "Maybe it's something we can finish at another time. What do you say?"

Nicole nudged him toward the edge of the ledge with her hand. "Let's get moving."

"You'll always wonder what you missed," he said in a smart-assed tone.

"I could say the same to you." She waited as he slid to the edge of the ledge and stood. Then she did the same. "One sip of water?"

He nodded and they both drank. There wasn't much left. They were either going to get out of the mountain caverns associated with the ancient monastery or find a way into one of the rooms on the other side of the rock wall. Hopefully they wouldn't get caught.

They continued their trek down the central corridor. Nicole felt a slight current of air coming from the direction they were traveling in. Maybe it led to the outside? Dear God, she hoped so.

Gradually, they heard movement in the distance, both from behind them and up ahead. Was it their kidnappers? Or their rescue team? She and Jaxson searched the rock wall carefully, looking for an opening to escape through. There was none. The faint sounds of other people in the tunnel were getting louder. She heard voices talking in Spanish and English. Was that good or bad?

Finally, Jaxson reached a point where he stopped moving. "This is as good a place as any to make our stand," he said, shining the light between them so that they could see each other's face. "This bend in the corridor will keep us hidden until they're right up on us."

Nicole nodded and whispered. "You've got the flashlight. What can I do to help?"

He leaned against the stone wall. "I'm going to turn off the light. You turn it on when they get close. If it's not our rescue team, we're going to fight like hell. The good news is that they probably don't want to kill us, at least not yet."

"Okay." Her breath hitched in her throat as she accepted the flashlight. For the second time in who knew how long, Nicole steeled herself for a fight. She heard the voices and footsteps coming from the direction she and Jaxson had been heading, getting closer and closer.

She switched on the flashlight when the men approaching in the dark sounded like they were just a few feet away. Not sure how effective she could be in her suit-sleeve-covered feet, but determined to give it her best, Nicole crouched in a ready position to fight and peered down the corridor.

CHAPTER FIVE

The sudden light revealed eight startled men with guns and flashlights. The gray-haired male in front of the group wore what looked like a long sleeved tribal-patterned shirt over dark pants. Nicole swallowed her scream. Her elated gaze zeroed in on the bruised face of her bodyguard. "Liam!" She ran to him and gave him a brief hug. "I was afraid they killed you!"

"It takes more than a few bad guys to keep me down," he quipped, with more than a little swagger. "They dumped me and Asher in the water unconscious, but we were lucky and got rescued by a local fisherman."

"I'm glad you're okay," she said, wincing at the thought of him in the ocean, unconscious with the sharks and other scavengers. They could have both been killed. "I-I'm sorry I got you into this."

"I could have told you no when they said no to the security team," he said magnanimously. "I thought I would be able to handle anything they had planned. Obviously, I was wrong. It won't happen again." He glanced at her feet. "Those are some shoes you're wearing."

"I couldn't run in the shoes I was wearing, so I left them where they had us tied up," she explained. "The floors in the tunnel are cold, so we had to improvise."

Nodding, Liam performed a quick examination of her. She had several cuts from her encounters with the sharp edges of the rocks, but a lot of the smeared blood was Jaxson's. Liam brushed the dirt off her face and gently moved the hair away from a lump on her head. "I'm so glad to see you and know you made it through okay! I couldn't have lived with myself if something had happened to you."

Not commenting, she thought of her mother, who was surely making life hell for everyone around her since her only daughter had been kidnapped. Nicole and her caustic parent weren't close, but sometimes she almost felt sorry for her. Her mother had ruined a lot of relationships, wasn't allowed to see one grandchild, and was on shaky ground with the parents of the other.

Liam drew two energy bars and a bottle of water from his pockets. "Are you hungry? Thirsty?"

Thanking him, she snagged both bars. Tearing into one hungrily, Nicole turned back to see two men talking to Jaxson Forest as he wolfed down an energy bar. They'd opened his shirt to examine the bloody cuts and bruises that marred his muscular six-pack.

"Isn't that Jaxson Forest?" her bodyguard asked, giving her a barely cloaked side-eye as she chewed and swallowed.

"Yes. They had us bound and gagged in one of those old chambers, but we managed to escape. This has been enough of an adventure to last me for a while! Did they ask for a ransom?"

"Twenty million, but your family was worried when the kidnappers couldn't produce you for a wellness check or proof that you were still alive. Both sides are stalling. Your brother Ben called in some favors to expedite your rescue. We've had help from the government, and even from someone undercover within the group of kidnappers. That's how we knew where to come in through this system of caves and corridors."

She turned to the gray-haired native. "Are you Juan's *abuelo?*"

"That I am, *senorita,*" he said with a nod. "My grandson has been misguided by others, but I hope he now sees the light."

Jaxson and the two men scurried back to the group. "Shh! Someone's coming from the other end of the tunnel. Let's get them!"

Determined not to lose their charges again, Liam and Jaxson's bodyguard, Asher, decided to start the trek out of the corridor right away. They gestured for Nicole and Jaxson to go first. Some of the men urged the old man to go with Jaxson, Nicole, and their bodyguards, but the old man was determined to save his grandson. Stooping low, they hurried as fast as they could. As Nicole and Jaxson rounded a curve with Asher, the flashlights of the men behind them winked out. A few steps more, and a gun went off. They heard shouting, then the sounds of fighting.

"I wonder who's winning?" Jaxson muttered in a low tone.

"Me too," Nicole said, straining her ears.

"We're not going back to check. You and Nicole are our priority," Liam said in a short tone.

"No stopping until you two are safe!" Asher confirmed.

They continued their hike for at least another hour. Nicole and Jaxson were breathing so hard that Asher had to relent and call for a stop. He took bottled water from his backpack and offered it to them. Nicole sucked hers down quickly, relishing the refreshing taste like never before. She saw Jaxson doing the same.

"You're both probably dehydrated," Liam said, studying them with the brightness of his flashlight. "Did you find water in this maze?"

"No," Jaxson answered as Nicole shook her head, "but we did take a bottle off one of the guards. It didn't last long."

Nicole's thoughts flashed back to that moment when Jaxson surprised her and let her have the last few sips of water.

He obviously wasn't the self-centered man she'd thought he was. She glanced around and found Liam studying her thoughtfully. "Let's get moving again!" he said.

Nicole forced her tired legs and aching feet to keep moving. Now she knew why her mother and some of her older female relatives always carried a pair of flats. Up ahead, she saw a hint of light. The air smelled fresher, too. And was that a slight breeze? The thought gave her energy she didn't know she had.

The pinpoint of light widened and brightened. They were close to the outside!

"We're on the home stretch!" Jaxson remarked just under his breath.

"It feels like we've been in here forever!" she said.

"Almost three days," Asher said from the rear.

Three days? It felt more like a week! Close on Liam's heels, Nicole picked up speed. Ahead lay the safety of her life, her family, and her career at Lady Zayne Cosmetics. While she'd been kidnapped, she'd been forced to draw on skills she'd never needed before to survive. It had taught her some new things about herself. She was a survivor. It had also shown her a side of Jaxson Forest she hadn't known existed.

With a gasp of unadulterated joy, Nicole reached the exit right behind Liam. She shut her eyes against the bright sunlight, and a warm breeze caressed her skin. Liam stuck a pair of dark sunglasses on her nose and nudged her to the side so that Jaxson and Asher could pass. Blinking behind the sunglasses, she saw them standing nearby. Asher had brought a pair of dark glasses for Jaxson, too.

Ahead, she saw the little drawbridge she'd trudged across on the way in. Someone was letting it down. A group of men and the local police were on the other side. As the bridge locked into place and the small crowd started across, a helicopter appeared.

"Shoot it down!" a man who like one of the local cops

yelled.

"No, it's about to land, and we have men on top of the mountain," another man, who was carrying one of the packs Jaxson's team wore, said.

Nicole thought about the conversation she and Jaxson had overheard inside the stone fortress. This was probably the helicopter that was coming for Andre and his henchmen. She didn't think he would surrender without a fight.

Right on cue, several shots rang out from above.

Asher and Liam drew Nicole and Jaxson back into the tunnel entrance. Still, they could hear more shots and the sound of the helicopter taking off. She stared at the helicopter as it rose from the clifftop. Was it bulletproof? she wondered as it continued to progress despite numerous rounds being fired.

Suddenly it hovered precariously, the cockpit dipping lower than the tail. She saw Andre seated in the back and trying furiously to get out. Abruptly, the helicopter exploded in a bright, glowing ball of gold and red. The men outside the cave scattered, some making it to the cave, others hunkering down to the ground as flying bits of shrapnel rained down from the sky. Molten metal sprayed the water, several particles reaching land and the men crouching there. Some of the men screamed in pain.

Heat from the explosion reached them at the cavern entrance. They edged further into the dark interior. Nicole strained her ears, listening for the crew they'd left to fight and hopefully capture their kidnappers. Surely, they hadn't been killed. She couldn't hear anything coming from the tunnel.

"That was a spectacular ending for the man who had us bound and gagged!" Jaxson said, as one of the local cops used a radio to call for ambulances.

Nicole blinked. The image of the helicopter exploding with Andre, his pilot, and whatever cargo he'd managed to load still singed her brain. She turned to face Jaxson. "Did you make the winning bid?"

His head lifted. Even in the semi-dark cavern she saw the arrogant look she hated transform his face. "Yes, but it was more than I ever expected to pay. It will impact the development budget and eventual cost of the drug we're developing."

"I'm thinking the plants were on the helicopter that just went down," she said with carefully muted satisfaction. She hadn't won the bid, but her company's money was still in the bank.

The corners of his wide mouth quirked upward. "We'll see."

Did he know something she didn't? She studied him for a few beats more, as if she could glean an answer. Why had she been thinking that there was more to Jaxson Forest than the arrogant ass she'd been competing with for rare plants and compounds? She edged a little closer to her bodyguard.

Liam turned toward her. He'd been furiously talking on his phone, but she'd been too stunned by the explosion to listen in. "We can leave as soon as the ambulances pick up the injured. Two police teams are already searching the cavern and the rest of the facility to see if there were other kidnap victims. They'll also check for any remaining kidnappers. There's a car waiting on the other side of the bridge to take us to the airport. You're going home!"

Nicole looked at the cavern entrance. "I can't wait!"

Liam extended a hand with his phone. "Your brothers want to talk to you."

Nicole gave the phone and Liam a wary glance. She didn't feel like being yelled at or hearing how stupid she'd been to put Liam and herself in danger for an exotic crop of a rare plant. When she got back to New York there would be hell to pay, but why start now?

"They've been worried about you," Liam said gently.

Despite their often-distant upbringing and sibling rivalry from time to time, she loved her brothers and knew they felt the same about her. Lifting her head and straightening her shoulders, Nicole accepted the phone. "Hello, I'm here in Cape Pacifica and I've been rescued," she announced, taking control of the narrative. "We're heading to the airport in a few minutes, and I don't plan on coming back."

Ben's voice came through from the other end of the line. "Nik, are you okay? Did they hurt you?"

"Not much. They attacked Liam and drugged me after the auction. When I woke up, I was bound and gagged along with Jaxson Forest. From there we had to work together to escape."

Hugo's voice held a mix of outrage and surprise. "They left you and Forest bound and gagged in the same room?"

"Yes, but I didn't know who he was until we escaped from the room. That was a hell of a surprise!"

"I know you two have a lot of negative history on the corporate side. It's a good thing you were able to work together," Ben said.

"I know how to put my differences aside when it comes to escaping a makeshift prison," Nicole said. She wasn't petty or stupid.

"We're really glad to hear your voice. When they couldn't prove you were still alive, we were worried sick. Mother's been giving everybody hell. Her doctor had to give her something for her nerves. We'll have a doctor check you as soon as you get back," Hugo said.

"I'm okay," Nicole insisted. She felt the sting of tears in her eyes. Her mother could be an overly dramatic wild card, but it felt good to get the assurance that her brothers cared. She'd spent a good part of her life feeling estranged and unloved. Now, Ben was happily married and had an infant son.

Hugo also had an infant son and was preparing to marry his longtime girlfriend, Ava. Where did that leave her, the last of the unlovable Zayne crew?

"Whatever it takes, we're going to get them for what they did to you," Ben promised.

"It looks like the local police already shot down the helicopter carrying the ringleader," Nicole said.

Hugo said, "If any of your kidnappers survived, they're going to pay. We've made arrangements for the corporate jet to get you, but there's an even quicker way to bring you home, if you'll agree."

"Why wouldn't I? Nicole asked, intrigued.

CHAPTER SIX

An hour later, she followed Liam across the bridge. Jaxson Forest walked behind her with several other men who carried boxes.

The Foreststone Pharmaceuticals corporate jet was already at Cape Pacifica's small airport when they arrived. The Lady Zayne corporate jet had been on the way, but it wasn't hard for Nicole's brothers to convince her to get on the Foreststone jet instead of waiting for family-owned transportation. She wanted nothing more than escape from the small African country, so she gave the okay for Lady Zayne's plane to return to New York.

Wearing a pair of woven sandals one of the team members had secured from a local vendor, Nicole boarded the plane.

On the Foreststone private jet headed back to New York, Nicole was elated to discover luxurious facilities to clean herself up. On board, she found clothing, makeup, and personal care products apparently purchased for Jaxson's family and friends. Grateful, she threw herself into the task of making herself look and feel better after her ordeal.

During a long, hot shower, she washed her short blond hair twice. Afterward, she toweled off, applied a healing lotion, and took a hard look at herself. Bruises, scratches, and even a few cuts covered her body. Makeup brightened and defined her classic facial features. Despite the damage, she smiled at herself in the mirror. She was free!

Going through the clothes, she slipped into the comfort of an off-the-shoulder blue sweatshirt dress. The soft, natural material felt good against her tender skin. The garment landed mid-thigh. Twirling in the mirror, she admired herself. She did have the legs for it. A scrape on one thigh and a bruise on the other prompted her to reach for a pair of leggings, but then she decided against them and applied makeup instead.

Briefly, she sat on the bed and bent over to cup her feet in the palms of each hand. They were puffy and still held a lingering chill. Massaging them, she pulled on socks and gratefully donned a low-heeled pair of booties.

With a backward glance at the soft, comfortable bed, she left her private suite and headed for the galley. Liam had brought energy bars, but she hadn't had a real meal in days. The rich savory aroma of bacon, eggs, and cinnamon raisin toast drifted in the air. Her stomach growled aggressively as she reached the entryway to the galley, where there was a dining area and a chef preparing food.

"You're in the right place!" a familiar voice exclaimed.

Nicole turned to see the handsome, cleaned-up version of Jaxson Forest, already seated with a plate of food. She hesitated, not certain she wanted to share a meal with the man who was still her nemesis. The past few days with him had her confused about her feelings.

His sharp golden-brown eyes took in her appearance, his gaze lingering on her face with something that almost felt like a caress. "You cleaned up just fine. I know your feet are a lot happier in those shoes."

A flash of heat went through her as he studied her and commented, but she stood her ground and pretended it had no effect. Right now, she wasn't ready to consider doing anything but fighting with Jaxson. Ignoring the comment about her appearance, she skipped to the one about her feet. "My feet are still cold, but it's nice to wear shoes again." She glanced down appreciatively at the designer booties.

"I could massage them for you," he offered with a sensual note in his tone.

Nicole's head came up, and she couldn't stop herself. "Stop it! We're not friends. We're simply having a temporary truce."

A wide, hungry smile transformed Jaxson's face. "We have several hours until we get back to New York. Our truce should last at least until then. We could see where it leads us. What better way to occupy our time and satisfy both our curiosities?"

Certain he had something much more physical in mind than rubbing her feet, she met his gaze with her no-nonsense expression on her face. "No, not happening." She glanced at the chef, who was busy chopping ingredients for omelets, and thought about enjoying her meal in the privacy of her suite. There would be no temptation or provocative conversation there. "Do you offer room service?"

The chef nodded politely. "Yes ma'am, whatever you'd like."

Jaxson pointed to the chair right across from him. "Please, have a seat. I promise to behave."

Her eyes narrowed. She took a few beats to consider. She didn't have to put up with crap from anyone. She was a big girl and shouldn't allow Jaxson Forest on a sensual bent to chase her out of the dining area like a frightened schoolgirl. This new side of Jaxson Forest intrigued her, and that was dangerous to the way she lived her life. It wasn't that she hadn't had men interested in her, it was that she always seemed to get the short end of the stick. She always ended up alone and regretting the relationships. Sometimes she considered emulating her mother by getting herself a boy toy to fulfill her needs until she tired of him.

Nicole drew out the chair and sat down. Jaxson was quiet as she ordered a Denver omelet with bacon, cinnamon raisin toast, and coffee. The chef poured her fresh brewed coffee that made her mouth water, then bustled away to the cook station to prepare her food. She felt Jaxson watching her as she added cream and sugar. She took a sip and sighed with pleasure. It was ultra-premium stuff.

"We do have good coffee," he said.

Nicole pretended to ignore him. She sat sipping coffee while she waited for her breakfast. Just a few days ago, sitting across the table from her nemesis for a meal would have been inconceivable. Somehow the trials and tribulations of the past few days had changed their dynamic.

Yes, she'd had to think twice about remaining in his company, but now she knew there was more to the man than the annoying, relentless, and cunning competitor who often snatched deals from the jaws of her victories. She worked hard to show her family that as a worthy addition to their cosmetics empire, she could run the various divisions of Lady Zayne Cosmetics and grow the business. Jaxson Forest added a significant amount to the already numerous challenges.

Jaxson appeared at ease as he sat across from her, occasionally glancing at her from the pages of the newspaper displayed on his tablet. "We made the front page," he said, holding up his tablet so she could see the display."

The kidnappers had confiscated her smartwatch, laptop, and phone, and they hadn't been among the things the local police found at the old monastery. Since her rescue, she'd only talked to her brothers on her bodyguard's phone. Not sure how to frame or even talk about her ordeal to others, she'd even ignored the brand-new replacement phone in her room. Now, like a deer caught in the headlights, she stared at the display on his tablet.

The headline read "Kidnapped Billionaires Rescued from Cape Pacifica Island." The black-and-white photo hid the dirt, dust, and bloodstains on their battered clothing. Wearing native rope sandals, Nicole saw herself mounting the steps to

Jaxson's private jet with him close behind. Both of them looked pretty good, considering what they'd been through. Several bodyguards and men carrying boxes surrounded them, making it a wonder that the photographer had managed to get a clear shot of them.

Nicole studied the men who held the boxes. It looked like Jaxson Forest had gotten something for his winning bid. Focusing on her face, she could only see and relive the immense relief she'd felt at the prospect of leaving the tiny African country and the proof of her serious lapse in judgement.

The corners of Jaxson's mouth turned upward. As if he'd gleaned something of her thoughts, he said, "I'm looking forward to hearing and approving the positive spin the marketing guys are going to put on this."

Nicole blinked and nodded. He was right. There had to be an upside to their kidnapping, something that could be exploited.

"For your team," he continued, "it'll probably be something like, 'Even the most trying times can't spoil the beauty of your Lady Zayne Cosmetics look."

A bit of a chuckle escaped her lips as she glanced up at him. His words sounded trite given what they'd been through, but her family was always looking to put a positive spin on everything that happened. Damned if she'd let them use her face, but a model with a similar look would get the point across. "Good call. I can imagine them proposing something like that."

His eyes glinted with amusement and challenge. "And what do you think my team will propose?"

Brows creeping upward, Nicole took a moment to collect her thoughts. "No fire, storm, flood, or abduction can keep Foreststone Pharmaceuticals from bringing you the best in life-saving cancer treatments."

Some of the humor leached out of his expression. "Not

bad!" His brown eyes pierced her, as if he was truly seeing her for the first time. Squaring her shoulders, she met his gaze with as much bravado as she could muster. Something in his avid gaze touched her as surely as a physical caress. She felt hot. A thrill of excitement pulsed through her. *No! Jaxson Forest is off limits!* It took everything she had to keep herself from leaning toward him.

The chef chose that moment to set a steaming plate of food in front of her. It broke the connection between them. The vision and the heady aroma of bacon, eggs, cheese, and wheat toast drew her senses. Her stomach rumbled and she didn't care. It had been too long since she'd had a real meal. Nicole lifted her fork and dug in. Her eyes closed at the melding of the different flavors on her tongue. She chewed, swallowed, and shoveled in more. Halfway through her meal she thought to glance at Jaxson.

He was watching her, an unreadable expression on his face. "I had a similar reaction to my first meal since our abduction, too," he confided.

She nodded and swallowed. The funny thing was that she usually skipped breakfast, opting for a bagel or muffin with her coffee. She opened her mouth to tell him that, but then caught herself. Clamping down on this weirdly chummy session with Jaxson, she continued to eat. Basic breakfast food had never tasted so delicious.

Nicole finished her breakfast. Setting the fork down, she patted her mouth with the linen napkin and lifted her coffee cup. "I appreciate your hospitality."

"You're welcome. What else do you appreciate?"

The provocative note in his voice drew her gaze from the milky caramel-colored liquid in her cup to his golden-brown eyes. "I appreciate the fact that despite our differences we were able to work together and escape," she said.

He nodded slowly. "We made a good team. But don't expect it to continue once we leave this plane and go back to who and what we are."

"And what's that?" she asked.

"Two strong-minded people who want the same things for different reasons."

"You got what you wanted this time," she noted, referring to the fact that he'd gotten some of the plants he'd paid so handsomely for.

His eyes glittered, his gaze covering everything visible from his seat across from her. Was she imagining the carnal note? "Not everything."

"What's left?" Nicole huffed. "I'm assuming that those boxes they loaded on this plane contained the rest of the plants you paid for."

"True, but that's not what I'm talking about. You're no shrinking violet. Do I need to spell it out?"

Nicole stared at him, abruptly aware that he was subtly proposing that she spend some of her remaining time onboard his jet in his bed. In return, she swept his form with a critical gaze. He'd shaved and his thick dark hair looked freshly cut. The pillowy lips on his wide mouth looked ready to mock her at any moment. What would it feel like to kiss them? It felt as if his golden-brown eyes could see clear through her pretense of being unaware of the sensual current running between them. An unexpected thrill of excitement shot through her.

Yes, somehow he'd dropped the sneer and the superior attitude during their abduction, and at times she'd found him downright attractive. He was a big hunk of a guy, and looked as good or better than any of the eye candy she'd seen at the events she attended. He was also known to have a high IQ, something that wasn't usually associated with someone as handsome as he was. No, he wasn't her type, but she'd been tempted more than once in the past couple of days to consider sleeping with him. Should she give in to her curiosity? Didn't she have enough problems waiting for her in New York?

"We're both adults," he murmured in a husky tone, "I pay my staff to be discreet, and they've all signed nondisclosure agreements. What happens on this plane, stays on the plane. Of course, I can't speak for your team."

"Everyone signed a nondisclosure agreement," she said.

"So?" His question hung in the air.

When she didn't respond, Jaxson pushed back his chair and stood. *Was he giving up that easily?* Nicole found herself standing and nudging back her chair. *He's not going to walk away from this!* Like a magnet to metal, she approached him, not certain what would happen when she got there. He waited, his eyes a wary blend of daring and desire as something within him drew her like a magnet.

Finally, she stood less than an inch in front of him, her body tingling madly with intrigue and longing. He was the forbidden fruit. The frantic alarm bells of common sense rang wildly at the back of her thoughts. They were easy to ignore, because following the rules and conventions had never netted her anything she didn't already have. Ready to push the boundaries, she lifted her hands to curl her fingers around his warm, freshly shaven cheeks. His scent, a complex blend of sandalwood, musk, amber, and man, beckoned her on.

Their gazes locked, his golden-brown gaze holding her mesmerized. The words he'd spoken when she wiggled her butt against his erection upon awakening repeated in her mind. *"Don't start something you can't finish."*

Her fingers slid over the shortened curls on his head to draw his head down to hers. On a whim, she touched her cherry-berry coated lips to his wide mouth in a chaste kiss. It felt *good*. Something akin to an electric charge surged through her at the contact.

CHAPTER SEVEN

She felt his quick intake of breath. Her tongue slipped out to taste his soft lips. It glided along the smooth curving surfaces to delicately dip inside his mouth. She tasted coffee and an indefinable something that made her want more. Their breath mingled with a mutual moan.

His lips parted, and she was in heaven. Drawing him closer, pressing her aching breasts into his sculpted chest, Nicole sank into the kiss. Her tongue danced with Jaxson's. The heat of his hands penetrated her dress as he caressed first her back and then the bare skin of her shoulders.

She strained to touch more of him, her hands skimming his wide cotton-covered shoulders, past his trim waist, to grab his firm rear covered in cotton slacks. The kiss grew more and more heated. They broke apart, breathing hard. His hand slid down her arm to clasp hers.

The searing look he gave her would have made a lesser woman blush. Nicole met his gaze, unflinching. She tossed him a hot look of her own and wet her lips with her tongue. His golden-brown eyes darkened.

"Come with me, Nicole," he urged in a tone that vibrated through her, stirring her senses. The pleading undertone added to the attraction.

This was her moment of truth. Was she going to scurry back to her room like a mouse or follow her desire? Her former nemesis took a step backward. She didn't pull her hand away. Jaxson turned and started walking. Nicole followed. They went past her room to the next. He opened the door and drew her inside.

Jaxson pushed the door closed behind her and pulled her into his arms. His mouth came down on hers with an urgency that had her legs trembling. She framed his face in her hands, her mouth busy with his. Then she teased his chest with her fingers beneath his soft casual shirt until he helped her pull it over his head and off. She stared. Jaxson obviously spent time in the gym. She liked his trim, well-sculpted body. He groaned as she threw her arms around his waist and pressed her mouth to his chest.

His fingers slid down her dress to curve around her butt and squeeze. *Yes!* They dropped lower to slip beneath the edge of her dress and caress her bare thighs. Fire consumed her when his fingers slipped beneath her lacy silk thong panties to caress her intimately. She moved against his warm fingers, imagining what it would be like to have all of Jaxson.

Fingers on the edges of her thong, he hesitated. Her eyes popped open. She glanced up to meet his fevered look with her own. "Sure you want to do this?" he rasped.

With a daring look, Nicole pushed her wet flesh against his questing fingers. "Can't you tell?"

In answer, he swirled his fingers in her moist heat. Then he slid the wet garment over her hips until it fell in a thin heap at her feet. *Yes!* Her fingers fumbled as she undid the button on his pants and pulled down the zipper. His pants and boxer briefs quickly followed. She helped him get them off. As she straightened, his sizeable, nut-brown member nearly hit her in the face. Nicole wet her lips. "Jaxson," she murmured approvingly, "this keeps getting better and better!"

When she started to drop to her knees, he caught her shoulders in a gentle hold. "I can't wait for that! I want to be inside you so bad I can taste it!"

"You can do that, too," she sighed, pushing her dress down and stepping out of it. Bending, Jaxson gathered her dress and the silk thong and playfully tossed them aside. They sailed across the room. She stood butt naked in front of him. He stared for a few blazing hot moments, obviously enjoying the view. The entire surface of her skin tingled as surely as if he'd physically caressed her. Then he grabbed her caveman style and carried her to his bed.

They tumbled onto the sheets in a frantic huddle of need and desire. Touching, kissing, biting, and caressing, they rolled together. He lingered lavishly between her thighs, and she insisted on returning the favor until Jaxson grabbed a foil package from the drawer beside the bed and opened it. She slid the condom onto his beautiful member. When he buried himself deep inside her, they both moaned in pleasure. Then Jaxson began to move in an earth-shattering rhythm that she struggled to match. Higher, harder, faster, until they clenched together at the peak and tumbled back to earth. Jaxson kissed her lips as they lay catching their breath.

He smoothed the damp hair away from her face. "Nicole, you are incredible. I've never met anyone like you. I've never had anyone like you. I want more. We could shower, start fresh, and take our time. Are you down for it?"

Something in his simple words touched her. She'd had sex before, but not like this. The second time they made love, Jaxson had spent a lot of time lavishing loving attention on every inch of her body and making her feel special. She'd clearly been more than another woman in his bed. It intrigued her that being with Jaxson was the closest she'd ever come to what her friends described as making love. She touched her lips to his. "Yes, I want to spend more time with you."

Later, Nicole awakened to Jaxson's hands caressing her breasts. He dropped a kiss on her navel. The man had stamina! "Are you working up to another round?" she asked incredulously.

"No," he said chuckling softly, "I just can't keep my hands off you. I could eat you up!"

"I like what you do to me," she said, her mind clouded with memories of him. "I was on the menu," she reminded him with a sensual giggle. He'd lingered between her thighs with a fevered intensity she would never forget.

"Oh yeah," he acknowledged, "and I hate that I'll probably never get a chance to be with you again."

"So, what are we doing?" she asked, something inside her hoping to be surprised by his answer.

"We're enjoying a special moment outside of our normal lives, where we stand on opposite sides."

"Does it have to be that way?" she asked, knowing that she sounded naive.

"If you can figure out a way for us to try this out for more than a few stolen hours, please let me in on the secret," he huffed. "I'm not giving up on my business or my life, and I'm willing to bet that you feel the same way."

"Do you even like me?" she asked in a slightly brittle tone. Inside, a small voice echoed her words, harkening back to her thoughts of being one of the unlovable Zaynes.

Jaxson drew her closer and surprised her with a kiss to her temple. "I like you plenty, Nicole, and not just because we've just had some of the best sex of my life. I love the way you kiss, the way you taste, and the way you smell. You're gorgeous, intelligent, sexy, and good backup when trouble comes calling, but you're not on my team. We don't have the same goals or aspirations. You're living your life to improve the bottom line for Lady Zayne Cosmetics."

"I wouldn't go that far," she said, objecting to his assessment of her life.

"We've only got another couple of hours until we're back in New York. Let's enjoy this time together," he urged.

"And when we get back to New York?"

"When we get back to New York, we'll go our separate ways."

Inexplicably, the words made her a little sad. She'd actually found someone who really seemed to like her, wasn't after her money, was great in bed, yet she couldn't explore anything with him because he was a serious business rival?

Fortunately, Jaxson with his magic hands was a great distractor. They stayed in his bed until the plane was about to make its final descent. Nicole slipped on her dress. She couldn't find her bikini panties, even though Jaxson helped her search for them.

"I'll find them and send them to you," he offered.

This was a first for Nicole. She didn't go around leaving her panties in different places. In fact, she was always in control of her encounters, except for the time when she'd been part of a blackmail scheme. She tried to shrug it off. "Just throw them away."

He nodded. After one last lingering kiss, she headed back to her room.

CHAPTER EIGHT

The plane landed smoothly at Liberty Airport in Newark, New Jersey. Showered and dressed, with her makeup perfect, Nicole made her way to the exit. Her bodyguard was there waiting for her. He looked infinitely more rested. She knew that the prospect of facing her family was enough to keep the wary glint in his eyes.

Her bodyguard held onto her arm, steadying her as she walked down the air-stairs to the ground. Cameras flashed, accenting the waning sunlight. She wondered what time it was, since she'd been on the plane for roughly twelve hours and there was a five-hour time difference between Cape Pacifica and New York. Nicole noticed trucks from some television stations parked nearby. Inwardly she shrank. She didn't want to make a statement and didn't want to talk to reporters. She'd been incredibly stupid and was lucky enough to have survived. She saw no need to revel in it.

By the time she reached the bottom of the steps, three people had completed the walk across the tarmac and were waiting for her. Warm wind tugged at the clothing of her two brothers and her mother. Apparently, they'd left their partners and babies at home. She smiled, knowing that the wind would make it difficult for anyone to catch or record anything they said.

Her youngest brother, Ben, pulled her into a tight bear hug. "Nik! You really had us worried!"

"I wasn't sure I was going to make it out of that one,

either!" she muttered.

"So glad you're home safe!" Ben kissed her cheek, then released her.

Hugo, her oldest brother, hugged her next. "I'm just so happy you made it back. Welcome home, Nicole. When you're ready to talk about it, I'm here for you."

Her chest tightened. She'd had to tell her story three times to the authorities on Cape Pacifica, plus sign a statement. It would be a long haul before she could relegate the experience to the recesses of her mind.

"Or we can agree to leave what happened on the island on the island," he said, apparently picking up on her apprehension.

She nodded, her eyes suddenly burning with the threat of tears. She wasn't a woman who cried a lot.

Hugo glanced down at her face and apologized. "I'm sorry, Nik. You're back home safe, and that's what counts," he added. "Whatever threats you faced are in the past now." He rubbed her shoulder and kissed her temple. "You do know that there's nothing you can't tell me and Ben?"

"Yes." Nicole stepped out of the circle of his arms to face her glamorous mother. Dressed to the nines in a filmy green silk designer dress with her blond hair coifed and cut into a wispy style that played on her Nordic looks, Pamela Zayne was scolding Liam. "My only daughter could have been killed! I've never seen or heard of such gross incompetence in a bodyguard. I won't tolerate this! You will never work for this family again."

Liam's face looked impassive, but she noticed the hard set of his jaw and a muscle working at his temple.

Nicole inserted herself in the conversation. "Mother, Liam works for me. He's the best bodyguard I've ever had, and I'm not going to give him up."

Her mother simply stared at her, her eyes taking in

the airy cotton sundress Nicole had donned and her flawless makeup and hair. When her mother failed to follow up with a caustic comment, Nicole looked harder. She saw that two tears were sliding down her mother's face and threatening to ruin her perfect makeup.

Nicole felt confused. She'd assumed that her mother was here with her brothers because it was what the world expected, and it was also an opportunity to put Lady Zayne Cosmetics in a limelight that would shine all over the world. In all her years, she'd only seen her mother cry twice. "Mother?"

Pamela Zayne reached out to draw Nicole into an unexpectedly emotional embrace. She felt her mother's body shaking with sobs. She felt the wetness where their faces touched.

"When I heard you'd been kidnapped, I didn't know what to do," her mother confessed. "I was afraid that we'd lost you forever and that I'd never get a chance to make things right between us."

Numb with shock, Nicole didn't know how to react. She hugged her mother back and patted her shoulder awkwardly. Her mother was not a sentimental person, and sentimental emotional displays were not her forte. So, who was the woman hugging her and crying? After all the well-documented fights with Hugo and his fiancée and Ben and his wife, had her mother finally lost it?

"I'm glad you're back safe. I want to spend more time with you. We can't let past mistakes keep us from getting closer. We're going to talk later," her mother promised. Pamela Zayne fished in her designer bag and found a tissue. She mopped her face delicately, careful not to further spoil her makeup. She gave Nicole a final squeeze, then released her.

As the Lady Zayne Cosmetics Public Affairs Director stepped to the impromptu podium set up on the tarmac and began to speak, Hugo took his mother's arm and led her to the waiting car. Ben closed in to sling an arm around Nicole. "What's up with Mother?" she asked.

"I think she was afraid she'd lost you," Ben said, "You're the only one she hasn't been fighting with."

"I'm the only one who doesn't have a baby, and I'm not married or slated to get married," Nicole said.

Ben squeezed her shoulder. "You'll get there."

Will I? She'd been infatuated a time or two, but Nicole had never met anyone she could remotely consider marrying. Despite what she'd witnessed with her brothers finding life partners, she suspected that she would never find anyone who would love her for herself and not for her family's money and powerful connections.

The men she met without money were jockeying to get hers. The men she met with money were usually as messed up as she was and unable to love anyone but themselves. Their love light wasn't big enough to shine on her. *Maybe love isn't for everyone...*

Sensing movement behind her, Nicole turned to see Jaxson Forest exiting the plane with his bodyguards. Tall, handsome, sexy, and formidably intelligent, the sight of him sent echoes of their time together reverberating through her body. She wanted a lot more of Jaxson Forest. Her gaze locked on him and she couldn't tear it away.

She saw Ben's questioning gaze bounce back and forth between her and Jaxson as the other man approached. Then Ben released her and went to thank Jaxson for helping her escape and for bringing her home to New York on his plane. The men shook hands.

"It was the least I could do," Jaxson said, his eyes on Nicole. "It was frightening and at times it seemed like we weren't going to make it. We had to work together to escape. Thank God we pulled it off and discovered that when the chips are down, we make a great team."

"Yes, we do." Nicole added in agreement.

"Well, I'm eternally grateful to you for bringing my sister home," Ben said. "Is there anything we can do to thank you?"

Jaxson grinned. "Maybe you can put in a good word for me the next time Nicole and I squabble over the rights to a new rare plant, compound, or process..."

"Or maybe you could let him have whatever it is?" Ben said to Nicole.

"No, I can't do that," she said resolutely.

Jaxson chuckled. Then his communications director came over and informed him that the press wanted a statement. With the Lady Zayne Cosmetics press secretary concluding her remarks at the podium, Ben and Nicole made a quick exit. Watching Jaxson speak from the podium and talk to the press as they drove away in the limo, she saw a woman run up to the podium and interrupt the session to throw her arms around Jaxson. Nicole decided that she would watch it on the news when she got home.

At her condo, she dismissed Liam and relaxed in the pleasure of being in her own luxurious space alone. When her curiosity got the better of her, she turned to the news. There were separate shots of her and Jackson descending the air stairs, with a running commentary about the leaked story of their kidnapping and rescue. She saw the video of her family welcoming her back on the tarmac.

When they got to Jaxson's interaction with the press, she learned that the woman who ran up to hug Jaxson was his sister, Charlotte. Jaxson's parents, Dr. Jack Forest and his wife, Camilla, came next with a heartfelt reunion with their son. Watching their touching reunion, Nicole wondered what kind of relationship Jaxson had with his family. It looked like it was much more peaceful than hers...

Her reunion with her family had looked somewhat the same, but who could know how startling it had been for her to see her mother cry over her? Was it any wonder that she couldn't imagine for herself the unexpected love and devotion she saw between her brothers and the women they'd chosen?

After a long, luxurious bath, she donned a silk negligée and climbed into bed. As her eyes closed and she drifted off to sleep, she felt Jaxson's big hands and hot mouth on her body, heard him murmuring softly to her in the dark.

CHAPTER NINE

Despite his ordeal and the long flight back to New York, Jaxson's family insisted on following him back to his place. They'd almost lost him, and they wanted to spend enough time in his presence to reassure themselves that he was all right. His mother and sister kept hugging him. His mother's eyes were shiny with tears. His dad held him in a bear hug for a long moment. This time the usual handshake and clap on the shoulder was not enough.

"You really had us worried," his dad said.

"I'll try to be more careful," Jaxson promised.

"You'd better," his dad countered. "We're getting too old for this kind of excitement. Your mother cried a lot, and neither of us could think about anything else. We expect you to be around to put flowers on our graves!"

Jaxson shook his head. "Dad, don't talk like that! I said I'd be more careful."

With a weighted sigh, his father squeezed his shoulder and released him.

He was tired because he hadn't rested. Especially since he'd spent most of the flight in bed with Nicole Zayne. What a wonderland that had been. He glanced at his sister. Charli and others would label what happened between him and Nicole as "cliche." After all, Nicole was the beautiful, blue-eyed, blond princess of the Zayne clan, and he was the dark knight from a rival family.

He'd wanted her on a primitive level since they'd been stuck in the corridors of the fortress, and she'd slept with her body close to his, unconsciously clinging to him and grinding that fine ass against him. After they'd escaped their captors and he'd made it clear he wanted her, she'd made every inch of her lush body available, and he couldn't get enough. When her eyes weren't clouded with desire, they'd held an unchecked look of wonder.

Jaxson stretched against the back seat of his limousine. He wasn't a womanizer. He didn't spend a lot of time on women, either. His dick had never gotten a workout like that, and Nicole had showered it with loving attention. It twitched at the thought of more. *Down boy, it's not going to happen.*

"You're different. What happened out there?" His sister's voice broke in on his thoughts.

"You mean other than being beaten, drugged, trussed like a Christmas turkey, and having to escape with no food and little water?"

She took his hand and massaged it between her own. "Jax, I know it was an ordeal. Don't you want to talk about it? Get it all out, so you can forget about it?"

He shook his head. "I won't be forgetting any of it anytime soon, Charli, and I don't really want to talk about it."

His little sister took his arm and rested her head on his shoulder. Her natural curls tickled his chin. "Then you'd better figure out what you're going to say when the press comes calling again. You and that Zayne chick have been the big news for the last couple of days. If the media is going to hound you, you need to figure out how you can get something out of it."

"I got the plants I wanted. Not all of them. Some were burned and went down with the helicopter," he said, wanting to change focus of their conversation. "They got greedy and there was a change in plans. They weren't able to load everything on the helicopter the guy who master-minded our kidnapping tried to escape on."

"That means you paid millions more for what you got!" Charli remarked. "I saw the bank transfer notice."

"The plants are very rare. I'm pretty sure we can find a way to cultivate them in the lab, maybe even synthesize the most important ingredients. They will save a lot of lives."

"Yes," Charli said with a sigh, "but will people be able to afford the treatment, seeing as you had to spend so much money on the plants?"

Jax gave his sister an affectionate look. "You know that I and Foreststone Pharmaceuticals have more than enough money to meet our needs. I'm more concerned with saving lives and giving people more time with their loved ones."

Charli put her arm around him and snuggled closer. "That's what I love about you, Jax. You will always be one of the good guys."

Will I? Jaxson wondered. He struggled with the bounds and constrictions of money, society, business, and how it impacted the availability of his life-saving treatments for the haves and have nots. His parents had been wealthy, but he'd surpassed them with his fascination with chemicals, compounds, and biology. His company was not a charity, but he had a foundation that helped make his company's products available to those who could not afford them.

* * *

After a few days of pampering at her favorite spa and spending rare time with her brothers, her sister-in-law, Mira; Hugo's fiancée, Ava; and her baby nephews, Nicole went back into the office. Her assistant, Casey, surprised her with a heartfelt hug.

"I was so worried that someone would muck things up and you would be gone forever!" Casey confessed with tears in her eyes. As if she'd suddenly realized the inappropriateness of her action, she quickly released Nicole and put some space between them.

Nicole swallowed, her eyes burning. Her family members made similar statements, but they hadn't penetrated the hard shell of numbness she'd felt inside. The unexpected emotion in Casey's words had gone deep. She drew in a shaky breath.

Concern filled Casey's gray eyes. "Are you all right?"

"Yes." Nicole managed a smile. "I just need a minute."

"Oh, of course!" Casey backed a few steps toward the door. "I left your appointment book on your desk, and there's an electronic copy online. I'll be at my desk if you need me."

Nicole nodded in response, but as soon as the door to her office clicked shut, she had a meltdown. The fact that she rarely cried didn't stop the tears. Box of tissues in hand, she mopped her face, filled a wastebasket, and blubbered like a baby. *What's wrong with me?*

Nearly five minutes had gone by when her brother Ben invaded her office. "Hey, Nik," he said, "you've been through an ordeal. I didn't expect to see you in the office so soon. You probably should have waited a little longer before you returned to work." Enfolding her in a bear hug, he let her cry on his blue silk suit. He drew a folded piece of flowery–looking paper from his pocket and pressed it into her hand. "Mira's been after me to give you the name of counselor she knows.

"I don't need a counselor."

"Says the woman who almost never cries. The hell you don't. You need to talk to someone, especially if you can't or won't talk to us."

Nicole released another flood of tears. "Did Casey call you?" she asked curiously as she patted her damp face with a tissue.

"No, I was passing by on my way to grab something to eat before the meeting and saw her hovering outside your door. Clearly, she didn't know what to do."

"What's the meeting?" Niclole lifted her head. She was determined to get hold of herself.

"The quarterly board meeting," Ben answered, his tone even.

She spared a glance for the open appointment book on her desk.

"I'm on my way to grab some breakfast before the meeting starts. You've got twenty minutes if you're going," Ben said helpfully.

Nicole straightened. "I'm going."

Ben flashed a half smile and pressed a kiss to her temple. "Good. I'll see you there. If it gets to be too much, no one will think any less of you if you decide to take off."

One of her hands formed a fist. She didn't plan on leaving the board meeting until it ended, period. "Thanks, Ben," she said as he released her and headed for the door.

Once the door closed behind Ben, she snagged her purse and used a mirror to assess the damage. Her eyes and nose looked pink and swollen, her face puffy. In the private bath connected to her office she splashed cold water on her face. Then she accessed the makeup bag she kept at the office and got to work.

With time to spare, she sat at her desk with her eyes closed until she felt more like herself. Minutes later, she left her office. She stopped to give a few quick, reassuring words to her assistant. Then, padfolio holding both her laptop and a notebook, she hurried down the hall and got on the elevator.

The twenty-fifth floor conference room was nearly full when she arrived. She met her mother's serene gaze, wishing she could match it. They exchanged polite greetings. There was no trace of the emotional woman who had embraced her and cried on the airport tarmac. Nicole greeted her brothers and several uncles, aunts, and cousins. Hugo enfolded her into an affectionate bear hug and welcomed her back. Quite a few of the others embraced her and told her how glad they were that she'd survived her ordeal.

Nicole held on to the nugget of calm control she'd found in her office and kept her tears at bay. Her Uncle Colton called the meeting to order and made a point of welcoming her back into the fold. The room filled with enthusiastic applause. She nodded and thanked everyone. Then the meeting started. Nicole scanned the agenda, making notes on questions she had and information she needed to provide. Her anxiety gradually eased as she fell back into her normal routine. Fortunately, she was not on the agenda. Neither was her disastrous attempt to secure the Poule plant for the company.

In a change to the agenda, house counsel reported a pending class action lawsuit over problems resulting from use of the company's innovative, age-defying formula, Lady Zayne Age Reversal Formula G. Nicole perched on the edge of her seat. This was one of her babies and one she and Jaxson Forest had both managed to reap miraculous benefits from.

She'd been present and involved with the study volunteers and the company scientists who had performed intricate tests on human cells to verify the safety of the product. They'd held off introducing the product until everything checked out. Because it did not contain color additives, its sale did not have to be approved by the FDA, but with complaints and an impending lawsuit it would be subject to regulation.

"Do you have more specifics on the nature of the complaints against our product?" Nicole asked.

The house counsel, one of her second cousins, peered down at her though a thick pair of designer frames. "I don't have all the details yet, but there are reports of a possible connection to kidney damage."

Wtf? Nicole bit down on her lip. She didn't believe that for an instant, and she'd dare anyone to prove that their product harmed anyone. Her voice rang out clear and strong. "I move that we form a team to investigate possible allegations against Lady Zayne Age Reversal Formula G and any basis for a class action suit. I also move that I head that team."

Hugo spoke from the other side of the conference table. "I second both Nicole's motions."

"Any discussion?" Ben, acting head of the board, asked, glancing around the room. When no one spoke, he said, "All in favor?"

There was a unanimous show of hands.

"The motion passes."

The rest of the meeting was a blur Nicole felt free to ignore. The agenda and the secretary's notes would be available if she missed anything important. With her laptop open, Nicole began to search through the complaints against Lady Zayne Cosmetics. There were a number, but most were grumblings about cost, product shades, fragrances, and targeted customers. The meeting ended before she could get through them all.

At the end of the meeting, both her brothers approached her. "I knew you wouldn't be able to help yourself when it came to defending the age reversal product," Hugo said with a grin.

"We know you fought hard to get the product in our mix and even found the manufacturer of the critical ingredient," Ben added.

"Would you like to go to lunch?" Hugo suggested.

Their mother's cultured voice interrupted the conversation. "Could you make it another time? I was hoping that Nicole and I could have a girl's lunch."

They all turned to see Mama Zayne standing behind them in an expensive silk print dress, sans the usual aura of power she cultivated. "Of course, Mother." Hugo patted Nicole's shoulder. "Let's plan on later this week."

"See you later," Ben murmured, following his brother out of the room.

"Do you mind?" her mother asked. "I want to spend more time with you, and we've got to start somewhere."

"No, I don't mind." Nicole smiled politely. She didn't know what was up with her mother, but this new version beat the negative, critical, strategic thinker Nicole knew, especially the one who rarely focused on her children in a positive way.

"I thought we'd go to Retanelli's," her mother said.

Nicole's brows went up. "Retanelli's? I didn't think they were open for lunch."

Her mother smiled, looking incredibly like a version of Ben and Hugo's babies without the chubby cheeks. "I called in a favor. Everything should be ready by the time we get there."

Nicole pushed back her chair and stood up. "Let's go."

CHAPTER TEN

Nicole returned from lunch with both a full stomach and a headache. The food had been excellent, but she didn't know how to react to the way her mother was acting. Most of all, she didn't trust her mother to continue to be the person she appeared to be. Pamela Zayne had been pleasant, supportive, and encouraging.

With no apparent knowledge of Mira's request that Nicole see a shrink, her mother had discreetly placed a business card on the table and suggested that Nicole talk to someone in an effort to put her traumatic experience firmly in the past. The woman named on the card was one of the best-known psychiatrists in the world, who authored books and frequently appeared on television.

Fingers grazing her forehead, Nicole spared a glance for the stack of papers in her inbox. There was more in the online company version. *Maybe I should have stayed home a little longer.* She was searching for a pain pill in her bottom drawer when her desk phone buzzed.

She lifted the receiver. "Nicole Zayne."

"Uh Nicole," her assistant, Casey, stammered, "I meant to tell you that your three o'clock canceled. Sorry."

The screen saver on the desktop showed two-fifteen. Nicole touched a key on her computer and her schedule appeared on the screen. "Barlow Labs?"

"Yes," Casey said, "They said that they'd decided to go in another direction. I've heard some rumors of a pending deal with Foreststone Pharmaceuticals. Maybe they're true."

Nicole growled in frustration. While she'd been pampering herself and recovering at home, Jaxson Forest had been buying what she considered a promising, but distant second possibility for what could be done with the Poule plant. Should she have bought the medium-sized company when she had the chance? She couldn't buy every company with a promising product.

"Nicole?" Casey's voice interrupted her thoughts.

"Yes?"

"I was asking if there was anything you wanted me to do. I know you had other options on the table."

Nicole lifted a gold pen from the canister on her desk and fiddled with it. "None of the options are as good as Barlow, but I want you to get Sterris-Hite in for a meeting by the end of the week. Tell them we're interested in a joint venture."

"I'm on it," Casey said. "I'll get back to you when it's done."

Ending the call, Nicole got up and paced her office. The need to get away, to just lay down and rest, pulled at her. Just as strong, the need to show her family that she was just as good or better than many of the family members running Lady Zayne Beauty kept her in the building like a mouse in a maze. She couldn't help herself.

On the third lap around her office, she reclaimed her ergonomic leather chair and got a notepad from a drawer. The *Mission: Impossible* theme song played in the back of her mind as she began to write names on her pad. She could do this.

***

Jaxson

In spite of his best efforts, Jaxson's toned body slammed down to the padded floor once more. His years of training ensured that he was not hurt. His trainer, an eighth-degree black belt who ran a well-respected karate school, gazed down at him, waiting to see what he would do next.

Jaxson hated to lose at anything. He glanced at the clock on the wall of his private gym. He barely had enough time to shower, dress, and get to the office in time for his early meeting with in house counsel. Apparently sensing that Jaxson was done for the day, his Sensei offered him a hand up. He took it.

His Sensei gave him a brief bow. "Not bad. You need to move a little quicker and remember the new maneuver I showed you. You are distracted."

Jaxson nodded. His focus had been off since the kidnapping. "More meditation?" he murmured under his breath. He knew his family, if they suspected something was wrong, would insist he talk to a psychologist.

"Whatever it takes," his trainer replied. His expression was inscrutable, but Jaxson felt as if the man could somehow sense that he had lost something on the African island and was struggling to cope with the fallout.

"I will see you on Wednesday," his trainer said, then quickly disappeared.

Jaxson gave himself a mental shake and headed for the shower.

Seated at his desk at Foreststone Pharmaceuticals forty-five minutes later, he opened the thick file in the center of his desk. Inside was draft of the paperwork for the purchase of Barlow Labs. He scanned all of the pages, a smile on his face. He had high hopes for the company he'd acquired, especially since his efforts to get the Poule plant had fallen short of his goals. The plant was rare, but more plants could surface in the future. He was not prepared to risk as much to acquire them.

He tilted his chair back and rocked a little. His thoughts touched on Nicole Zayne. He imagined that she was having a disappointing day. It hadn't brought him any pleasure to cancel the Barlow Labs appointment with her, but what would have been the point? That company was his now, and their promising formula would be used as an alternative to the one they were developing with the Poule plant.

Nicole was a worthy competitor, but he'd beaten her to the prize this time. The rich scent of the Arabica coffee in his mug heightened his senses. He savored his victory with a rare shot of cognac in his premium roast coffee.

Before he could finish his coffee, someone knocked on his office door with an annoying amount of energy. The possibilities were limited, since his secretary stopped all outsiders. The only people aside from her and his assistant with access to his door were his family. His gaze swerved to his desk drawer and confirmed that he'd replaced the bottle of cognac and closed the drawer. Jaxson straightened in his chair. "Come in," he called.

The door opened and his executive assistant, Marcus, stood in the entryway along with Forestone's corporate attorney, Blake Cochran. "Sorry to bother you, boss, but I thought you'd want to hear this right away."

"Come in and take a seat," Jaxson said.

Marcus and Blake stepped in and closed the door. "There's a pending class action lawsuit that involves some of our products," Blake said.

Jaxson swiftly moved his chair out of recline mode. His feet met the floor. "Which products?"

"All the ones containing DSEG."

DSEG was shorthand for a product that was used to bind and heighten the effectiveness of other ingredients in their formulations. Mentally, Jaxson ticked off all the products involved. It was a hell of a list. "That's nearly two-thirds of what we offer."

"Exactly," Marcus confirmed, "and it's a naturally occurring compound whose properties haven't been altered in any way."

Jaxson considered his assistant's words for a moment. "You do know that many naturally occurring compounds have trace amounts of harmful elements, though. We tested the crap out each of the ingredients in the final formulations."

Marcus's head bobbed up and down in agreement. "Since we're ahead of the curve, I thought you might want me to get a team together to check all the facts, see where this is coming from, and make sure it doesn't bite us in the ass."

Jaxson's fingers closed on the edge of his desk. "You're right. We're forming a team to address this issue. You and Blake are on the team, but I'm heading it. Your first task is to figure out who's masterminding this thing."

"I'm already on it," Blake assured him.

Marcus, I want you to draft a list of all the companies that may be affected," Jaxson said, drumming his fingers on his desk. "I'm assuming that we'll be one of the big fish they go after, but there may be others. We need to get going on this, so the sooner we form our team the better." He glanced at his assistant and corporate attorney and began naming people to be contacted. He named the head of the product testing teams, the company public relations director, and a clerk to keep things documented and orderly. Blake and Marcus left the office, anxious to get things started.

Chin resting on his palm, Jaxson sat staring off into space. In his head, he mentally checked off the companies that used DSEG. It didn't take long for him to get to Lady Zayne. Should he let Nicole Zayne in on the coming avalanche? An automatic *no* came to mind, but if this thing became a harsh reality, he might not have a choice.

It didn't help that at the back of his mind he still remembered the intoxicating scent of her skin, could still feel the silky glide of her body against his and hear her throaty cries of satisfaction. Too bad she was on the wrong side of the mix. Was he really going to let a good time in bed sway his opinion of a dedicated rival? Although to be fair, she'd also been great as an escape partner. She'd more than held up her end.

Leaning forward, he lifted his heated cup for another long sip of his concoction. *Think with the right head, Jax!*

***

Nicole

Instead of sleeping in, since it wasn't one of the days her bodyguard worked her self-defense skills, Nicole got up early to work out in her gym.

Nicole scoured all her notes and information on Sterris-Hite prior to the meeting. She even knew the company's estimated value on the market. She also brainstormed with Lady Zayne's research and development director for ideas of what could be done to maximize the value of a Sterris-Hite purchase if their product could not be made to perform as needed for Lady Zayne Cosmetics. She'd already determined that purchasing the formula and trying to improve it with her company's laboratory talent was not a good idea due to already committed company resources, knowledge base deficiencies, and the required learning curve. With the help of one of the guys in the investigative firm her brother Ben recommended, she discovered that one of the targeted company owners was going through a personal crisis and was hard up for cash. The revelation eased her anxiety. Jaxson Forest already had the number one alternative to the Poule plant. Surely, he wouldn't waste his time beating her to number two.

For the meeting, she wore her pink power suit. She loved the color, and she'd discovered that it was great for getting people to underestimate her. For a big part of her life, she'd been viewed as just a pretty face waiting for an advantageous marriage, until she'd shown her family that she was more than a match for most of her relatives involved in the family business.

Ready to get things done, she arrived a few minutes early

with Casey and Drew, the corporate attorney assigned to her, and made sure they were ready for any contingency. When the Sterris-Hite team arrived, everyone was cordial. Nicole sat through their proposed joint venture discussion, then made a generous offer to buy them out. Surprised, they took a recess to discuss. She fully expected them to take a few days. They surprised her by accepting her offer, contingent on the continued employment of their people. She readily agreed, and they signed the paperwork declaring their intent that Drew had prepared in advance.

Nicole was going over her notes from the meeting with Sterris-Hite when she saw the text from Ava, Hugo's fiancée: *I'm on my way.* It took a moment to remember that she'd agreed to have dinner with Ava at Ariana's restaurant to help Ava with the guest list and other family-related questions for her wedding.

CHAPTER ELEVEN

Calling for Liam and the limousine, Nicole packed up her things and headed out. Thirty minutes later, she and Liam stepped out of the limousine at the restaurant on the Upper East Side. Ava was waiting for her in a private room in the back.

"I hope you don't mind meeting here," Ava said as they settled down and started looking at the menu.

"No, this is good," Nicole assured her. "I've been too occupied with work since I got back. It feels kind of nice to be out among people."

Ava flashed that brilliant smile again. "Good! I already took the liberty of ordering champagne for both of us."

Puzzled, Nicole looked up from her menu. "What are we celebrating?"

"We're celebrating you!" Ava said. "I'm so happy that you made it off that island in one piece."

"Me too," Nicole huffed, "but we don't need to celebrate."

Ava put down her menu and gathered Nicole into her arms. "We don't have to talk about it," she said in a low tone, "but I want you to know that you were truly missed. Besides Hunter and Hugo, you're my favorite member of the family."

Nicole smiled at Ava's warmth in speaking about Hugo and their son. Ava had been through the wringer with the Zaynes. Hugo had kept Ava dangling for years. Nicole's mother had often been cruel once she realized that Ava was in love with her son and Hugo had feelings for Ava. Nicole had suspected long ago that if any of her siblings married, Hugo would marry Ava. She just didn't expect it would take so long to happen. Thank goodness they had found each other again, and that Hugo discovered Ava had given birth to his son, Hunter.

The waiter brought the champagne then. Nicole saw that it was her favorite Dom Pérignon. Nicole glanced at Ava in surprise. She knew that the fiercely independent Ava, prior to her engagement to Hugo, had been struggling with her finances because of the costs of maintaining her mansion in St. Thomas.

Ava laughed as the waiter made a production out of opening the bottle and pouring the golden liquid into the delicate champagne flutes. "Don't worry, I can afford it. Besides, Hugo and I are already one in almost every sense of the word," she murmured, "and we both want the best for you."

Nicole gave her an appreciative look. "Thank you." The waiter offered the first glass to Ava, but she pointed to Nicole. With a nod, Nicole accepted the glass and took a small sip. "It's good."

After giving Ava her champagne, the waiter made himself scarce. Ava lifted her glass, her gaze meeting Nicole's. "To your return and a future filled with everything you desire!"

"Oh, yeah!" Nicole said, clicking her glass against Ava's and taking a deeper sip of the sparkling champagne. Tiny bubbles sizzled against her tongue as the fruity liquid with hints of vanilla cream exploded in her mouth. "I love this stuff!"

The waiter returned briefly with a couple of small plates and a charcuterie board filled with meat, cheese, and fruit, and an assortment of bread and crackers. Ava assured him that they weren't ready to order yet.

Setting her glass down, Ava put ham, beef, cheese, olives, and a small sprig of grapes on her plate. "I'm a little hungry because I skipped lunch," she explained, "but I'm trying to keep my weight down for the wedding and the honeymoon."

"Hugo wouldn't care." Nicole spoke for her brother in a confident tone.

"I'd care," Ava replied. "I've got the perfect dress, and I've lived for this wedding. I don't want to look at the pictures and wish I'd done anything differently."

With a smile, Nicole held her tongue. Ava's body sported generous curves. Although she would never be slender, she was everything Hugo wanted. Nicole knew that Hugo was all in because Ava and her mother wanted the big wedding, but he'd have been just as happy with a simple ceremony in a church with immediate family members only.

"Ava?" a familiar masculine voice called from the entrance to their dining room. "I thought that was you. It's been a long time! How are you doing?"

Oh, hell no! The world just isn't that small! Nicole craned her neck, hoping to get a glimpse of the visitor. The uniquely curved entrance to the room hid the male who'd spoken.

"Oh, I'm so happy to see you!" Ava jumped up from the table and ran to the entrance. "Your timing is on point!"

Nicole could hear the lowered buzz of their conversation from just outside the room. She told herself she was being paranoid. When she could stand it no longer, she got up and went to the entrance to peek out.

Ava and Jaxson Forest were releasing each other from a friendly hug. "I know you've heard that I'm getting married," Ava said, straightening.

Jaxson held on to her hand, giving it a congratulatory shake. "He finally realized what a good thing he had with you, huh?"

Ava smiled and nodded. "Yes, but it wasn't easy. I almost lost everything."

"You deserve every bit of happiness that comes your way,"

Jaxson said, his observant brown eyes catching sight of Nicole lingering in the doorway.

Something sizzled in those golden-brown eyes. Nicole felt the weight of his gaze like a physical touch. Her thoughts slid back to a sensual time filled with soft sighs, gentle caresses, and vigorous sex. She gave herself a mental slap. "Hello Jaxson, how are you?"

Thanking him, Ava's gaze followed the direction of Jaxson's. She spotted Nicole and gestured toward her. "Nicole and I are having dinner."

Jaxson gulped audibly and his head dipped. The look he gave Nicole let her know that she'd been seen in every sense of the word. "Hello. It hasn't been that long since I saw you, but it feels like an age. How are you doing, Nicole?"

Because it felt more comfortable to face him from a distance, Nicole forced herself to approach Jaxson. She stopped a couple of feet away from him. "Things are different since I got back, but I'm okay." The minute sizzle in his eyes let her know that he agreed about things being different. "And how are you?"

"I've been better," he said, surprising her with his honesty, "but I'm working on it."

"If you figure out something that brings everything back to normal, let me in on the secret," she said, realizing that she'd given him more of a hint about her pain than she'd intended. She knew what he could do to help her feel better.

In her peripheral vision, Nicole saw Ava's glance bouncing back and forth between her and Jaxson. She looked puzzled.

Nicole shifted on her feet. She was puzzled, too. Despite her anger and fury at Jaxson's business tactics, something drew her to him. She wanted to get in his face but didn't know what she would do when she got there. Somehow, she managed to hold her ground. "I'm sure you'll work your way through it," she said.

"I wouldn't have it any other way," he said with a confident note that Nicole envied. She was still at odds with what happened on the island.

Ava smiled at Jaxson. "Would you like to join us, or were you meeting someone?"

"I wasn't meeting anyone, but I wouldn't want to intrude."

"You wouldn't be intruding. If anything, you might be a little bored. We were going to go over the guest list for my wedding."

Jaxson threw Ava an affectionate look. "Am I on the list?"

"Of course you are!" Ava laughed, adding, "Especially since you and Nicole made that grand escape from that island."

The interchange between them hit Nicole like a slap in the face. She was going to have to put up with Jaxson Forest at her brother's wedding, too? "We're *still* business rivals." Nicole's mouth snapped shut at the sharpness in her tone.

Ava's golden-brown eyes widened. "Oh, Nicole, I'm so sorry. I just assumed that since you and Jaxson worked together to escape, you also buried the hatchet."

"Temporarily," Jaxson and Nicole said at the same time.

Jaxson centered his gaze on Nicole. She couldn't have moved if she wanted to. Her heart fluttered in excitement. "I certainly wouldn't want to make you uncomfortable," he said.

Was she being narrow-minded and petty? And why should she care? Nicole darted a glance at Ava, who seemed to be at a temporary loss for words. She liked Ava and knew she'd gone through a lot to get Hugo to realize he loved her, and to get their dragon of a mother to back off. Should she have just kept her mouth shut? "It's Ava's wedding," Nicole reasoned out loud, "and you're obviously one of her good friends. I can certainly agree to put our differences aside for one more day."

"I can do that, too," Jaxson said. What surprised Nicole

was that something in the depths of those brown eyes told her that it would not be easy.

Ava stepped closer to Nicole, her face a study in conflict. "Are you sure?"

Mentally bracing herself, Nicole nodded. She could do this. She *would* do this.

"Whew!" Ava exclaimed in relief. She turned to Jaxson. "I guess I shouldn't push that one-day truce you and Nicole agreed to. Maybe you and I can have lunch or dinner some other time."

"That sounds fine." Jaxson lifted an eyebrow. "But Hugo won't mind?"

Ava laughed. "Of course not. He's not the jealous type. You'll be seeing him again soon."

"I'll call you." Jaxson stepped closer to press a kiss on Ava's cheek. "And I'll be looking for my invitation."

The glow of happiness surrounded Ava once more as she said, "They're going out in a couple of weeks. It was good to see you."

"Good to see you too, Ava." Jaxson gave Nicole a polite nod. Then he turned and walked away.

Ava darted more looks of intrigue toward Nicole as they returned to their private dining room. "Do you want to talk about it?" she finally asked.

Nicole's "No" echoed in the room. "I'll tolerate Jaxson Forest for the sake of a smooth and harmonious wedding, but I don't want to talk about him."

"Okay." Ava opened a folder and drew out her list. "I need you to go over this and tell me if I missed anyone. I also need to know if there are people who shouldn't be on the list."

"*Now* you ask me?!" Nicole cracked.

Ava laughed.

"Did you want to give Mother an opportunity to view the list?" Nicole asked.

Ava twisted her lips. "It's *my* wedding. Hugo says I can have whatever and whoever I want. Your mother already gave me the list of who she wants to invite, and it's incorporated with mine. I've also made my wedding planner available so your mother can provide her thoughts and suggestions, but I'm not going to fight with her or stress about meeting her requirements."

Nicole nodded. "Smart move."

***

Nicole decided to leave work at lunchtime the next day. She planned to shop for a wedding gift for Hugo and Ava after getting some lunch, but after hours of looking and not liking anything, she called Mira and asked for the name of the shrink her sister-in-law had recommended.

CHAPTER TWELVE

With big, serious gray eyes that oozed sympathy and a manner that invited confidence, Dr. Minerva Walters sported a tawny colored pixie cut reminiscent of Kris Jenner's. The doctor had dismissed her receptionist and had been preparing to leave herself when she'd gotten a call from Mira about Nicole's visit.

After asking Nicole a few questions, she suggested they have a formal session. The doctor ushered Nicole to a comfortable leather couch in a room decorated in gray and blue.

Nicole took a seat on the dark blue leather couch. When her head reached the cushioned back, her eyes closed. She felt weird, tired, confused, sad, and numb, all at once.

Dr. Walters's voice prompted her from the other side of her lids. "This is a safe space. Anything you say remains here, unless you decide otherwise. You can talk about anything that's on your mind, but I think you need to talk about what happened on the island."

Eyes still closed, Nicole's fingers went to her forehead, massaging the ache that wasn't quite an ache. For several beats, the room was silent. Then Nicole began to talk. She explained her drive to succeed, her need to prove to her family and herself that she was just as good or better than the other family members involved in the business. She talked about her arrival at the meeting place on the island and how she'd gotten the group's leader to agree to let her keep one of her bodyguards.

When she talked about losing the bid for the Poule plants and then being ambushed and drugged as she attempted to leave, her eyes stung with the threat of tears. Then she described waking in the dark, tied and gagged, and how she'd managed to free herself and her co-captive. By that point her tears began to fall. By the time she reached the part where the helicopter crashed in a hail of bullets with the head kidnapper and most of the plants, her face was wet.

Dr. Walters pressed a wad of tissues into her hands. "I sense there's more," she said in an encouraging tone.

Mopping her face with some of the tissues, Nicole nodded. "I haven't been myself since. I feel like I'm isolated and alone, even when I'm in a room full of people."

"Do you live alone?" the doctor asked.

"Yes, I have a condo. I can't take the intrigue and drama that comes with staying at the family mansion. I have my own life."

"But after your traumatic experience, you probably need the comfort of family and home. Perhaps there's a family member you could stay with?"

Nicole thought for a moment and shook her head. "One brother recently reconciled with his wife after nearly getting divorced, and the other is getting married soon. Both are deeply in love and have babies, and it's a sensitive time for all of them. I'd be the third wheel, the third pimple on a donkey butt." She neglected to add that she didn't relish the thought of seeing up close and personal just what she was missing in the romance department. Her brothers, both of whom had vowed never to add more children to the family empire, had each fallen like a ton of bricks. Even Ben, who could be fickle, now spent a lot of time making sure Mira was happy.

"What about cousins, aunts, or uncles?"

"We're not that close, and they're too competitive, anyway. I-I can't show them any signs of weakness. Do you have another suggestion?"

"After something like this it's always good to pamper yourself, do the things you like. Perhaps you could spend time with your mother?"

Nicole laughed. "You don't know my mother!"

The doctor's gray eyes were sympathetic. "People can change, and we all deserve second chances. She might surprise you. At least think about it."

"I will," Nicole said.

"Do you feel a little better than you did when you came in?"

"Yes." Nicole breathed out with a heavy sigh. "I needed to talk about it without being judged."

"This is a judgement-free zone," Dr. Walters agreed. "Are you ready to tell me the rest?"

Nicole speared her with a look. "What makes you think there's more?"

"I've been at this awhile, so I'd say from your manner of speaking, the glimmer in your eyes when you talk about the island, and a shadow in your voice, you're holding back something you need to discuss."

Nicole tossed her used tissues into the trash can by the sofa. "Not today."

"You're safe. There's nothing you can't discuss here," the doctor reminded her.

"Next time." Intent on escaping, Nicole reached for her purse.

Dr. Walters opened her tablet, and her fingers flew across the keys. "Tomorrow? I have an opening at noon."

"I need at least a day," Nicole confessed.

"The day after tomorrow, then? Noon?"

The fact that Dr. Walters was probably offering up her

lunch hour wasn't lost on Nicole. Still, she hesitated. Did she really want to talk about Jaxson Forest and what happened between them? What she'd done wasn't her norm and despite their business rivalry, she hadn't been able to let it go. "Okay," she finally agreed.

Dr. Walters smiled encouragingly. "It gets better, Nicole. I promise."

Nicole stared at her for several beats, wanting to believe that. She wanted to be happy in and with herself once more and suspected that it would take more than a couple of visits to a shrink. "See you the day after tomorrow," she said. Then she got up from the couch and headed for the door. Liam was waiting for her outside the office.

***

After his meeting with the psychiatrist his sister Charli had wheedled and begged him to see, Jaxson had to admit that the load of stress and worry that he usually carried around felt lighter. As a result, he'd spent a week at his parents' home, and their love, companionship, and caring had taken the edge off the numbness and the secret guilt he harbored for endangering himself so recklessly. Now he felt more like his old self and ready to immerse himself in his business. He hoped the feeling would last but couldn't bring himself to be that optimistic.

Jaxson arrived on time for his meeting at the Corrigan Health and Beauty Offices. Several of the other corporate presidents and VPs were already seated in the conference room. This first meeting would set the tone and the processes for the meetings to follow for their industry group. The difference was that the next series of meetings would be attended by their staff members.

Outside the room, as the clerk signed Jaxson in and gave him a badge, he saw Nicole Zayne seated near the end of the large conference table. His gut clenched at the sight of her in a deep red power suit. Her hair was swept up in blond wisps around her face, her wide blue eyes mesmerizing as she pursed pouting, candy-red coated lips. She was getting her share of attention and seemed totally unaware.

Finding his nameplate, he set his laptop on the table and made his way around the room greeting those he knew and introducing himself to others. Speaking Nicole's name politely, Jaxson nodded when she looked up from her laptop. Hypnotic blue eyes hit him with the impact of an electric charge. The alluring tones in her voice drew his attention away from the business at hand. "Mr. Forest, good morning."

He returned the greeting, then forced his gaze away. He didn't consider himself to be a player, but he was an equal opportunity date, and he'd had his share of beautiful women. What made Nicole Zayne so special? Whatever it was, he hadn't been able to get her off his mind. As he stepped away, the president of a health and beauty company asked her a question.

Jaxson took his seat closer to the middle of the table, edging his nameplate closer to his water glass. The president of a competing pharmaceutical company seated next to him greeted him pleasantly, introduced himself, and shook Jaxson's hand. "There's a lot of money on the meter in this room," the man remarked, "and they need to get started soon. I don't like anyone wasting my time."

Jaxson agreed. Sometimes, he could feel Nicole Zayne's gaze boring a hole through the side of his face. Reminding himself that he was here for business purposes only, he opened his laptop and got into the proper software. It took everything he had not to look back at her.

Clint Bowers, the president of Corrigan Health and Beauty, came in shortly afterward and began the meeting as the acting president of the newly forming group. A quick vote among the attendees confirmed his status. An assistant summarized what had happened to date. Then, an investigative member of the staff informed them that a man named Julius Carmichael was behind the class action lawsuit. His wife died of cancer, and because she'd used products containing DSEG for a number of years before developing the disease, he was convinced that DSEG was the culprit.

"Why zero in on DSEG, when there are so many more obvious substances for causing cancer?" someone asked.

"That would be something only Mr. Carmichael could answer," the investigator replied. "However, he has been able to obtain a qualified drug injury attorney and have his lawsuit certified in a California court. In essence, you're all being sued for pharmaceutical fraud. Carmichael's lawyers have just begun putting out their calls for other plaintiffs to come forward and join the suit."

"How do we know this isn't just a lot of noise?" someone in the back of the conference room asked in a loud voice.

"We don't," Clinton Bowers answered, "but that doesn't mean we shouldn't band together and do everything we can to make sure we don't all end up paying millions or even billions."

One of the few women in the room, Nicole Zayne's sweet, sultry voice cut through rough yet restrained male voices. "It might help to educate the public about DSEG and what it does and does not do."

Heads turned, all eyes focusing and lingering on the curvy blonde. She was industry royalty and well worth looking at. Taking a much-needed sip of the water provided, Jaxson noted that she held her ground. "Gentlemen," she said with a nod. This resulted in a mixed chorus of "Morning," "Ms. Zayne," and "Hello." Then she repeated her statement.

Many in the meeting, including Jaxson, agreed with her words. Educating the public could only help their cause.

"Perhaps we could meet with Mr. Carmichael?" another

leader suggested.

"I wouldn't recommend it," the investigator said, looking uncomfortable. "It could easily be construed as an attempt to coerce him to drop the lawsuit."

"I suggest that we make this group a formal entity, funded by all, and charged with the task of educating the public about DSEG," Jaxson said.

Representatives of a few of the smaller companies grumbled that paying into the industry group was not fair to them since the lawsuit would most likely go after the largest companies to get the biggest payout. Their objections eased when another leader suggested that all support to the entity to be formed be based on market share and sales.

Then someone expressed the opinion that the entity should be a resource repository for all the information each company had on DSEG, to be shared by all. By the time the meeting ended they added another goal: to set up a customer service line to answer the public's questions on DSEG.

As they prepared to end the meeting, Milton Conrad, a friend of Jaxson's who had been peppering him with questions about the kidnapping, remarked, "Since Jaxson Forest and Nicole Zayne were kidnapped, their names have remained in the spotlight. They're both part of this group. I think the two of them should represent this group in the ads to educate the public."

Jaxson's mouth opened and closed in surprise. He didn't think that suggestion would go over too well with Nicole. Before he could come up with an appropriate response, several other voices chimed in in agreement. Clinton Bowers asked if he would be willing to represent the industry group in a few ads to educate the public about DSEG.

"Of course," Jaxson said. "Anything I can do to get this issue resolved." His pulse sped up at the prospect of spending more time with Nicole, but he suspected she would find a reason to say no.

The attention in the room shifted to Nicole. Bowers said, "How about you, Nicole? Would you be willing to represent us in a few industry ads to educate the public about DSEG?"

Shoulders stiff, back straight, Nicole gazed back at the group with exaggerated calm. "I'll do what I can, but I need to check my schedule first."

"The production team we hire will be required to work around you and Jaxson's schedules. We're simply asking for a commitment from you."

She hesitated momentarily then nodded. "I'll do it."

Echoes of approval accompanied her words.

Bowers thanked Nicole and Jaxson and then promised that a packet of the proposed structure, bylaws, and standard operating procedures would be mailed to each member of the group within the next few days for legal department review and comments.

As Jaxson reached the exit, he turned to look back at Nicole. She was surrounded by a group of people. She looked in his direction at that moment and her challenging gaze met his. He was playing with fire, and he knew it, but damned if he didn't like watching Nicole light up a room. He already knew she wasn't a woman who was easily forgotten. Lifting an eyebrow, she turned away from him to talk to someone else.

CHAPTER THIRTEEN

Nicole left the meeting a little shaken but covered it with bravado. Was she going to be seeing Jaxson Forest everywhere? She was glad about her upcoming appointment with Dr. Walters. She needed it after sitting in a room with Jaxson Forest for hours. She could feel his presence, even when she couldn't actually see him. No one else had mattered. *Will it always be like this? Why was I dumb enough to climb into bed with that man?*

Nicole drove herself and Liam across town to Dr. Walters's office. She went through the registration process with the receptionist who was now present. When Dr. Walters came to call her back, Liam followed. After a brief hello to Dr. Walters and a sharp glance around the office, he ducked back into the waiting room.

Dr. Walters greeted her, her big gray eyes not missing a thing. "You seem a little tense. Do you want to talk about it?"

Nicole told her about her meeting with the industry group and seeing Jaxson there.

"It upsets you to see Jaxson Forest."

"Yes, and lately he seems to be everywhere I go!" With anyone else, Nicole would have mediated the strong negative energy in her tone.

"Why does he upset you?"

"We're business rivals," Nicole said in a calmer tone.

Dr. Walters leaned toward her. "But that's not the problem, is it?"

"No."

Dr. Walters waited patiently until Nicole told her that she'd been intimate with Jaxson on his company plane.

"You're both adults," Dr. Walters observed. "Do you want more of Jaxson Forest?"

"I-I don't know." Nicole's teeth hit her bottom lip as her back reached the rear cushion of the sofa. "I want to get in his face and make him see me for who I really am. He makes me feel confrontational, and yet I know that if he kissed me, I'd melt like butter."

"Is there a reason you can't explore this with him?"

"Yes!" Nicole's incredulous gaze zeroed in on Dr. Walters's calm face. "We're business rivals who've made our relationship personal. He also made a point of telling me that all bets were off once we returned to New York. Then there's the fact that he's from a different world, he's been in the gossip columns and society pages with several women, and it was just sex with the nearest body for him. He doesn't really like me."

"Did he tell you that, or is that your assessment of his feelings?"

Nicole thought for a minute. She'd used the words with him offhand, but had he said them? "No, he didn't actually say that."

"Then maybe you could give it a shot?"

"No." Nicole shook her head. "No, he's got to come to me, and I want him on his knees!"

"Then how will you handle your...frustration?"

Nicole's head snapped up at the question. "You think he's got me sexually frustrated?"

Dr. Walters allowed herself a small smile. "What do you think?"

Nicole's hands went to her face, covering her nose and mouth. *How can I be so clueless?* "You may be right. I-I think I've been out of touch with my feelings. If it's only about sexual frustration, I have a number of options that don't include him."

"I'm glad I was able to bring that to your attention." Dr. Walters's smile widened. "Is there anything else you'd like to talk about?"

"Yes. I still don't feel like myself. I'm not comfortable in my world or with all the things I did before. I push myself and get things done, but I feel numb and alone. I'm an outsider."

"Spending more time with your brothers didn't help?"

Nicole's head dipped. "I actually felt more alone. Maybe I'm selfish, but seeing their circles of love just made me see everything I've missed."

"What about your mother? I remember reading about problems at the company when your father died, but it seems like she's managed to make a success of her life."

"Huh!" Nicole swallowed a snarky comment. "You don't know my mother."

"No, I don't," Dr. Walters said calmly, "Tell me about your mother."

"My mother is power hungry, manipulative, vindictive, and controlling. She's not a warm person, or someone you could discuss your feelings with. We were raised by nannies and the household staff. We have always been more like chess pieces in her game than her children."

Dr. Walters brows lifted. "She didn't welcome you back from your ordeal with open arms?"

Nicole paused, remembering her mother's emotional reaction to her return and the caring she'd been displaying ever since. "Actually, she was pretty emotional, and she's been trying to connect with me, but I don't trust this sudden change."

Dr. Walters smiled. "Maybe she really does want a closer relationship with you. Maybe there are parts of her that you don't know."

"I know all I need to know," Nicole assured her, "but just to settle any possible doubts, I'm going to see what she has to say."

Dr. Walters gave her an encouraging smile. "You might be surprised."

"Oh, I would be." Nicole laughed.

Dr. Walters's gaze covered Nicole's face. "Do you feel better than you did when you came in?"

"Yes. You've given me some things to think about."

"It's going to get better," Dr. Stone promised.

"I'm counting on it," Nicole said, rising from the sofa. "Same time next week?"

"See you then," Dr. Stone replied.

***

Nicole was in her office at headquarters, finishing some paperwork, when her mother strolled in, dressed in one of the latest Valentino fashions. She gave Nicole her no-nonsense look. "I've tried to give you some space to work through getting over your ordeal and get back to your life, but now I'm thinking that you need more."

She gazed at her mother in confusion. "Excuse me? I-I don't know..."

"We're going to lunch at the house where we can talk. I had Chef Oliver prepare a special meal."

"Lunch is fine," Nicole said with a nod, "but I don't know what you mean about getting over my ordeal or my needing more."

Pamela Zayne's cool blue eyes assessed her. "I think you know exactly what I mean. My focus hasn't always centered on you, but don't think I haven't kept track of you and the things going on in your life. I don't want to fight with you, Nicole. I just want to do better as your mother."

"You don't think it's a bit late?" Nicole asked, biting her tongue as an afterthought. It was foolish to taunt the dragon, but she'd often felt that she would have been better off as an orphan.

A hint of regret softened Pamela Zayne's tough demeanor. "I'm simply asking for a chance to connect with you. I may not always have been the mother you needed, but I'm the only one you have."

In response, Nicole simply bobbed her head and bent to retrieve her purse from her bottom desk drawer. Then she pushed back her chair and stood. As they walked toward the exit together, it struck her, as it always did, that her tough, beautiful mother looked more like her sister.

Nicole discovered that her mother had cleared both their schedules for the day. The drive to the mansion was uneventful. As the driver helped them out of the car, Nicole stood and stared at the place where she'd spent so much of her life. When she moved to her own place, it had felt like an escape from a prison. Now, she was able to look at the Tribeca brick and glass structure with a sentiment that bordered on grudging affection. It had been her home and was a part of who she was.

Inside, they took the elevator to the second floor. As soon as the door opened on the marble tiled great room, they stepped onto a Persian area rug.

The scents of butter, chicken, bacon, and onion assailed her senses. Nicole's stomach rumbled in response. Yes, she was hungry after all. The intimate breakfast room was surrounded by a lush garden on the other side of the glass wall. A white tablecloth and the best silver and glassware graced the table. Feeling somewhat like a guest in her childhood home, she went to freshen up for lunch. When she returned, her mother was already seated, sipping a glass of white wine.

Taking her seat, Nicole lifted the glass of wine next to her place setting and took a sip. The crisp, fruity taste of her favorite Riesling exploded on her tongue.

"Good?" her mother asked, her expression indicating that she knew the answer.

"Excellent," Nicole replied, taking another small sip.

Pamela lifted her glass for a toast. "To family!"

Echoing the words, Nicole touched her glass to her mother's.

"How does it feel to be back in the house?" her mother asked. "I know you weren't very happy when you moved into your condo."

That was an understatement. When she'd left home, Nicole had been upset by her mother's controlling ways and the lack of privacy despite the home's multiple floors. "I can acknowledge that there were good times and bad times here," Nicole said. "Despite our Thanksgiving dinners, it feels a little weird and...uncomfortable, but there's so much here from my childhood that tugs at my memories."

Her mother set her glass down. "I hope you understand that you were young and you needed to be protected, whether you wanted it or not."

"I do." Nicole took another sip of wine.

Pamela leaned forward to make her point. "If you were here now, things would be entirely different from before."

Nicole's eyes widened. Did her mother know about her sessions with Dr. Walters? The thought of having to drop the person who had been a Godsend since she got back from her ordeal made Nicole's head pound. She caught herself. The doctor was bound by law and ethics not to discuss her case without permission. "What makes you think I want to come home?" she asked.

Pamela let out a small sigh. "I've been seeing a psychiatrist and working on myself ever since I messed up with Ben and Mira. Ava avoids me, and I'm not allowed to see Hunter without Hugo or Ava present. I don't want to lose any of my children. Maybe I don't love you the way you think I should, but I do love you, Nicole."

Nicole noticed that her mother's eyes were shiny. She was uncomfortable with this uncharacteristic display of sentiment from her mother. A blend of sympathy and guilt assailed her, making her feel as if she should do something. But her mother wasn't the sort of person you freely hugged when feeling emotional. She was rarely in a vulnerable emotional state. "We're all adults now, Mother, so does it really matter?"

"It matters to me." Pamela's voice sounded hoarse. "I can't change the past, but I can do better in the future."

Nicole reached for her water and took several sips. "What do you need me to do, Mother?"

"Just give me a chance. Lunch or dinner once a week?"

Nicole suppressed a frown. That was a lot of expected face time, coming from a woman who hadn't spent a lot of time with her through the years.

Pamela's sharp eyes didn't miss a thing. "Just until we establish a better relationship."

Nicole felt pressured but didn't see a graceful way out. She reasoned that with her schedule, some of the proposed lunches or dinners wouldn't be possible. "Okay."

"Thank you." Pamela's voice rang with relief. The chef chose that moment to enter the breakfast room with steaming bowls of chicken consommé with root vegetables, black truffles, foie gras, mushrooms, and puff pastry. It was Pamela's favorite soup.

Chef Oliver placed the bowls of soup in front of them, and waited while they tasted it.

"Mmm, delicious as always!" her mother declared.

Nicole tasted hers. She hadn't had this French soup in a long time. The different flavors danced across her tongue. "It's really good!"

With a pleased nod, the chef went off to finish preparing their second course.

Pamela finished her soup first. "I guess I was very hungry," she murmured, setting down her spoon. She was silent for several beats, but Nicole could see by the way her mother fidgeted in her seat that she had something else on her mind.

"What is it, Mother?" Nicole asked, finishing her soup and placing her spoon on the tablecloth.

"You've been different since you came back from that island. My counselor tells me that it can take time to get over an ordeal like the one you had, but I want to make sure you're okay."

"I'm okay," Nicole said, meeting her mother's gaze. The words felt like a lie on her tongue, but she really couldn't point to a specific problem. She simply felt like a stranger in someone else's life.

"You're okay, but not as good as before?"

Nicole shook her head.

Her mother's facial expression softened. "Can we talk about it?"

"No." The word came without conscious thought.

With a little sigh, her mother fiddled with the stem of her wineglass. "No judgement or censure here, but I hate that you were held against your will. My imagination has been quite vivid about what you must have gone through."

Nicole closed her eyes, opened them, and blinked twice. "I

fought and got hit when I realized that they weren't going to let me go, and they...they drugged me, but I wasn't assaulted in any other way. That's all I'm going to say. You were there when they checked me out at the hospital."

"Yes, I was there," her mother said, her expression a mixture of concern and relief. "I gave you my counselor's recommendation for someone to talk to and I've heard that Mira recommended someone too. You are talking to someone?"

Nicole shot her mother a direct look. "Yes. You didn't know already?"

"No, I've been trying to respect your privacy as much as I can."

"I like the sound of that," Nicole said. She glanced up and saw Chef Oliver with their second course. He set plates of hot, enticing food in front of them. Nicole recognized *fricassée de lotte,* another of her mother's favorites. The concoction of monkfish, shrimp dumplings, marble potatoes, pickled onions, and button mushrooms smelled heavenly and looked like something out of a magazine. It was one of Chef Oliver's specialties.

Again, he waited until they'd tasted their food and pronounced it delicious. Then he took their soup bowls and disappeared into the kitchen to perfect the third and last course of their meal.

Tired of wondering what was next on her mother's agenda, Nicole asked, "Can we just enjoy the rest of our lunch?"

Pamela Zayne managed to smile. "Of course."

***

CHAPTER FOURTEEN

Jaxson finished his lunch and made the obligatory small talk with his staff and their vendor. As everyone prepared to leave to return to work, he chose to stay and pay the bill.

He should have felt a bit odd, sitting at the large table alone, but he was glad the lunch was over, and everyone left happy. Giving the bill a quick scan, he gave the waiter his company credit card. That was when he saw her. In one of the booths sat Nicole Zayne across from a man he didn't recognize. Her companion was the ardent, lover-boy looking type in a gray suit with a pink shirt.

The man leaned forward, clasping her hands in his. Long blond hair dusted his nape as he bent to kiss her hand. Jaxson noted a Tom Cruise-like nose and thin lips. This was the French playboy who had been chasing Nicole in several newspaper photos. Jaxson reached for a name. It sounded something like "Idiot," and that was precisely what he thought of the fool.

Jaxson shifted his gaze to Nicole. She was a beautiful woman. She'd brushed her short blond hair away from her face and done something to make her blue eyes look enormous. He stared. Her blue and black dress lovingly caressed what he could see of her curves. Yes, Nicole Zayne was always worth looking at.

When the waiter returned with Jaxson's card and receipt, he decided to order another drink and watch the show. Sipping a glass of cognac, he gradually realized that instead of fascination, Nicole's expression seemed more a mix of boredom and determination. Lover boy appeared to be oblivious.

Observing all from his vantage point, Jaxson told himself that he wasn't jealous. As time wore on and he felt somewhat tense, he realized that he *was* jealous. He'd told Nicole that whatever happened between them would be done once they returned to New York, but his body wasn't having it. Watching them made him feel tense and combative, especially when lover boy tried to slide to the other side of the booth with her.

Nicole offered a comment and a steely smile that stopped the other man in his tracks. Then she picked at her salad. Jaxson couldn't help wanting to be next on her menu. She'd found him very appetizing on the plane.

He decided not to wait for his bill. Jaxson set his empty glass down and placed enough money on the table to cover his drink and a tip. It wasn't like him to sit at a restaurant and watch a woman who interested him interact with another man. He had to do something. He rose from the table and headed for the booth where Nicole sat. She looked up as he approached, eyes wide with the shock of seeing him. Jaxson inclined his head to the side, indicating that he wanted to speak with her privately. Then he passed her table and kept walking through the still busy restaurant until he reached the empty coat check area between the men and women's restrooms.

It wasn't long before he saw her, bag swinging on her shoulder as she headed his way at a brisk clip that he interpreted as anger-fueled. It was all he could do to suppress a grin. He loved messing with Nicole.

She stopped a foot away from him, folding her arms in front of her body. "What are you doing here? Are you spying on me?"

"Actually, I had lunch with my staff and happened to see you with lover boy as I was paying the bill."

"Don't call him that! His name is Éliott." Nicole narrowed her eyes. "What do you want? Why are you even talking to me?"

"I think we made a mistake," he said.

"Which mistake are you referring to?" She lifted an eyebrow.

"The one where we said that everything would end when we got back to New York."

She shook her head. "As I recall, that was something *you* said. Are you admitting that you were wrong?"

Jaxson hesitated. He was rarely wrong about anything, but he needed to get Nicole Zayne out of his head. The best way to do that was to get her back into his bed until they grew tired of each other. "I was wrong when I said that everything would end when we got back."

He saw some of the stiffness in her shoulders ease, but something close to anger glinted in her eyes. "And?"

He realized that she wasn't going to make it easy for him. Jaxson straightened, glad for the miracle that no one was close enough to hear their conversation. "And I apologize. What we had was good, and I haven't been able to get you off my mind."

"I didn't like how that ended," she admitted, "and the more I think about it, the more I think that you made the right decision. It's over."

Jaxson barely held on to his disbelief. Nicole Zayne was turning him down? This was a first for him, and he didn't like the feeling. The women he dated were usually around as long as he wanted them. No woman had ever walked away from him. Glancing around to make sure they were virtually alone, he came to another decision. "Let me I show you something?" he said, extending a hand to Nicole.

There were elements of mistrust in her expression, but Nicole was no coward. Gazing back at him in confusion, she gave him her hand. In no time flat he drew her to the barely lit area behind the curtain that partially covered the empty coat check booth.

His mouth came down on hers in a hot, sensual exploration. The scent of her skin and the vanilla musk fragrance she wore filled his nostrils. Pouring all the pent-up emotion and need he'd been working to ignore since their time on the plane into his actions, he made love to her mouth with kisses that alternated between soft and stinging. His tongue dove into her mouth, sliding, teasing, and promising more. Clutching her soft body tightly to his hardened frame, he let his hands shape, mold, and caress every curve she possessed.

"Jaxson," she murmured between fevered kisses.

She undulated against him. Her hands moved restlessly on his chest. He felt little tremors shake her body as she leaned into his kisses and bit his lip and his tongue.

Standing in the semi-darkness, making out with Nicole under the imminent threat of being discovered, he loved the thrill and the opportunity, but realized that even if there was no chance of someone walking in on them, he was not the type of man to take Nicole Zayne against the wall in a restaurant. "Come with me," he whispered as his mouth slid down her neck.

Nicole froze. Abruptly, her soft hands pushed against his chest, putting more space between them. She looked discombobulated, as if he were the last person she expected to be kissing in the semi-darkness. "No, no!" She shook her head, taking a few steps backward. "I'm not doing this!"

Turning away, she glanced back at him with an oddly mixed expression he couldn't decipher. Fear? Need? Dislike? Maneuvering her way around the curtain, she briskly walked away.

Jaxson's body was hard with excitement and his emotions at a gallop. He took several deep breaths and calmed himself before drawing back the curtain. There was no one on the other side. He strolled to the entrance and left the restaurant. Outside, he climbed into the waiting company limousine.

His thoughts ran rampant on the ride back to the office. He didn't know what he'd been expecting, but somehow, he'd failed. It seemed that Nicole had made the decision to stay away from him. He could move on, or he could try to change her mind. Pride urged him to move on. Plenty of women would jump at the chance to be with him. Why was he stuck on the Lady Zayne cosmetic empire's princess?

***

Freshening up in the ladies' room, Nicole made it back to the table as soon as she could. She'd straightened her clothes, but her face was flushed, and her emotions were too close to the surface. Éliott studied her with evident concern and a barely hidden note of wounded pride. "I was afraid you'd left," he confessed.

"I wouldn't do that!" she said, taking his hands and giving them a squeeze in a silent apology. "It's just that my stomach isn't very happy with me today," she added.

"Sorry to hear you're not feeling well." He leaned forward. "We could stop at the Pierre instead of you heading back to work, and I could make you feel much better..."

"I'm really not up to it," she said, pointedly ignoring the disappointment in his eyes. "Can I get a raincheck?" After those hot, tantalizing moments in the coat room with Jaxson, there was only one annoyingly distracting man on her mind. She gazed back at Éliott and realized that there was no way he could make her forget about Jaxson Forest. Yes, he was handsome and charming, but those attributes were not enough to truly interest her. She couldn't even summon the desire to satisfy the needs Jaxson inspired with Éliott.

"Nicole, you run hot and cold on me. Today, more cold than usual, especially after your trip to the ladies' room." His eyes narrowed. "I think it will be a while before we do lunch again."

You've got that right! Nicole struggled to keep her facial expression neutral. "I apologize if you feel I've wasted your time," she said, palming her clutch and getting to her feet. "I thought you enjoyed sharing a meal with me."

"You led me to believe there would be more," he said, rising to stand beside her. "I was looking forward to being with you."

She was starting to get annoyed. Reining in her tone, she said, "I didn't plan on getting a stomach issue."

He flashed her a tight smile filled with disbelief. She was rapidly getting to the point where she didn't care. "Let me walk you to your car," he said.

Nicole was silent during their walk out of the restaurant. Her gaze swept the dining room. She didn't see Jaxson. *That's a good thing, isn't it?*

At the limousine, Éliott kissed her on both cheeks and placed a lingering kiss on her mouth. *"Au plaisir,"* he murmured in his sexiest tone.

"Until we meet again," she said, repeating his words in English. Éliott helped her into the car. He gave a little wave as her limo pulled off.

***

Coffee mug in hand, Jaxson sat at his desk reviewing the script for the informational sessions he would be taping with Nicole. He knew the studio would use teleprompters, but he'd learned that reading went smoother when he was familiar with the material. He took a long sip of coffee, careful not to get any on his print shirt or sable-colored suit with its cream silk pocket square. The company media advisor, Mary, tried to talk him into wearing blue, which always looked good on camera, but Jaxson insisted on this particular suit. As he set the mug down, one hand went to his breast pocket to fluff the beige silk hanky there.

Dressed in a berry-colored business suit with her thick

sandy hair pinned up in a conservative style, Charli burst into Jaxson's office just as he was preparing to leave for the videotaping session. "Are you sure I can't come with you today to watch the taping process?"

Jaxson shook his head, his hand making a downward motion. "This will be the first taping, and we'll need to get everything straight. Neither Nicole nor I have a lot of time to devote to this, so the sooner we get it over with, the better."

"I'll be quiet. You won't even know I'm there." Charli's voice held a pleading note.

He gazed at his little sister. A recent high school graduate, she'd already started college and was trying to navigate her way to a bigger role at Foreststone Pharmaceuticals. "Things are already tense between Nicole Zayne and me. I don't want to add you to the mix."

Charli tilted her head. "Tense? You two just escaped together from that island. What's there to be tense about?"

Jaxson smiled at her naivete. "We've been business rivals for some time."

Incredulity crept into her tone. "And you didn't bury the hatchet?"

"Only long enough to escape our kidnappers and get home." Jaxson pushed back his chair and stood. Clicking his briefcase shut, he lifted it from his desk. "If we have to do another taping, and I sincerely hope we don't, I'll let you come along."

"But Jax—" Charli began, abruptly stopping when Jaxson, ignoring her, kept on walking to the door. Outside, the driver held the limo door open for him and his bodyguard. As they took off for the studio, his hand dipped into his suit jacket pocket and came out with a balled-up bit of silk that closely matched his pocket square. He usually carried an extra handkerchief.

He held the soft material to his nose and inhaled its

aroma. It still held Nicole's exciting scent. He'd found her panties in one of his shoes. He hadn't followed through on his agreement to trash them but would eventually. Not normally a vindictive person, he wasn't above pushing her buttons, especially since she'd turned him down.

CHAPTER FIFTEEN

Jaxson and his bodyguard arrived at the studio a few minutes early. Several people walked past the car. A few entered the building. There was no sign of Nicole or her company's limousine. Once his bodyguard gave the okay, he exited the limousine, and they went through the revolving doors of the mirrored glass and steel skyscraper.

Building security eyed each entrant. People who worked in the building flashed their badges and kept on moving to the elevators. A thin, gray-haired woman with a narrow face and oversized red glasses sat behind an information desk in the middle of the lobby, verifying identities, directing traffic, and handing out elevator passes. Once she successfully identified Jaxson and his bodyguard, she gave them passes to the tenth floor to meet their studio contact person.

The elevator doors opened on the tenth floor to a lobby decorated with the faces from many of the studio's hit shows plastered on the walls. Jaxson was not a television fan, but he still recognized the famous faces of the stars of the popular soap opera, *There Will Always Be Tomorrow.*

A heavyset man with beady black eyes sat at a desk with a computer and phone in the center of the room. He eyed them curiously. A slender, attractive brunette in a form-fitting gray dress that matched her eyes smiled and came forward as they stepped off the elevator. "Mr. Forest?"

"Yes, and this is my bodyguard, Asher Sinclair," Jaxson said, guessing that she was an intern.

"I'm CiCi Ballinger, a studio assistant." She shook hands with both men, and they exchanged hellos. Jaxson could tell that his usually reserved bodyguard was quite taken with CiCi. Asher's eyes lit up and he smiled widely.

CiCi turned to Jaxson. "If you'll follow me, Mr. Forest, I'll take you to Studio D. Mr. Sinclair, you're welcome to come along and check things out, but once the taping begins, we prefer that you wait outside."

Asher agreed. Then they followed CiCi past the contemporary sofas and chairs, a few clusters of group working areas and offices, and doors marked Studio A, Studio B, and Studio C. Some people looked up to smile, some waved, but most kept on working. Finally, they arrived at Studio D. CiCi opened the door and ushered them inside.

Dressed in a prim and proper blue power suit, Nicole sat in a tall studio chair with her shapely legs dangling above the floor. The color made her blue eyes more electrifying and created a nice foil for her blond hair. The sight of her hit Jaxson like a punch to the gut. He didn't understand her effect on him. He'd been fighting Nicole on a business level for years and had always thought her attractive, but not enough to lose sleep over. Now, the only word he could use to describe her was gorgeous. His chest tightened.

Her red-coated mouth opened at the sight of him, then quickly closed. He thought he detected a hint of vulnerability, but when he looked again, her strong, unreachable persona was firmly in place. Her gaze locked with his and they both nodded and spoke politely. Then her eyes zeroed in on his cream silk pocket square and stayed for several beats. He fought the urge to laugh. *Wrong bit of silk, Nicole!*

While CiCi took Asher around Studio D, the man who had been talking to Nicole came and introduced himself as Connor, their producer and director for the shoot. Then he explained that the studio staff wanted to put a little makeup on him to ensure he looked his best during the taping. Jaxson agreed and was shown to a corner of the room with a makeup artist. There, a girl named Julia seated him in a comfortable leather chair, covered him with a black cape, and made quick work of applying makeup. When she finished and gave him a mirror to inspect her work, he was a bit relieved to see that although she'd accented his features, she'd done nothing too overt.

Returning to where Connor and Nicole were discussing the setup, Jaxson added his opinion. The proposed upholstered chair and loveseat setup was good. He thought it would be best if Nicole took the loveseat and he took the chair.

"Well, you two are in agreement." Connor's gaze bounced back and forth between them. He grinned. "But I'd like to try something a little more intimate. Let's start with both of you sitting on the loveseat. If it doesn't work, we can do the taping with one of you on the loveseat and the other in the chair. Can we try it my way?"

Damned if I'm going to make this harder than it needs to be. Jaxson walked to the loveseat. Nicole carefully scooted over to give him more room. Still, as he settled into place, their bodies touched. Something akin to an electric current shot through Jaxson, startling him. Had there actually been a spark? Maybe he'd been dragging his feet? He'd felt Nicole jump, too. "Excuse me," he said.

She didn't respond, but he felt her body stiffen where they touched, as she carefully wet her lips. He couldn't help feeling like a sixteen-year-old forced to sit next to his crush and behave under the beady eye of her father. He glanced at Connor, who looked pleased with himself.

"You two look less formal this way," Connor said, "and I can sense a chemistry that's going to draw in the audience and make them listen to everything you have to say."

Jaxson decided to give Connor something else to think about. "Where is my teleprompter?"

Connor pointed to a screen on the other side of the camera operator. "You'll be able to read it. Dusty isn't in position yet. Nicole's is to the right of yours. We're going to take a few minutes for you to practice looking and speaking naturally as you read from it. We may have to adjust the font sizes."

The camera operator moved into position. Jaxson squinted at his teleprompter screen. "I need the font to be at least two sizes bigger."

"Done." Conner signaled to a staff member, who got it done. "Nicole?"

She concentrated on her screen. "Mine is fine."

Connor stood in front of them, rubbing his hands together. "All right, then. Lights!"

At Conner's signal, Jaxson and Nicole were bathed in bright, hot light. "Let's do a practice run to see if we need to adjust anything," he said.

Nicole started off, introducing herself to the camera. Then Jaxson joined in. They stopped and started taping several times as the team adjusted the teleprompters, their positions, and the lights. A trickle of sweat ran down Jaxson's temple. To head off another round with the makeup artist, he reached into his jacket pocket for the handkerchief that should have been there. His fingers closed on silk, and he used it to lightly mop his face. Nicole's signature perfume and her scent filled his nostrils. Then he remembered.

Nicole stared hard. Her brows lifted in disbelief. Color flooded her face. With all the work they'd been doing on the informational spot, he'd completely forgotten about his plan to push Nicole's buttons. She made a strangled sound in her throat, her blue eyes shooting twin flames of fire at him.

Conner flashed Nicole a look of concern. "Nicole? Are you okay? Can I get you something?"

"Water!" she said in a strangled tone. "And I need a

minute."

"Of course." Conner hurried to a chilled bottle of water from one of the tables. He gave it to Nicole. Twisting off the top, she took a sip, her gaze still on Jaxson.

No one else seemed to have noticed that he'd mopped his face with a pair of silk panties. He wasn't laughing. His plan to push Nicole's buttons seemed childish now. "Where's the wastebasket?" he asked, ready to follow through on his promise to toss her underwear.

Nicole's eyes got even bigger. If they were lasers, he would be dead. She shook her head with a quick jerk, an almost pleading note seeping into her eyes. She didn't want him to toss her undies in the studio trash? Jaxson didn't know why she would care. He would be following through on his agreement. After all, he and Nicole were the only ones who knew the undies were hers. He stuffed the silky material back into his pocket.

"Wastebasket?" One of the studio assistants lifted a plastic basket.

"I'm good for now," Jaxson said, covering his actions, "but how about something to mop my face. I'm starting to sweat."

Julia, the makeup artist, ran over to examine his face. "Yes, you are." She held one hand beneath her brush to protect his suit while she lightly dusted his face with powder. "That should do it."

She glanced over at Nicole. "I think I'm good," Nicole said.

Stepping closer, Julia studied Nicole's face. "You're fine, but your face is a little flushed."

Nicole stood.

Jaxson studied her soft curvy body and her shapely legs. It took effort to stop his body from responding. He really needed to get Nicole Zayne off his mind.

"Excuse me," Nicole said. Her heels clicked as she briskly

walked to the door and ducked out.

Good idea. Trailing her out of the studio, he found the men's room he'd seen on the way in. He considered tossing the undies in the trash in the men's room, but the mischievous streak rose again, and he decided to mail them to Nicole. Then she could dispose of them any way she saw fit. When he came out, Nicole was nowhere to be seen. He hung around the hall for a few minutes, then went back into the studio. She wasn't there, either. Then the door opened and she returned, looking refreshed and prepared to finish the taping. He felt ready, too.

At the end of the day's work, Conner asked for time to review and edit the tapes and nailed down time on both their schedules for one last session. Nicole was first to leave with a slow but determined strut out of the studio with Liam, who'd been waiting outside. Jaxson didn't know what he'd been expecting, but his interaction with Nicole emphasized her decision to stay away from him.

Jaxson left the studio with his bodyguard. His wandering gaze took in several beautiful women who eyed him with interest. He smiled politely. They returned his smile, but he kept walking. He needed a bit more time to readjust his focus, but his decision was already made. *I'm done with Nicole Zayne.*

Lost in thought, Nicole sat in the back of the limousine. The sight of Jaxson Forest mopping his face with her panties had been a shock. She'd been angry and embarrassed, but beneath it all—although she'd die before admitting it—she'd also been turned on. Memories of their time together still filled her dreams. Did he have to be such an ass? Did he have to enjoy being her business rival so much? Jaxson was hot, handsome, and boy, did he know how to get her panties wet without half trying.

Panties! Nicole covered her nose and mouth with her fingers. *I should have retrieved my panties. What can he do with them?* Her mind composed a list of all the embarrassing ways he could use them. Post them on the internet? Put them up for auction? Show her brothers? She was being ridiculous. Still, her teeth worried her bottom lip. There'd been little opportunity to retrieve them without further embarrassment. *I'm going to have to let this go. We're the only ones who know that what he has is not a random piece of underwear.*

CHAPTER SIXTEEN

Nicole

Nicole mentally prepared herself for the next taping session. Nothing Jaxson did would upset or shake her. And why should it? They'd gotten together and now it was over. They'd both moved on.

Like the last time, she was first to arrive at the studio. The team sent her to hair and makeup to touch up what she already knew to be flawless. Julia, the makeup artist, applied a thick set of long eyelashes that she insisted would look better on camera. Nicole disagreed, but decided to let the results speak for themselves. The door opened, and Nicole heard Jaxson's voice. She also heard a soft, feminine voice and the clicking of a woman's heels on the studio floor. She tried to move her head to see who it was.

"No, I need you to hold still for a few moments more," Julia said. "I'm almost done."

Nicole kept still, but her senses were on high alert. Jaxson had brought another woman to the taping? Then again, she reasoned the voice she'd heard could have belonged to one of the studio assistants.

"Okay, all done. What do you think?" Julia held up a mirror for Nicole to check the results.

Nicole assessed her reflection in the mirror. "It looks better than I thought. Hopefully, I'll get used to wearing them."

"Oh, you will," Julia said with a little laugh. I thought they were a bit much when I first started wearing them. Now my lids don't look right without them."

Tilting the mirror so that she could see behind her, Nicole saw Jaxson in a custom gray-blue suit that complimented his tall athletic frame. To his right, she spotted a slender, but curvy woman in a navy suit. She was more of a girl, Nicole decided, and much too young to be with Jaxson. She also looked vaguely familiar. A wave of negative emotion hit her. Jealousy? Straightening her shoulders, she reminded herself that she really didn't care who Jaxson was with.

Julia unhooked the cape from the back. It took a few moments for Nicole to realize that Julia was waiting for her to return the mirror. She placed it in her hand. Before she could exit the chair, Jaxson was there with the girl, giving Julia a friendly hello and greeting Nicole more formally. She coolly played along.

Jaxson addressed both her and Julia with his hand on the younger woman's shoulder. "This is my sister, Charli. She's just started college, but she's been working part-time for Foreststone Pharmaceuticals for the last several years and she's looking to learn every aspect of the business."

Nicole assessed the younger woman with new eyes. Charli possessed a very pretty version of Jaxson's features. The hair piled up on her head should have made her look more mature. It didn't. She was clearly very young. Acute intelligence lit those brown eyes that were so like Jaxson's. Nicole felt as if she were being assessed too. "Hello, Charli. It's nice to meet you," Nicole said. Julia echoed her words.

"I've been looking forward to meeting you," Charli said, "especially since you and Jax went through that ordeal and managed to escape together."

Jax? Somehow the name suited him. "I was grateful for the clothes you had on the corporate jet. Mine were in bad shape by the time we boarded the plane, and there was no time or place to shop."

Charli laughed. "You're welcome. I keep a lot of clothes and makeup on the plane for me and my girlfriends. You look like you're just about the size of my friend Keisha."

Jaxson pointedly cleared his throat. Charli gave her brother a quick glance, then apologized for taking up studio time.

"No problem. I just need to let him have this chair so Julia can get to work on him." Nicole stood and got out of the way.

As Jaxson settled into the chair and Julia smoothed a cape into place, Charli asked Julia, "Can you make my brother look beautiful?"

Jaxson lifted an eyebrow while all three women laughed.

"Your brother has beautiful features," Julia answered, still smiling. "I simply accent the most important ones to show his handsome face on camera."

"Good answer," Jaxson said.

Nicole excused herself and headed to the area set up for the taping. Conner, the producer and director, was there. "Are you feeling better today?" he asked after they exchanged greetings.

Nicole set her purse down. "Yes, I'm fine. Thank you for asking."

"Good. Having Jaxson's sister here isn't going to interfere with the taping, is it?"

"No, I don't anticipate any problems," Nicole said. She took her place on the sofa.

"Any issues with today's script?"

"No, I got a chance to review it last night. I'm just counting on this being the last session."

"It should be. Most of the taping we did last time was good. I could tell when you started having some problems, though.

Remember, the camera sees everything."

Did it capture what Jaxson mopped his face with? Nicole gave Conner a sharp glance.

Conner shrugged. "If you start feeling ill, just stop the taping. That's all I'm asking."

Nicole shook her head. "I want this to be the last session. I'll do everything I can to make today a success."

"Understood. Excuse me." Conner stepped away to speak with the lighting tech.

Jaxson came to the set with Charli trailing close behind him. Nicole was ready for the accidental brushing of his body against hers. Last time he must have been dragging his feet because she got a little shock. He settled beside her on the love seat without contact. Nicole focused her attention on her teleprompter.

The session taping began and moved along smoothly. Nicole interacted with Jaxson, and they generated a smooth vibe as they went through the industry group's information. After an hour, they took a break. Nicole headed for the restroom.

Long ago she'd learned to refresh herself with catnaps and meditation. She was sitting on the sofa in the ladies lounge with her head resting on the back and her eyes closed when someone came in. She blanked out the sounds of them using the facilities and washing their hands. Heels clicked lightly on the tile floor as they approached her. Nicole opened her eyes to find Charli studying her.

"Are you okay?"

"Just a little tired," Nicole said, willing her to go away.

"Jax has been having trouble sleeping, too," Charli said.

So, Jax had been having trouble sleeping, too? What else did they have in common? Somehow, they'd never gotten a chance to really discuss how the kidnapping had changed their lives.

Did he have more than the scratches, gashes, and bruises she'd seen on his brown skin impacting his life?

Lifting her head from the back of the sofa, Nicole sat up and eyed Charli with new interest. Apparently, she had more to say.

"Are you and Jax fighting?" Charli asked on a soft note.

Nicole smiled. "We're business rivals."

Charli's head tilted as if she was trying to understand. "You two have got this weird vibe going, but I...I think he likes you."

"Does he?" Nicole considered the thought. You didn't have to like the people you had sex with. Sex was about getting and giving satisfaction. You could turn off the lights and what was left to specifically identify a person? Nicole rejected the thought. She'd know Jaxson in the dark, no question about it. But what did she really know about Jaxson Forest?

"Ah, I should get back," Charli said, turning abruptly. "See you in the studio."

Nicole noted that Charli hadn't answered her question. Did it matter? Did she even care? Deep inside, a part of her did. She'd always been one of the unlovable Zaynes. Some of the men she'd dated had been more for show than anything else. Of course, they'd mutually benefited. Others had wanted something, whether it was money, power, or influence. Somehow along the way, she'd convinced herself that this was how relationships were supposed to be...and then along came Jaxson Forest. The truth was that she wanted him to like her.

***

Back in the studio, Jaxson, Charli, and Conner sat talking. They glanced up as she returned, and Conner asked her if she was okay. She assured him that she was fine and ready to finish the taping.

The rest of the session went like clockwork. Afterward, Conner thanked Nicole and Jaxson. He promised to have a clean version of the sessions for them to watch before he labeled the final version. Nicole gave Charli one of her business cards with her private number scrawled on the back. "In case you need any of your business questions answered from the female perspective," she said.

Charli thanked Nicole and gave her a professional-looking card of her own. Underneath the Forestone Pharmaceuticals name and logo was her full name, Charlize Forest, and the title, "Business and Technical Development Intern." "It was nice meeting you, Nicole. Maybe we can have lunch sometime."

"I'd like that," Nicole said, aware that a lunch with Charli was unlikely, especially if Jaxson had anything to say about it.

They met their bodyguards outside the studio, and everyone went on their way.

***

In the back of the limousine with Charli, Jaxson saw Nicole climb behind the wheel of a pink Mustang with her bodyguard, Liam.

"Oooh, I like her car," Charli said.

"You want a pink Mustang for your birthday?" Jaxson asked.

Charli looked thoughtful. "Let me think about it. Maybe I should ask Nicole for a ride to see how it feels."

Jaxson couldn't help the growl that escaped his throat.

Charli looked at him. "She said you were business rivals. Being rivals means you're not on the same team, but you don't have to hate each other. Don't you like her?"

"It's complicated," Jaxson said, his voice still more gravelly than he liked. Charli's knowing little giggle didn't help. He and Nicole had done a good job of playing nice. Since one of his deputy directors was now attending the industry meetings and the taping for the industry informational spots was done, he would not see Nicole again until Ava's wedding.

CHAPTER SEVENTEEN

Jaxson

He could have trudged down to the Bio Lab, but he preferred the privacy of his office. Jaxson tugged at the knot of his tie, loosening it. He'd already removed his jacket due to the tropical-like warmth in the room. A mixture of relief and anticipation filled him as he sat at his desk studying the small potted shoot reaching toward the ceiling.

Tiny leaves had already begun to form close to the head of the stem. The green shoot represented hope for the future products of Forestone. He'd left Cape Pacifica with a little more than half of the crop he'd paid a fortune for. From what his investigators and the police had been able to determine, the rest had been destroyed in the burning helicopter with the man who'd led his kidnappers.

Jaxson had dabbled extensively in botany during his early teens. That meant he had enough knowledge of the process needed to nurture and reproduce the Poule plant to be dangerous. Luckily, he knew his limitations. Now he had a world-renowned botanist, Dr. Stanley Reynolds, on his payroll. He gave his expert two of the precious Poule plants he'd brought back from Cape Pacifica and uttered a few prayers that he hadn't thrown millions down the toilet with his bid at the auction.

Just as he was beginning to fear that he'd wasted product development funds, his expert came through. This promising new seedling and several others were proof that it was possible to get the plants to grow in the United States. His company expert had done wonders duplicating the native habitat of the Poule plant. Now, all they had to do was mature the plants and determine if they still possessed the same properties and potency as the plants grown in their native habitat.

He rotated the pot in the light of his office lamp. Soon a lab assistant would come to return the plant to the greenhouse. He thought of Nicole Zayne. It had been months since he'd seen her. He'd thought the memories and the desire to get back between the sheets with her would disappear. It hadn't. With his business and interests, women had never been at the top of his list. Somehow, Nicole had managed to work her way up his priority list without even trying.

He didn't need the therapist his family had begged him to see to tell him that he should just get it out of his system. After all, the need to fornicate was Biology 101. He knew what she wanted more than anything, and he now had the means to give it to her without endangering his plans. It would change the dynamic between them.

He turned the plant in the light once more. An idea formed in his head. He knew how to get Nicole's attention.

When the lab assistant arrived, Jaxson quizzed her about creating a short-term environment for the plant that would protect it during a special shipment. Then he verified the requirements with Dr. Reynolds and notified him that he would have to make do with one less seedling.

***

Nicole returned to her office and flopped into her chair. She'd had a long morning with the laboratory staff from Sterris-Hite. Several questions remained about their process and materials that jeopardized the possibility of them providing a replacement for the Poule plant. She'd been guiding and nudging them along, but it was hard. Science wasn't as easy to deal with as manufacturing and business issues. Her product schedule was shot, and the probability of producing anything close to what she'd wanted with the Poule plant seemed more remote than ever.

Her ears were still ringing from the criticism she'd received at the last board meeting from an uncle and one of her cousins. Now that she was back and presumed okay, her uncle harped on her risking herself and the product development budget with no payoff. Then her cousin questioned Nicole's judgment and fitness to be on the board.

Nicole readily admitted her mistake and told the board that the bottom line was that the development budget was secure. Furthermore, she informed them that she had several mitigating options at play and would brief them soon.

In her office, she had shifted her focus to the view outside her window. The skyline of Long Island City across the East River wasn't as legendary as the one of Manhattan, but it was impressive just the same. With all the building going on, she was lucky to have an unobstructed view of the river. Her reverie was interrupted when someone began rapping on her closed door with an energy that could not be denied. She glanced at her phone, her preferred mode of interruption. Her assistant and the secretaries knew that she was not to be disturbed. This was probably urgent. "Come in!" she called out.

The door opened and her assistant, Casey, stood in the entryway with a delivery man pushing a rolling cart that held a large white cardboard box. "Special delivery for you!" Casey announced. "And the carrier has orders not to leave it with anyone but you. You have to sign for it personally."

"Really?" Nicole eyed the carrier and the box with a hint of suspicion. "Who is it from? Are we sure it's safe for me to open it?"

"J.F.?" Casey pointed to the initials scrawled at the top along with a printed return address. Then she inclined her head.

"Security x-rayed it and checked it out. They said it was okay."

Jaxson Forest? That was the only J.F. Nicole could think of. The address listed matched one she'd seen for Forestone Pharmaceuticals. Then she saw the Foreststone Pharmaceuticals logo. What he'd sent seemed much too complicated to be a bouquet of flowers.

The deliveryman stepped out from behind Casey. "If you could just sign, Ms. Zayne, I'll be on my way."

Nicole extended her hand, and the man came forward and gave her a tablet. She scrawled her signature in the indicated spot with her fingernail.

Casey hovered close by. Virtually holding her breath, Nicole used her letter opener to cut through the clear tape. There was foam inside and an envelope on top of the glass box with a lighted top that made her think of a terrarium. Casey helped her lift the glass container out of the foam. It felt warm against her fingers. Her eyes touched on what looked like a digital display along one side of the top.

Inside the glass enclosure was a small potted plant with tiny leaves just beginning to form. Nicole took a deep breath, her chest suddenly very heavy. She was no botanist, but she recognized the plant. Jaxson had sent her a Poule plant.

Her eyes burned with the threat of tears. The thing was worth millions, more if it lived. Why would Jaxson do such a thing? Her heart pounded her chest. In a strangled tone she instructed Casey to get her Harry Marshall, the reknowned botanist she'd hired after the one Poule plant she'd been able to procure in the past had died.

She stared at the plant, glad that Jaxson had the foresight to provide a controlled environment. It was precious. Her fingers shook as she used her letter opener to open the white envelope that had been on top of the glass enclosure. There was a plain white card inside with the name 'Jaxson Forest' emblazoned on the top in an ornate script. When she opened the card, a Ritz-Carlton room key card fell into her lap.

Grasping the room key, she read the short note: Champagne *lunch and... Tomorrow, noon, room 2402. Jaxson*

The nerve! Does he think I'll just fall back into bed with him because he sent me a plant? Her first instinct was to get mad. She wasn't for sale, multimillion-dollar plant or not. But her lips curved into a smile. The gesture was the most gutsy, romantic, and expensive gift she'd ever received from a man. It meant more than any jewelry, candy, flowers, or champagne. It would help her save face at Lady Zayne after losing the Poule plants to Jaxson and getting kidnapped, too.

Hearing the click of her returning assistant's heels, Nicole opened her desk drawer and slipped the card and hotel key card into her purse. She didn't know what she was going to do, but between the gift of the plant and Jaxson's offer, her heart was pounding and her hands were shaking. Heat pooled between her legs.

Harry hurried in ahead of Casey. Seeing the plant inside the glass enclosure, he let out a low whistle. "Holy moly, what a gift! And this portable stabilized environment they provided for it is something I wish I'd thought of."

Nicole couldn't contain the smile that transformed her face. "It's what I think it is, right?"

"Sure is." Harry lifted the box, examining the contents. "I need to get the greenhouse in Westchester set up for this ASAP. If we can preserve it and get it to thrive, maybe we can grow our own."

"That would put me on top for the rest of the year," Nicole said, "and there would be a large bonus in it for you, too."

"I'm on it," Harry huffed. "Mind if I take it to the lab now?"

Nicole shook her head. "Go ahead. I don't want anything to happen to it."

"Wow! Is that a Poule plant?" Casey asked as Harry picked up the enclosed plant.

"It is," Nicole answered gleefully. Then she added, "If anyone wants to know how we got it, you don't know. I don't want anyone to hear about this delivery, understand?"

"Yes ma'am," Harry and Casey answered in unison. As soon as Harry was out of sight, Nicole told Casey that she was taking an early lunch. Hadn't she earned it? After her stressful morning and the excitement of receiving the Poule plant, she didn't think she could do much more.

***

Jaxson

The next day, Jaxson arrived at the Ritz-Carlton more than an hour early for his time with Nicole. He hadn't asked Nicole for an RSVP but suspected she wouldn't give him one. If he knew Nicole like he thought, she wouldn't decide to come until the last minute. He could almost laugh at himself. He'd had a little taste of Nicole Zayne on the plane, and it had obviously blown his mind. Now he was waiting in a hotel room for her to show up and give him another fix.

He liked this hotel his company used to accommodate out-of-town guests. The room was perfect. Luxurious, but not too big. The enormous bed looked like an inviting adult playground with a surplus of pillows, Egyptian cotton sheets, and opulent coverings. The hotel staff had already placed a table for two in front of the large glass windows and covered it with a tablecloth and a bouquet of fresh roses. They'd even set the table with gold plated silverware, their finest porcelain, and the good crystal. A bottle of champagne he hoped she would like was chilling in a bucket on the table.

He'd already removed his suit jacket and tie but decided it would be too presumptuous to slip on a robe. He caught a glimpse of himself in the mirror. His white cotton shirt and dark gray slacks looked less formal. This was it. If Nicole Zayne didn't climb back into his bed today, she never would.

Standing at the expansive windows, he studied the lush greenery of Central Park, surrounded by residential buildings. It was something he sometimes did in his office to give his hard-working mind a break. He was high up enough to alleviate any concerns that there could be witnesses to his time with Nicole.

A knock sounded on the door. Jaxson checked his watch. *Too early for Nicole.* "Yes?" he called out.

A male voice responded. "Room service, sir."

Jaxson opened the door to an immaculately groomed waiter dressed in a white coat and black pants. A hotel badge fastened to the front of his jacket identified him as Myles. Jaxson widened the opening and beckoned him into the room. The waiter rolled in a linen-covered cart ladened with several silver serving dishes on a warming tray. "Where would you like me to set up, sir?"

Jaxson pointed to the table set for two.

Myles's gaze went to the cart ladened with dishes, then back to the small table set for two. "I'd be happy to serve you."

Jaxson shook his head. "No, not necessary, Myles. My guest has not arrived yet."

"Sir, there isn't enough room for the serving dishes and dinnerware. Would you like me to bring a larger table?"

Food was the least of Jaxson's worries. He was hoping to work up an appetite with Nicole. "No. Can you leave the cart? We can push it into the corridor when we're done. Would that work?"

"Yes, sir. If it's not too much of an inconvenience, please call when you're done so that the cart does not remain in the corridor too long."

"Yes, I'll do that." Jaxson reached into his pocket, drew out a bill, and gave it to Myles.

The waiter smiled. "Thank you, sir. Would you like to check the food before I go?"

Jaxson lifted the covers of several of the dishes. Not knowing what Nicole liked, he'd ordered a little bit of everything. There were fresh oysters, filet mignon, seared salmon with garlic-lemon sauce, shrimp, lobster rolls, Caesar salad, a seafood bisque, and French bread. The rich, combined aromas of the food filled his nostrils. His stomach rumbled. "Everything looks good."

With a little bow, Myles exited the room. Jaxson closed the door behind the waiter. He usually controlled his appetite and kept his body in top shape. Today was a day he fasted intermittently, so he hadn't eaten until after twelve. When his stomach rumbled once more, he ate one of the lobster rolls.

CHAPTER EIGHTEEN

Jaxson dropped down into the cushy chair near the windows. He didn't expect Nicole till at least twelve-fifteen. He'd brought a proposal to read while he waited, but his thoughts were jumbled. At five to twelve, someone knocked on the door. Jaxson got to his feet, anticipation surging through him. "Yes?"

No one answered, but he heard a key card in the lock and the resulting electric hum. The door opened and Nicole nodded to her bodyguard and stepped into the room on four-inch heels. Blond hair formed a bright halo around her oval face, and her short red dress lovingly caressed every curve of her body. She looked beautiful. Her intense blue gaze met his, a smirk on her face. She closed the door behind her.

He had a hard time holding back his smile. "Nicole, I'm glad you came."

"Jaxson." At his words, her smirk widened to more of a cocky grin. Yes, he'd said, *glad you came.*

Jaxson stepped closer. "Can I take your things?"

She gave him her designer bag and he placed it on the desk near the rear wall. When he returned, she circled him on a light cloud of her signature scent, the heels making her tall and statuesque and highlighting her shapely legs. Damned if she didn't know how to turn a man on. *Ooh, baby!*

"Champagne?" he asked, pointing to the champagne chilling in the bucket by the table.

"No. All I can think of is you," she said with a mischievous glint in her blue eyes. "Maybe later." Her bold gaze covered him from head to foot. It lingered on the bulge in his pants. She licked her lips.

The bulge got bigger. *Down, boy!* Jaxson swallowed hard. He reminded himself that he couldn't just grab her and throw her on the bed. "If you're hungry, I ordered lunch."

"Maybe much later," she said in a husky voice. Her intense gaze returned to his lips. When he started toward her, she halted him by holding up one perfectly manicured hand. "I wore something special for you."

With her other hand, she unfastened the sash on her red dress. The sash dropped to the floor. The dress slipped from her shoulders and quickly followed the sash. Nicole stood in front of him in a nude-colored bit of silk and lace that technically covered everything but hid absolutely nothing. Her lush, curvy form drew him like a beacon in the dark.

"Damn!" He stared, covering her form with his heated gaze. "I like it."

She gave him a sassy smile. "I like that you like it. There's more where that came from, or less, depending on your taste... I...I just need you to know that I'm not looking for a husband and I don't need a boyfriend, but I haven't been able to forget our time together on the plane. I don't want to want you, but I do. It was good. You were the best I've ever had."

"I've been thinking the same thing and trying to deal with it," Jaxson said, stepping closer until he reached her. "I'm yours. Whip it on me. Give me everything you've got."

She reached out to touch his cheek. "Just you and me, getting whatever this is out of our systems. Our secret. No strings...no press...no drama. Agreed?"

He grinned in amusement. "I couldn't have said it better." He pulled her into his arms at last. His mouth came down on hers in a hungry kiss that went on and on. She tasted like chocolate mints. Her fragrance teased his senses.

"Jaxson!" she moaned in between kisses, like she was begging for something. His mind filled with all the things he wanted to do to her. An afternoon was not enough. Nicole Zayne was hot. Drawing him closer, she sank into him, her fingers at his nape. His tongue danced, sliding sensuously against hers. She drew him tight, clinging to him, pressing her soft body against his.

This woman went to his head like no other. He could think of no one he wanted more. Clawing need drove him like never before. With a frenetic edge, his fingers skimmed her soft, warm curves, molding the globes of her bottom, caressing her abundant breasts, squeezing, and making her his. She moaned low in her throat.

Her restless fingers fumbled with the buttons on his shirt. He took his hands from her body long enough to shake it off. Then she was pressing hot, open-mouthed kisses to his chest while she fumbled with his belt. Touching, kissing, tasting her soft skin as best he could, he failed to hold on to her. As he began backing her toward the bed, she unzipped his pants and dropped to her knees... "I could never forget this." Grasping him in her hands, she dispensed with his briefs and stared down at him. "So big and beautiful!" She covered him with her red coated lips and closed her eyes.

He'd had fellatio performed on him before, but nothing like this. She lovingly administered to him with a skill and enthusiasm that rivaled his dreams. He threaded his hands through her hair, trying not to overwhelm her. He needn't have worried. She knew what she was doing and apparently loved it. Control slipped as his body came alive with sensual energy and delight. Before he knew it, he was melting like an M&M.

Mmm." Nicole rose to her feet, licking her lips. She grinned, grabbed his hand and ran it down her body. "I've got faith in you, Jaxson. All this is here, just waiting for you."

Damned if it didn't work. She was all but climbing his body as he stepped out of the clothing pooled at his ankles and lifted her into his arms. He carried her to the bed and placed her on the soft pillows and premium sheets. There, he eased the slinky garment from her form and covered her body with kisses. He laved her pink-tipped breasts with his tongue, drawing each soft mound into his mouth. His tongue traced the curve of her waist and her soft thighs. He paused between her thighs, lifting his head to meet her gaze. "I could never forget *this*." Then he intimately kissed and licked her until she was a pile of quivering flesh.

They came together, rocking, thrusting, straining from the edge of the big bed to the center and back. Still panting, they lay entwined between the luxurious sheets. Jaxson's stomach rumbled. The lobster roll had not been enough. Or was it the fact that he'd been expending so much energy since she came into the room? "Hungry?" he whispered close to Nicole's ear.

Nicole's soft sultry laughter reverberated through him. Her blue eyes sparkled. "For you, Jaxson, more than anything, but let's break for lunch."

Minutes later they were draped in thick cotton robes and seated at the table. "I could have more food delivered since most of this is probably cold," Jaxson said.

Steel laced Nicole's soft voice. "Today is between you and me. I like what you have here. I don't want to see anyone else in this room. I'll serve lunch." She removed several of the silver covers on the dishes, "What would you like? The bisque is still a little warm, and the filet looks wonderful."

The thought of Nicole, who probably never lifted a finger to do anything, serving him pleased Jaxson. Nicole never ceased to surprise him. "I'm a surf and turf sort of guy," he said.

She filled a plate with filet mignon, seared salmon, shrimp, and a lobster roll and placed it in front of him. "Good?"

"Yes." Jaxson smiled.

Nicole's glance strayed to the bottle chilling in the bucket. "Will you pour the champagne?"

"Yes." He retrieved the bottle from the bucket and turned it so that she could see the label.

"My favorite!" she said happily.

"I'm glad you like it," he said, opening it while Nicole fixed her plate with a sampling of all the seafood. As he poured champagne into their glasses, Nicole filled two bowls with Caesar salad. They settled down to eat.

Nicole put her fork down. "Jaxson, I really want to thank you for the plant. It was incredibly generous of you, and your timing couldn't have been better. No one has ever done anything like that for me and I'm beyond grateful."

Jaxson grinned back at her. "You're welcome. We both went through hell trying to get those plants. I know you needed something for your efforts, and I wanted to provide that and get your attention."

"You've got all of my attention," she said in a low, sultry tone. Lifting her glass, Nicole made a toast. "To working this out of our systems."

Repeating her words, he touched his glass to hers and drank. Then they both dove into their food.

With his appetite for food satisfied, Jaxson set his fork down. His gaze focused on Nicole as she sipped her wine and finished her food. Apparently sensing his attention, she wet her lips and threw him a provocative look. Then she let her robe fall open. The was all the encouragement he needed.

Pushing back his chair and getting to his feet, he came for her. She got up and stood by the table, naked and ready for him. "You're insatiable!" she said just before his mouth crashed down on hers in a sensual exploration that had them both moaning in anticipation.

"You love it!" he virtually growled, drawing his tongue down her neck and backing her toward the rumpled bed.

"I do," she confirmed, the backs of her legs reaching the bed. She let herself fall backward and drew him down on top of her. Her legs wrapped around his waist. "Tell me what you want," she said.

"Let me show you," he shot back. That was the start of round two, a heated down and dirty session with no holds barred. They took turns acting out their fantasies and rutting like two animals in heat.

Afterward, they lay together, caressing each other and dozing. Late afternoon light trickled into the room. "Can you stay?" he asked. "We could go for round three. I have this room for as long as I want."

She sat up in bed, checking her watch. "I have to go. Liam is coming for me, and I have a Zoom meeting with our facility in India that I can't miss."

Jaxson wanted more. "When can we do this again? Do you want to?" He trailed his fingers across her side.

Nicole shivered. "Yes."

He pressed the issue. "Next week? Same time, same place?"

"Yes." Nicole fused her mouth to his in a carnal kiss. He latched onto her, holding, caressing, skimming her body like he would never let her go. Her hands clasped his, halting his sensual exploration. "I've got to go."

Nicole leapt from the bed and virtually ran into the bathroom. She closed the door. Jaxson fought the urge to run after her. He wanted to, but they had spent most of the afternoon in bed. Besides, he'd already pinned Nicole down to return next week.

Showered and dressed in no time, she came out of the

bathroom. Sitting on the side of the bed, he watched her slip the bit of silk and lace back on and cover everything with her wrap dress. Approaching the bed, she kissed his lips. "Thank you for an exciting afternoon, and again, thank you for the plant. It meant more than you can imagine."

"I wouldn't bet on that," he said.

She simply smiled. "I'm looking forward to next week."

"Next week," he echoed. Then he walked her to the door and let her out. Her bodyguard was already walking down the hall. Afterward, Jaxson showered in the luxurious bathroom. His body brimmed with barely constrained energy. His spirits were high. He could have danced around the hotel room.

When Asher, his bodyguard, arrived, Jaxson was ready. Asher glanced into the room, obviously taking in the rumpled bed and the remains of the meal Jaxson had shared with Nicole. "Looks like you had a great afternoon," he said.

Jaxson grinned. "It couldn't have been better."

Asher nodded. "I haven't seen you this relaxed in a long time."

Not bothering to answer his bodyguard and friend, Jaxson struggled to wipe the telling grin off his face. He'd had enough of Nicole Zayne to fuel a million fantasies, and now he didn't need them. His thoughts were already skipping forward to next week.

***

Nicole forced herself to focus and be mentally sharp during her meeting with the facility in India. The notes and questions she'd put together earlier served her well. Still, she caught Ben watching her with a curious expression more than once. With the policy change explained and agreed upon, the meeting ended. Her brothers wanted to stop for drinks on the way home and invited her along.

Nicole hugged each of her brothers. "I'm going to have to

take a raincheck on that. I'm tired. I'm going to go home and go to bed."

"Alone?" Ben asked, being too nosey for her comfort. She didn't answer.

Hugo gave her an astute look and laughed. "She's got a bit of a glow going on." He turned to Nicole. "Honey, you've even lost that stressed and edgy look that had me worrying. Sure you didn't spend the afternoon in bed getting filled with delight?"

She suppressed a gasp. *Am I that transparent?* "Don't be crude. I'm not discussing my love life with either of you!" She began to gather her tablet and paperwork.

"Who said anything about love?" Ben countered defensively. "If you think Hugo and I just fell into it, think again. I want you to know that it's not easy, especially for us."

"Stop it. Discussion over," Nicole said, heading for the door.

"Whatever you did," Hugo said, his voice following her all the way into the corridor, "you need to do it again."

Walking back to her office alone, she allowed a grin to escape her lips. She wanted to spend more time in bed with Jaxson Forest. Who wouldn't? Her body thrummed with energy. He had the gorgeous, toned, trim body of an athlete, and she loved it. She could still feel Jaxson's hands on her body, his big, beautiful member pounding into her, making her dizzy with need. She wanted more.

It was going to be a long week.

Soon, meeting Jaxson at the Ritz-Carlton became a weekly thing, sometimes even twice a week. Weeks stretched into months. She told herself that each time would be the last, but damned if the man wasn't downright addicting. When she allowed herself to think about what it meant, it scared her. Her best defense was that what she did with Jaxson Forest was still kept in the dark. No one but their bodyguards knew about it, and she was determined to keep it that way.

CHAPTER NINETEEN

Nicole and Jaxson enjoyed a pleasing result from their DSEG infomercials when most of the class action lawsuit participants dropped out. Eventually, Julius Carmichael's lawyers convinced him to drop his case.

The unforeseen need for her to go to Europe to help settle a licensing issue with their European divisions put a stop to her times with Jaxson for longer than she could have imagined. Nicole was gone for three miserable weeks. She needed Jaxson more than she could bring herself to admit. To add more hardship, he'd purchased a private island in the Caribbean and had been busy making it meet his requirements. He would be staying there for a while and invited her down. She was happy to accept.

Liam checked out the Foreststone private jet, talked with Jaxson's security team, and OK'd Nicole's four-hour trip to Jackson's new island. She needed the break and looked forward to spending time alone with Jaxson.

During the flight, she tried to relax and nap. Briefly she surfed the internet. There, she saw pictures of Jaxson with Olivia Henry, a prodigy who was working on a new cancer treatment with him. The woman was both brilliant and attractive. Nicole wanted to scratch her eyes out. She knew that Jackson was fascinated with the woman's gifted mind.

Nicole switched off the internet and tried to focus on the book she'd brought. She'd told Jaxson many times that she wasn't looking for a husband and didn't need a boyfriend. Those words were coming back to haunt her. She wanted him. She needed him. He was hers.

She didn't care what he did with his days as long as he wasn't giving himself to another woman. She'd seen him on the Science Channel and on medical news television shows with Olivia Henry, and it was obvious the woman was working her way under his skin. Men were so blind! By the time he woke up he'd probably be married to the bitch. Nicole ran a hand through her short hair. She knew what was wrong with her. Settling the governmental issues troubling the Lady Zayne European Division had taken an excessive amount of time. She'd been too long without Jaxson.

The jet landed on the island's small airstrip. She got off and the attendant brought her bags. Jaxson was waiting for her, looking delicious in an open white linen shirt displaying hints of his muscular chest and matching shorts that showed his toned, lean-muscled body to its full advantage. Her mouth watered. She wanted Jaxson with a passion that just wouldn't go away. Playing it cool, she walked toward him as his driver gathered and loaded her bags.

A warm wind blew his shirt, displaying his sculpted honey brown chest. He stared at her, an intense look on his face as she approached in her breezy print sundress. The high splits on the sides furled in the wind to flash her tanned legs and matching shorts. The heat in his gaze lifted her spirits and sent heat pooling in her core. He started walking to her. It took everything she had to keep from running to him. Reaching him finally, she dropped her expensive purse and designer jacket to fling herself into his arms.

"Nicole," he groaned, his lips crashing down on hers. His tongue teased and tasted her, promising many sensual delights to come. She leaned into the kiss, thirsting for more, holding his head down so that she could kiss him back with enthusiasm.

The kiss went on and on.

"It's been too long. Miss me?" he asked when they broke apart to catch their breath.

"Mm-hmm. Too much!" Gazing up into his brown eyes, she stood on tiptoe to brush her lips against his once more. "I could jump your bones right here."

"Or the back seat of the Land Rover?" Jaxson flashed her a grin. "Not necessary. I've got a luxury air-conditioned villa, several big beds, and all the sun and water you could want. We've got the whole weekend with minimal staff except for security." He grasped her hand as the driver recovered her purse and jacket from the ground. "Ready for the weekend?"

She rested her head on his chest for a moment, inhaling the clean, masculine scent of him mixed with the fresh, sensual notes of his cologne. "I'm ready for you."

His hands dropped to her hips, pressing her close and gently grinding against her. She moaned softly. The hardness of his body beckoned to her, flooding her core with a fissure of heat. "You really want me to take you on the back seat of the SUV?" he whispered close to her ear.

She smiled up at him in the sunshine, biting her lip. "Yes, but I can wait and live that fantasy another day."

The moist heat of his breath tickled her ear. "Know that once you're in my bed, you're not getting out until you beg me."

She laughed. "Do you promise?"

"Have I ever gone back on a promise?" Tugging on her hand, he led her to the car. Jaxson's assistant held the door open while they got into the back then shut the door and got in the driver's seat to make the short trip to Jaxson's mansion.

The car began a slow, measured drive up a hill. Island palms and lush greenery with a backdrop of crystal blue water and fluffy white clouds over an azure sky filled her view as she sat in the circle of his arms. His hands caressed her restlessly, and sometimes she felt his warm lips on her neck and at her temple. It made her feel loved, not that that word had ever come from either of their mouths.

Did she want real love? Did she want it from Jaxson? Nicole didn't know if she was capable of the emotion. It scared her, especially when she saw how it had changed her brothers who had fought it, but ultimately caved in. They were both ecstatically happy, but at what cost? Their lives were hopelessly intertwined with those of Mira and Ava.

The car rounded the bend, and Nicole took in the glorious sight of his island villa. It was a large white sprawling structure that reminded her of the *Scarface* mansion from that old movie. Cigar-shaped columns dotted the immense front porch. Four rectangular reflecting pools injected plumes of water into the air. She saw evidence of tennis courts and an Olympic sized swimming pool in the distance. There was even a dock with a sailboat and a luxurious yacht.

"Wow," Nicole breathed, admiring his new acquisition but wondering what he would do with a place this big. "It's a lot for one person."

Jaxson flashed her a heated grin. "You're here, and my family will be visiting on occasion. I haven't decided if I'll ever use it for business. I want to relax and have fun here."

The car stopped in front of the mansion. Not waiting for his assistant, Jaxson opened the rear door and climbed out, drawing Nicole with him. Stepping between the rectangular water fountains, they bounded up the formal-looking steps and passed the wicker couches and recliners at the top to pause at a glass door accented with gold.

The door opened and a plump, grandmotherly-looking woman opened the door and ushered them into the cool interior. "Welcome back home, Mr. Forest."

Thanking her, Jaxson introduced Nicole to his housekeeper, Mrs. Martin, and told her that his assistant would be bringing in Nicole's bags, and they did not want to be disturbed. Greeting Nicole with a sweet smile and warm words of welcome, Mrs. Martin told Jaxson that nearly everything was ready for the weekend and lunch was in the oven. "I've got another twenty minutes of things that need doing and then I'll be on my way," the housekeeper said, bustling off.

Nicole took in her surroundings. The luxuriously relaxed interior was decorated in blue, white, and gray, with thick accent rugs and high-end island furniture on the hardwood floors and ceramic tiles as far as she could see.

Still holding Nicole's hand, Jaxson leaned close and asked in a husky voice, "Are you hungry?"

"Only for you," she answered, pressing her lips to his. He had beautiful lips. Everything about Jaxson Forest was beautiful, and she appreciated him now more than ever.

With a tug on her hand, he led her to the rear of the house. Nicole followed him into a masculine-looking room with an enormous bed, and Jaxson shut the door behind them.

They came together, kissing furiously and tearing at each other's clothes. Moaning, she reveled in the taste of his mouth, the feel of his tongue sliding against hers, and the scent of his skin. Her fingers burrowed inside his open shirt to touch his smooth, muscular chest. Somehow managing the fastenings on her dress without her help, he slipped it off her shoulders and down her arms. It dropped to the floor. Her shorts quickly followed.

Stilling her hands on his body, he took a good look. Suddenly she was standing beneath Jaxson's heated gaze in her tiny bra that made her breasts look like they were on a platter, and barely-there lace panties. "Nikki, you never disappoint me," he said with a sexy grin.

THE BILLIONAIRE'S SECRET LOVE

She tilted her head, her brow lifting. "Nikki?"

"Can I call you Nikki? You've been Nikki in my mind for a while now."

"My brothers call me Nik sometimes, but I like you calling me Nikki."

"Nikki, you look and smell good enough to eat."

"I try to keep things interesting." Heat flooded her core at the compliment, knowing that he was sure to follow through. With his big, beautiful body, Jaxson was a hot, sexy, and demanding lover who never failed to satisfy her. She wanted to jump him, kiss him all over, and ride him till he made her see stars. She reached for him, her fingers fumbling with his zipper.

Jaxson's hands and mouth traced the curve of her breasts, lingering on the tips. She shivered against the moist heat of his mouth through the thin fabric. His palm slid across her stomach and down into her panties. His expert fingers stroked and twirled her sensitive flesh. Nicole moaned. Her body clenched around his fingers, drenching them.

"Mmm, I guess you did miss me," he murmured, his fingers squeezing the fullness of her butt and curving around it to lift her. Her legs clenched around his trim waist. He carried her to the bed.

She rubbed herself against him, feeling his hard heat through his shorts and her panties. She ran her tongue along his chest and pressed an open-mouthed kiss against it. "Jaxson, I want to see all of you. I want..."

He laid her on the soft sheets. "You've got me. It's my turn, and I'm going to give you all of me. I'm going to make you scream." In short order, he dispensed with the tiny bra. With a ripping sound, her panties followed. Then Jaxson's mouth was on her body, tasting, teasing, and kissing, like she was a treasured treat...

***

Hours later, Nicole stretched, rotating her butt against Jaxson's hard body spooned behind her. His hand covered her breasts, caressing them. "You want some more of me?" he asked in that husky tone that usually made her want to jump his bones.

He'd had his turn, making good on his promise to make her scream in pleasure. Then, she'd had her turn and she'd gotten to do everything she'd dreamed of doing to and with him since they'd been apart. Afterward, they made love in the shower and again in the hot tub. Her body hummed and ached with satisfaction. She'd fallen asleep, partially from exhaustion. Not ready to answer, she turned, reveling in the warmth of his body, his scent, and the feel of his arms closing around her. She lay her head on his naked chest. Her stomach rumbled. Surprised, she snuggled closer to him.

Jaxson pressed a kiss to her temple and laughed. "I guess that answers my question. There's food in the kitchen. Security is keeping us safe, but there's no one in the house."

He sat up, his gaze darting to the late evening light filtering through the shutters, then to her discarded dress and the remains of her underwear on the floor. A hint of amusement colored his face. "I'll get your bag, unless you want to wear my shirt or one of my robes for now."

"I'll take the shirt," she decided. It fit like a dress when she rolled up the sleeves. It felt good to be enveloped in his scent.

CHAPTER TWENTY

They padded barefoot through the semi-dark house, Jaxson leading the way. Her bags were outside the bedroom door. Nicole glimpsed breathtaking views through several windows. Hidden sensors turned on the lights as they went from room to room. Finally, they arrived at a spacious room with a bar that surrounded an open, industrial-looking kitchen.

She plopped down on a stool as Jaxson ducked into the kitchen. He checked the oven, shaking his head at the meal that had been in the oven for hours. Then he turned back to her, extending a hand. "Lunch is no longer appetizing, so let's go to plan B. I need my sous chef," he said in his sexy baritone.

She stood, a smile on her lips. "I'm willing to substitute."

Jaxson shook his head resolutely. "Nikki, you are an original. You could never be a substitute for anyone." He grasped her hand and twirled her around, reeling her in until she was right in front of him. Then he kissed her lips.

She wasn't an affectionate person, but Jaxson was, and being around him made her feel good. He gave her a little hug. "You can dance. Want to go dancing after dinner?"

Confused, she said, "I thought you had the island to yourself."

"I do, but I know some people on a nearby island that my pilot can bring when I want outside entertainment. We could also fly to one of the other islands for a night out if you want."

Nicole gazed up at him. "I've spent hours on a plane to get

here. I don't want to leave the island."

"But you'll dance with me?"

"Of course." Nicole was suddenly grateful for all the social dancing lessons her mother had forced on her. Jaxson was good at everything he did, and she wanted to show him what she could do.

"Good. I'll talk to my pilot, and we can set it up for after dinner." He found his phone and made a quick call. Then he opened the fridge and drew out roast beef, bread, lettuce, tomatoes, and cheese. "I can slice the roast beef and make the sandwiches if you make a salad for us. The fridge is fully stocked."

"I'm on it. She reached into the refrigerator, gathering additional vegetables. As she stood at the sink, washing the vegetables for the salad, she turned to find him watching her. "You're not too tired, are you?"

"No," she lied, shooting him a perky glance, "I'm good." She was a little tired, but she'd missed him and wanted to make the best of the short weekend.

"Good." He continued slicing the roast beef.

Instead of the bar surrounding the kitchen, they ate on a screened terrace surrounded by palm trees, exotic flowers and lush greenery. The flowers' scent and the sound of the water crashing to the shore provided a romantic backdrop. She sipped red wine and ate one of Jaxson's delicious roast beef sandwiches with her garden salad.

Jaxson sat across from her, enjoying his food in companionable silence. He pushed his plate away. "Ready to slip into your sexy dancing dress?"

She thought about the things she'd packed: mostly bikinis, shorts, sandals, sexy nightwear, a nice top, and a pair of slacks. Did she even have a skirt? "Um...shorts, my sundress, or a bikini?"

Jaxson quirked an eyebrow. "I've got something for you."

"You do?" His answer surprised her. She knew he could be quite the ladies' man with his good looks, personality, and killer intellect, but despite her stated preferences for keeping their relationship between the sheets, she wasn't seeing anyone else. She suspected it was the same for him. Her chest felt tight. "Something your sister left?"

"No, something new, a dress just for you."

She blinked, curiosity making it impossible to feign indifference. "How do you even know my size?"

Jaxson gave her one of his panty-melting looks. "I know."

She didn't question him further. He'd had his hands, lips, and mouth on every inch of her body. Maybe he'd figured out her size that way. On a less romantic note, he could have seen the tags in her clothing during the times they'd been together. She helped him gather their plates and dishes and place them in the kitchen sink. "I'd like to see that dress now."

He led her to the bedroom next to his. There, nestled in the closet, was a royal blue, asymmetrical silk ballgown with a beaded bodice and cutouts. It was the stuff that fantasies were made of. There was even a pair of beaded matching heels. Fingering the silky material, Nicole held the dress close to her body. It was her size. She checked the shoes. Same result. "Wow."

"Do you like it?" he chuckled.

"I love it!"

He shifted on his feet. "Before you get back into to the how and why, Charli guilted me into attending a 'Dancing With the Stars' fashion show. I saw this number paired with those shoes and thought about you."

She stood on tiptoe and kissed his lips. "Thank you! I can't wait to wear them." The open door of bathroom beckoned to her. "I think I'll get ready in here."

"I have double sinks and a larger shower in my bathroom," he reminded her.

She let her gaze caress his body from head to toe. "Yes, but I might forget that I'm trying to get dressed if we're in your bathroom at the same time."

"Noted." Jaxson's hot gaze slowly perused her body. "If you see something you like, it's yours, anytime."

Nicole tilted her head to look at him. "Promise?"

"Promise. We've got unfinished business." Then he turned and went into his room next door. Nicole stared after him, enjoying the stimulating view of his rear. Then she dragged her bag into the spare bedroom and got to work.

While they freshened up and dressed, Nicole heard a plane. Shortly thereafter, she heard Jaxson leave his bedroom. Leaning into the lighted makeup mirror, she reapplied her makeup and used drops to brighten her eyes. *Why am I nervous? It's not like I haven't had training in every kind of social dance there is.*

"Jaxson?" she called as she left the spare bedroom and headed toward his kitchen. In the distance, she heard people coming into the house. Before she could reach them, Jaxson appeared in a fitted white suit. He grasped her hand and twirled her around.

"Scorching!" he said, reeling her in to kiss her lips. He looked so sexy in the suit that she could have swooned.

"You look hot, too." She let her hand slide from his trim waist to his firm butt.

Heat sparkled in his eyes. "Would you rather we just danced on the sheets?"

His words sent heat rushing through her. She couldn't contain her grin. It was still hard to accept how hot and sexy Jaxson was in addition to his extreme intelligence, and that he wanted her as much as she wanted him.

"Don't we have time to do both?"

"We do," he whispered close to her lips. "I thought it might be more entertaining if we highlighted our extended time in bed with a few activities."

She locked her arms around his neck. "I'm not complaining."

"Good." He kissed her hard, his mouth promising more to come. Then he released her and took her hand. "Let me introduce you to the band."

He led her to an area in the back of the house with floor-to-ceiling windows and a stunning view of the water. The large room had a few tables and a gleaming hardwood floor. A group of men were setting up their equipment at one end. Their name, "The Island Runners," was highlighted on the drums.

Jaxson introduced her to Tony, Derrick, Philip, and Hano. The good-looking and friendly band members seemed to know him well. They greeted her warmly, and she enjoyed their easy closeness. As Jaxson led her away, Derrick began a slow reggae song on his guitar and Tony joined him on the drums.

When Jaxson drew her into his arms for a slow dance, she realized why she was nervous. He was so good at everything. She wanted to show him that she was good at some things, too. She wanted to impress him and let him know that she was more than the Lady Zayne Empire princess.

The slow dance didn't last long. The music melded into a lively salsa that was soon followed by a cha-cha. Jaxson whirled her around, twisting and moving his hips in intricate steps that she managed to mimic and follow. The man could dance! It was fun and romantic, but she didn't have the luxury of watching him and his sexy moves. She had to keep up.

With the unmistakable sounds of a tango beginning, Nicole called on all she could remember. Jaxson dipped and swayed with her, his lips close to her cleavage, his body virtually covering hers. She wanted to be the tall, slinky, sexy femme fatale she'd seen in movies, but the reality was that she was of average height and despite her dance lessons, not a pro. The room was cool, but by now she was hot and parched.

"Break time?" he murmured close to her ear.

"Yes." She let him lead her to a table and chairs. They sat down.

Like magic, a man in a black suit appeared with a tray full of glasses, half filled with a frothy white liquid garnished with a pineapple slice and the other half containing a red beverage. "Since we already have the band, I thought a bartender would be acceptable. These are pina coladas and rum punch. If you'd like something else, Colin would be happy to fix it for you," Jaxson said.

Selecting one of the pina coladas and thanking him, she asked for a glass of water on the side. Jaxson did the same. "You're getting tired," he said, "Can you give me another two dances before we quit for the night?"

"Yes, but I plan to be in charge of everything that happens afterward," she said boldly.

His eyes lit up, his fingers caressing hers. "I'm looking forward to it."

***

Nicole awakened to the soothing sounds of birds singing and waves crashing to the shore. She was lying naked next to Jaxson's big body, and it felt wonderful. She gazed upward for the magnificent view of his square jaw, full sensuous lips, and long, dark, curling lashes. His thick head of kinky curls covered the pillow, making him look almost boyish and innocent. He was a beautiful man, and who and what he was with her was more than she'd ever dreamed.

Last night she'd tied him up and had her way with him.

She'd played out several of her fantasies on his ripped brown body and then she'd rode him into oblivion several times. What more could a girl want?

Apparently, more. She stretched her body against his and felt him hardening even more. "Good morning," she murmured, looking down at the big, thick, glorious length of him. Her mouth watered.

Jaxson chuckled. She felt the vibration of it beneath her. "Good morning. Did someone say I was insatiable?"

She gazed into golden-brown eyes rapidly clearing from the traces of sleep. "I admit to making the statement, but I think we might be in a competition. I never wanted anyone as much as I want you."

"Struggling with a similar problem here, but I'm flattered." He delivered the pithy words in a teasing tone.

"You should be," she said, sliding down his sculpted chest and fully defined six-pack to cover him with her mouth. *Mmm...* It wasn't something she usually did, but Jaxson was different. He inspired her to explore a sensuality she'd never known. She enjoyed the fresh, clean scent of his body and the taste of his skin. His groans deepened, spurring her on.

Just when she was really enjoying herself, he pulled away and drew her upward like she weighed next to nothing. Then he pushed into her wet core. She gasped with pleasure, always surprised at how well he fit inside her. Jaxson was a big man in every sense of the word. He rolled her onto her back, settling himself between her legs. Then his hips began rocking with piston precision.

After an extended time in the shower, he made her breakfast in the kitchen. Appreciating his respect for her wish to be alone with him as much as possible, she helped by making the coffee, the toast, and washing and slicing fresh fruit. This was the most domestic she'd ever been, but she liked doing things with Jaxson. His mere presence made everything worth it.

After breakfast, he gave her the choice of hanging out on the beach, taking the yacht for a spin, or sailing away for a private picnic on a different island. Nicole peered at the yacht—she estimated its length at sixty feet—docked where it could be seen from the breakfast patio. Despite the tall mast on the sleek sailboat, the yacht dwarfed it. "Do you have a captain for the yacht, or do you take it out on your own?"

Jaxson laughed. "Don't you trust me? I can captain the boat, but I have a guy who does it for me. If you want that up-close-and-personal experience with just the two of us on the water, we can take the sailboat. I've had lessons and I'm pretty good."

"So am I," she said. "My brothers race sailboats. I used to crew for them and their friends."

His finger lightly traced the curve of her jaw. "So, between the two of us we should be just fine on the sailboat?"

"Yes." She smiled up at him, waiting for a kiss. "I'll check the weather forecast."

His lips grazed hers, then returned for a deeper kiss. She slipped her tongue into his mouth, savoring the taste of him and the sensation of his tongue sliding against hers. She sighed as his hands slid down to grip her butt. "Want to stop by the bedroom first?"

His words tempted her more than she was willing to admit, but she knew he was an active person, mentally and physically. She wanted her time with him to be more than an extended booty call. "Only if there's something we can't do on the boat."

"That gives us a lot of leeway." He chuckled. "Let's gather our things and head off before it gets too hot."

CHAPTER TWENTY-ONE

Nicole changed into a bikini and threw on a coverup and sandals. Jackson pulled on a T-shirt over his dark blue swim trunks and boat shoes. Half an hour later they boarded the boat with a picnic basket, a cooler full of drinks, and their life jackets. Jackson insisted that they don the life jackets immediately.

As they put on their life jackets, she heard a power boat. She turned to look. The yacht wouldn't be that loud. Then she saw the power boat close to the dock with three men on board. She glanced at Jaxson when he murmured something about security.

"After what we've been through, you can't be too careful."

She quickly agreed. "They'll keep enough distance to give us privacy but keep us safe," he said.

Jaxson gave her a quick tour of his B42 sailboat. With its hydraulics and electronics, it was easy to operate. She was glad to see the head, sofas, and small galley below. Hopping off, Jaxson untied the boat and then climbed back aboard. Then they set sail.

With the warm wind in her hair and the smooth motion of the sailboat cutting through the water, Nicole was in heaven. Sun sparkled on the blue water, creating a glittering diamond-like effect. Cushy clouds floated overhead, dotting a sky of Disney blue. Jaxson, looking hot and handsome at the helm, made the view even better.

After about an hour, he let her man the boat until she'd had enough. Just when she thought he was going to drop anchor in the middle of the ocean so they could swim, he angled toward a small island.

"Did you plan on coming here?" she asked as he dropped the anchor then swung his dinghy over the side of the boat and winched it down.

"It was in the back of my mind. I've been here with my sailing instructor and my family. It's a good private spot for a picnic when I'm not on the island." He lowered the picnic basket down to the dinghy just as Nicole finished climbing down. "I would have helped you down," he murmured under his breath.

Gazing up at him, she laughed, then balanced her weight in the dinghy with the picnic basket. "I'm good. I know my way around a boat. Why don't you get the cooler? I can help set it down."

Jaxson lowered the cooler and Nicole placed it on the floor of the dinghy. She shifted as Jaxson climbed down to the dinghy to join her. Grasping the lines, she untied the dinghy while he started the motor. The ride to the lush little island with a white sandy beach was quick.

They unloaded the dinghy in companionable silence.

Jaxson surveyed the beach and the tree-lined area along the edges. "Where would you like to sit?"

Nicole found a spot on the beach with a mix of sun and shade. "How about this?"

"Perfect. Can you unpack our lunch while I get the chairs?"

"Sure, but don't go to all that trouble for me. I don't need a chair."

"No chairs it is," he said, wrapping the dinghy's lines around a tree and making a knot.

Nicole flipped the latch and opened the top on the wicker basket. Inside she found hand sanitizer, bug spray, a blanket, a tablecloth, a couple of plates, wine, wineglasses, grapes, assorted cheese slices, crackers, chips, and an assortment of sandwiches. He helped her spread the blanket and place the tablecloth in the center. Then they unpacked the basket.

"Is it okay that we don't have a table?"

She turned to meet his gaze. "I'm not as high maintenance as you think. This is fine. Don't you usually picnic with a blanket on the grass or sand?"

"I do, and then I lounge on the blanket, or the chair if I see ants."

"Sounds like you've got everything covered."

"Everything except you." He sat beside her on the blanket.

She climbed onto his lap and pressed her lips to his. The kiss went on for several moments. The taste of him exploded on her tongue. She couldn't seem to stop kissing him.

"I like it. I like kissing you, too." He spoke against her lips. Had she spoken her thoughts out loud? His hands caressed her bare legs, inching upward until they reached her bikini bottom. His magic fingers slipped inside, and soon it wasn't enough. And just like that, they had a quick coupling on the blanket right beside the food she'd just unpacked.

"I like being inside you," he said in a deep, sexy tone when she held onto him, her body still clenching.

She shot him a devilish grin. "I like you being inside of me."

She put her bikini bottoms back on, and then they ate lunch and sipped wine on the blanket in the shade. Afterward, she insisted that Jaxson apply suntan lotion to her sensitive skin. He had her naked in no time flat, and that inspired another round of lovemaking. The sand, the sun, the wine, and the man went to her head. She felt like she was floating on a sea of sensation.

Nicole opened her eyes. The sun was angled much lower

on the horizon. She looked up to find Jaxson's brown eyes watching her. "Why didn't you wake me up?"

His boyish grin pulled at her heart. "I think you earned your rest. Besides, I like watching you."

Nicole shook her head. "You're going to make it awfully hard for me to go home tomorrow."

His expression turned serious. "Stay with me."

"What are you asking?" The possibilities frightened her. She'd never been with any man like she'd been with Jaxson. The one time she'd thought she'd been in love had turned out to be a man pretending to be someone he wasn't, and he'd blackmailed her.

His eyes narrowed. "You look frightened. Does the thought of staying with me scare you that much?"

"No, of course not!" She blinked, shaking her head.

He didn't look like he believed her. "Who hurt you?"

The question penetrated deep down into her soul, and suddenly Nicole the tough businesswoman was nowhere to be found. A tear slipped down her face. Jaxson repeated the question, his finger wiping away the tear.

"Someone who will never get the chance to do it again."

"Can you talk about it?"

"No, not right now."

"Because you still have feelings for him?"

She forced herself to meet his gaze, willing strength into her expression. "Because it hurts that I let myself be so weak and vulnerable. I was too stupid to see right through him."

He reached for her, a blend of curiosity and shock transforming his face. "Does your family know?"

She shook her head. "Just Ben. He helped me fix it. And this is between you and me."

"I won't tell anyone," he said, drawing her into his arms. "You can trust me."

"I'm stronger than this!" she muttered, hating the need to burrow her face into his chest and cry for something that had been over for a long time.

"I know how strong you are," he said with conviction, "You're the woman who was by my side when I escaped from that island hell. You can let it out, whatever it is."

Somehow his words opened the floodgates. She blubbered like a baby. Jaxson simply held her, occasionally patting her back and comforting her with his presence. Since when did she find Jaxson Forest so comforting? Sometimes she didn't recognize herself.

When she had calmed, he kissed her forehead. "We should head back."

She sat up and pulled on her bikini and coverup. Despite spending most of her time in the shade, her skin now had a sun-kissed look.

"It looks good on you," Jackson said, stepping into his trunks and drawing his shirt over his head, covering that sculpted bronze chest and washboard abs. She hated to see him cover his toned and trim body. The man was a feast for the eyes.

They gathered their things, loaded the dinghy, and returned everything to the boat. As they headed back to his island, the sun was sinking fast on the horizon. She surveyed the surrounding area with concern. Other boats sailed in the distance, but getting back would take at least an hour. She didn't like the prospect of sailing at night.

"We're not as far out as you're probably thinking. We'll get back before dark," he said, obviously gleaning some of her thoughts, "and don't worry, our guys are nearby." He was silent for a moment. "If you really listen, you can hear their boat."

She strained her ears and was rewarded by the faint sound

of an engine. A smile lit her face. "Thanks."

It was almost dark when they made it back to the island. The power boat with the security team pulled in just behind them. "Do you think you'll want dinner?" Jaxson asked as he tied the boat.

"Believe it or not, I don't usually eat this much. Lunch was more than enough. If you're going to eat, I'll have a glass of wine."

Jaxson chuckled. "Wine is fine with me, too."

They sat on the screened patio, drinking wine, listening to music, and talking until she could barely keep her eyes open. Then Jaxson took her to bed and made such slow sweet love to her that she felt certain he cared for her. She'd never gotten this far in a relationship with anyone. This was real...but was it a relationship?

She fell asleep and dreamed about Jaxson.

***

Jaxson awakened to a deliciously cool breeze and the sound of the ocean. Nicole was cuddled up next to him, her lush rear resting on his package. Without her family's trademark makeup brand, she still looked beautiful with a golden tan on her normally pale skin, straight nose, graceful brows, naturally pink pouty lips, and delicate cheekbones. The contrast between her light golden tan and his rich mahogany skin drew his eyes.

He had just begun to get into enjoying his newest acquisition, his estate. Somehow, her presence had made it even better. When she left later today, he would miss her being in his space. It wasn't just the mind-blowing sex, he reasoned, his gaze touching on the barely covered lines of her body. He more than liked Nicole, and her time away in Europe had really brought it home. He'd missed her more than he should a woman who had been secretly heating up his bed once or twice a week for months.

She moaned in her sleep. He caressed her back until she quieted. Her tears and the revelation that she'd been badly hurt by someone had shocked him. Nicole was tough and demanding. She had to be, to survive her family.

From all he'd gleaned from Ava and the news, the Zaynes were all about the business and keeping it ahead of the industry. There'd been snarky press resulting from her mother's very emotional reaction to Nicole's escape from the island. Being close to his mother, he'd found the remarks insulting and difficult to understand. Then, Ava gave him the inside track on Pamela Zayne and her turbulent, controlling relationships with her children.

Nicole stretched, rotating her butt against him. His body's reaction was immediate. He cupped her bare breasts with his hands and slid them down to her hips. "Is that a request?"

Her lids opened, and her head turned. Ocean blue eyes gazed at him, rapidly losing the traces of sleep. She smiled, turning her body to lock her arms around his neck. "Can't get enough," she said, drawing his head down for her kiss.

By the time they got up, showered, and dressed, delicious aromas were wafting through the house. "I asked Mrs. Martin to come in and cook for us today," he explained as they made their way to the breakfast room. "I want you to enjoy your last day."

Glancing up at him, she took his hand. "I can stay another day."

The words made him ridiculously happy. He squeezed her hand, enjoying its softness. "Good. Stay as long as you want."

She shot him a teasing look and laughed. "I have meetings scheduled, I didn't bring enough clothes, and we both have things we have to do elsewhere."

"That just means you'll have to come back." He drew her into the breakfast room, noting that Mrs. Martin had already set the table outside on the lanai.

She nodded, pleasure and excitement lighting her eyes. "I will. I can't tell you how much I've enjoyed myself."

Jaxson lifted the tops off the silver serving dishes covering the table. They heaped crisp waffles, bacon, strawberries, pineapple, and eggs onto their plates and settled on the lanai. Mrs. Martin came out with freshly brewed coffee and filled their cups. They chatted while they ate.

Afterward, he suggested that she walk the two-and-a-half-mile length of the island with him. She surprised him by agreeing. "We have bicycles, if you would rather ride," he said, amending his offer.

"I jog and walk all the time," she said. "I've been studying martial arts, too."

He'd suspected as much from the way she'd handled herself during their kidnapping and escape. "I have a sparring session scheduled for tomorrow morning, if you'd like to join in."

"Yes, please! I didn't get to do much while I was in Europe."

They donned their sneakers and walked the island. Jaxson took time pointing out the things he loved most about his island: the location, the privacy, the remote lab and office at the house, and the ability to work and play away from his company's New York offices and the paparazzi.

After the walk, they spent the rest of the day lazing around on the beach and then the pool. Mrs. Martin served a light lunch by the pool and left a delicious island dinner for later.

The next morning, they got up early and sparred with the martial arts expert Jaxson used, who boated in from a nearby island. As he'd gleaned, Nicole was in great shape and could spar with the best of them. He sparred with her, both working up an appetite that landed them back in his bed.

The one appointment that he hadn't been able to cancel was with Olivia Henry, the medical oncologist and biochemical expert he'd hired to work on a new cancer treatment. Nicole surprised him by asking if she could sit in on his meeting if she was quiet and promised to keep anything she learned confidential.

"Are we competing for a new formula or raw ingredient I don't know about?" he asked, giving her a guarded look.

"None that I'm aware of," she said. "Jaxson, I'm not trying to dig into your secrets. I'm more interested in seeing how you operate in your business environment. All I've ever known is Lady Zayne, and I know that each corporation has its own culture. I'm trying to get to know you better."

Jaxson weighed her words. He could almost hear his corporate information security chief shouting a loud *hell no!* Still, Nicole's explanation sounded reasonable, even if her request was a bit outrageous. Was it really all about getting to know him better? He knew that most of the sensitive information had already been handled and discussed on the project. He was meeting to get a status and be assured that the project issues had been resolved and his product development was proceeding as planned. "I'm all for you getting to know me better," he said. Knowing what he had on the agenda, he agreed to let her sit in.

CHAPTER TWENTY-TWO

Nicole was impressed with Jaxson's office in the west wing of his mansion. It was compact and efficient, yet could accommodate six guests at his conference table. There was even an attached communications center, panic room, and remote laboratory he could use for limited work on his projects away from the office. He ushered her into his office and pulled out a guest chair at the conference table for her.

She noticed that her chair and its position were not in line with his computer's camera. The cameras mounted above the conference table were off. A screen hung down from the ceiling over his small conference table and projected what was on his computer screen. Unless Jaxson outed her, no one on the other end would even know she was present.

The meeting started. Nicole's gaze focused on the beautiful and exotic-looking Olivia Henry's almond-shaped eyes, thick brows, cute nose, and wide, sensual lips set in a honey brown complexion. Her white lab coat, unbuttoned, revealed a scoop-necked blouse that showed a little cleavage and hinted at a curvy figure. From the article she'd read on the plane, she knew that Olivia was a mix of Asian and black, and considered a genius. *Was it enough to snare Jaxson?*

Nicole's gaze slid back to him. Already greeting Olivia and the two people on her team, Jaxson flashed his boyish grin and a wide smile. *Maybe?* Nicole already knew that the well-known oncologist had attended a few events with him. With their interests and work relationship, it could be nothing, but Nicole found herself gritting her teeth. Jaxson was hers, but nevertheless, she felt threatened. *Were Jaxson and Olivia more than friends?* She needed to know.

Jaxson immediately informed Olivia and her team that he had a guest who was listening in but would not be otherwise participating in the meeting. He also told them that he'd reviewed all the agenda items for discussion, but anything additional should wait for the next meeting.

Olivia briefed him on her team's progress with product X957. They'd seen promising results on a cellular level, with the product causing a sharp decline in cancer cell reproduction. They were still gathering data, but had concerns about damage to healthy tissue, something common in cancer treatments. She went on to list the ingredients of concern.

Nicole listened raptly, surprised that the information was so interesting and delivered in a way she could understand. The subject matter wasn't that different from many meetings she'd attended, but the impact of saving lives versus preserving youth and beauty wasn't lost on her. Jaxson asked questions, using terms Nicole didn't always understand, but Olivia answered them easily and introduced a few of her own.

By the time the meeting ended, Nicole knew she was in trouble. She knew she'd been blessed with good looks, but no one had ever called her an exotic beauty. She might be highly intelligent, but she wasn't a genius. Add to that the fact that, unlike herself, it was unlikely that Olivia came from the type of messed-up family background that made it difficult to form and maintain a relationship.

The official part of the meeting ended. Jaxson talked and joked around with Olivia and her team about an upcoming conference, its requirements, and the arrangements that had been made. Then he said his goodbyes and shut off the conferencing system. "What do you think?" he asked as she approached.

He was pushing back his chair and standing when she

reached him. "I'm impressed with the things you do. I hope I never get cancer, but if I do, you're one of the first people I'll be talking to."

Jaxson flashed her that boyish smile. "Saving and preserving life when the prospects for a future seem bleak is the biggest reward of this job. I started down this road when my favorite uncle died of cancer when I was twelve. It was brutal."

She grasped his hand, giving it a squeeze. "I'm sorry you lost your uncle."

He nodded. "So am I." As they exited his office and closed the door he asked, "What do you want to do with the rest of your last day?"

"Can we just enjoy being together?"

Surprise flickered in his eyes and quickly disappeared. "Sure," he said on a light note. Then he led her outside to the porch swing on the breezy side of the house.

They'd been in the swing for more than an hour when she decided to ask her question. "Are you interested in Olivia Henry?"

She felt his body tense momentarily beneath the side of her face on his chest. He straightened in the swing, pulling her up with him till they faced one other. "I like Olivia, and she's done wonders for the projects we've been working on," he said, "Why are you asking?"

Trying to pull her reasons together, she felt like a fool, especially under the intense look in his eyes. "The papers and some magazines have you two down as a couple," she began.

"Does it matter? You were clear when we first got together. You don't want a husband or a boyfriend. That we even get together remains a secret. You said you want to work out whatever this thing is between us and move on."

She felt her face burning with something that felt like

acute embarrassment. And why did his words hurt like arrows piercing clear through to her heart? She couldn't picture herself walking away from him. "This...this thing between us doesn't seem to be going away," she managed to say. It was difficult to keep meeting his gaze and not show the emotion tearing at her.

"What are you saying?" His tone softened. "Do you want to change your mind?"

Her pulse sped up. The thought frightened her. Jaxson already had more from her than she'd willingly given any man. "I don't know," she said honestly. "Jaxson, I suck at relationships."

He chuckled. "And how long have we been sleeping together?"

"At least six months," she said. That had actually been a record for her. "What do *you* want?"

"I want to try something new." His gaze held hers, unflinching, ready to press his point.

No! His words made her catch her breath. "With Olivia?" she managed to ask.

"With you," he said, his hands grasping her shoulders. His mouth covered hers in a soft kiss with a sensual edge.

Abruptly relieved, she allowed herself to breathe. Jaxson still wanted only her. She could feel it, but she wasn't out of the woods yet.

"You have to give me something more, Nikki. I like you a lot, more than that, if I'm honest. I'm not getting any younger, and I want to share my life with someone. My family is pushing marriage candidates at me regularly. I'm not ready to marry anyone, but I need to at least start looking around if your feelings for me don't extend past my bed."

Her heart thumped like crazy, and her head swam. She felt like she was going to pass out. She was about to blow everything with Jaxson, but getting herself to move forward was an insurmountable task. Her head hurt, and she searched for something to say.

"Nikki?" His fingers gently framed her face, silently demanding an answer.

"I have feelings that go way past just sleeping with you," she confessed, hating her weak tone and the way her body trembled with the simple admission. It wasn't as if she was confessing undying love for him.

Jaxson drew her into a warm embrace, his lips on her temple and the side of her face. His hands massaged her back and slid down her waist to cup her butt. "I just had to hear you say it."

Nicole's outwardly tough persona raised her head, standing up for her against Jaxson's implied demand. "You have to give me some time."

"I've been patient," he said. "I can last a little longer, but not forever. I want you with me. I want people to know that you're mine. That is, if you want to be. Do you?"

"Yes." Nicole surprised herself by answering without any reservations. "You just have to give me more time before we go public. This is new for me."

"This is new for me, too."

The rest of her time with Jaxson was spent cuddling and making love. She didn't allow herself to worry about defining their relationship, going public with it, or what she would have to do to make it work. She convinced herself to live in the moment.

***

Ava and Hugo's wedding preparations were the talk of the town. Nicole flew down to Maui with Ava, her maid of honor, Lindsey, and the other bridesmaids ahead of the rest of the bridal party to celebrate and prepare. She loved Maui but didn't come often because of the distance. The wedding hotel, the Royal Hawaiian, had everything she'd come to expect as a Zayne, plus gorgeous views and sumptuous food.

Ava seemed happy and excited during the lunches, parties, and pamper sessions. This had to be her lifelong dream, because Ava had been in love with Hugo since they were kids. Nicole celebrated with her and the others, happy for Ava and Hugo.

At times, though, Nicole saw a pensive look on Ava's face, and she wondered what caused it. Was Ava worried that Hugo wouldn't show up for his wedding? That would be crazy, since Ava was the only woman he'd ever admitted to loving after years of loving his bachelorhood. Their toddler son, Hunter, had been instrumental in helping Hugo to settle down.

The day of the wedding came and in keeping with tradition, Ava did not see Hugo. Ava grew quiet, laughing a lot less. The rest of the wedding party and the guests had arrived the night before. Nicole went to the nanny's room to play with Hunter. He was a beautiful baby; his strong resemblance to Hugo and their mother always fascinated her.

Hugo came in as she was leaving, looking relaxed and happy. Nicole hugged him. "Ready to leave being a bachelor behind forever?" she teased.

Lifting Hunter into his arms and nuzzling his face against his son's downy cheeks, Hugo smiled. "Yes. I bet you thought this day would never come."

Nicole laughed. "Me? What about Ava?"

Hugo nodded. "Yes, it took me a while, but I got here."

"No reservations or regrets?"

"None." His tone was definite and resolute.

"How do you do it?" she asked on a softer note. "Are you

really ready for everything it means to be a married man with a family?"

Hugo's gaze locked with hers. "I know we all said we'd never have children, and marriage was the last thing we wanted, but I wouldn't send Hunter back even if I could, and I can't lose Ava. I came close to that, and you have no idea how miserable I was. I would do anything to keep her, and she wants and needs to be married. I didn't want to be a father, either, but here I am. There's no going back. No man, and I mean, *no man* other than me is going to raise my son."

Nicole blinked and nodded. "I hope you know how happy I am for you both."

"Sure." He bounced his son up and down in his arms. Baby laughter filled the air. "That was a heavy conversation for my wedding day. Are you going through something?"

She nodded, thinking of Jaxson. She hadn't told her family about him and didn't know if she wanted to. Nicole reveled in being free to do as she pleased without considering anyone else's needs and desires.

Hugo gave her a knowing look. "You can't buy into that unlovable Zayne crap. People either love you or they don't. It's as simple as that."

"And you love Ava," she murmured under her breath. Hugo had been the brother to sow the most oats and the one most opposed to marriage.

"Yes, I love Ava. It took a while for me to own it, and I may not shout it from the rooftops, but I do."

"Does it hurt? Does it scare you?" she couldn't stop herself from asking.

"Yes, and yes," Hugo said, drawing her closer for a group hug with Hunter, "but the alternative is an emptiness creeping over an endless line of women. None of them alleviated my feeling of being all alone in the world. I'm the happiest I've ever been." He released her, but not before Hunter grabbed a handful of her hair.

"Ow!" Nicole pried his baby fingers out of her hair.

"He has a thing for hair and he's pretty good with his hands," Hugo said proudly. He studied her for a moment. "You're still getting some counseling, right?"

"Yes, but a lot less of it," she said.

"If you think you're in love, go for it. You're definitely more lovable than me and Ben put together."

She wasn't in love with Jaxson, was she? She shook her head. "I wouldn't go that far."

Hugo fixed her with a determined look. "When I get back from my honeymoon, you and I are going to talk, so get ready."

"Okay." She pressed a quick kiss to Hunter's forehead and squeezed Hugo's shoulder. "See you at the wedding."

**

Nicole immersed herself in the wedding day activities. Ava's stylist brushed Nicole's short hair upward and curled it into a style that didn't look much different from the elegant updo some of the other bridesmaids wore. Both a nail tech and makeup artist were on hand to give personal attention to each of them. Ava had selected beautiful purple dresses for them all. Nicole's crisscrossed at her breasts and hugged her figure like a glove. She loved it. Slits on both sides gave tantalizing glimpses of her legs and helped her walk gracefully on her three-inch heels.

Because of her upbringing, Nicole didn't have a lot of friends, and she wasn't used to the easy camaraderie the other women enjoyed. Between Ava and her maid of honor, Lindsey, Nicole was included in everything. She felt very comfortable.

CHAPTER TWENTY-THREE

The procession began with an instrumental rendition of Whitney Houston's "I will Always Love You." Hugo entered the church with the minister, while Ben escorted his mother followed by Ava's mother and a family friend. The wedding party lined up. Nicole sensed trouble. The time for Ava's appearance was rapidly approaching and there was no sign or signal from her or Lindsey. Standing outside the door where the bride had prepared herself, she heard the sounds of Ava crying and Lindsey talking to her.

From a side door, Nicole peeked into the chapel. Her mother was whispering something to Ben. It was past time for Ava to appear. Mira also sat in the front row with her nanny and little Ben sleeping in his carrier. Ava's nanny held a very wiggly Hunter, who obviously wanted to get down and run around the chapel. Hugo stood at the front with the minister and Ben. He looked confident, but his gaze focused inward, and Nicole knew that the hand in his pocket was probably shaking. Was Ava having second thoughts?

Ava's father, a no-nonsense type of guy who had obviously gotten tired of waiting for her to appear, banged on the door. Lindsey came out and stood with the bridesmaids as he went in.

"How is Ava?" Nicole whispered, certain everyone heard her.

"Nervous," Lindsey answered brightly, "but hopefully her dad can do a better job of calming her down."

Nicole knew that brides sometimes got very nervous

when it came to walking down the aisle. She took another glance at the chapel full of people. Many of them were fidgeting and glancing back at them, obviously getting restless. She tried to put herself in Ava's shoes and failed. Her day, if she had one, would be all about her. If she ever managed to get married, she didn't want a big production like the one Ava had planned.

Nicole spotted Jaxson in a middle row, sitting close to the aisle. Her heart did a few flip-flops, calming when she saw that he'd brought his sister Charli as his plus one. She couldn't really see above his broad shoulders, but imagined he looked like something off the pages of a men's style magazine in his black tux. She guessed he'd arrived today because she hadn't seen him.

His demand for more weighed on her. She worried that she was going to mess things up. She'd never felt this way about anyone. It scared her enough to seriously consider backing away to where she only had to deal with herself. Could she imagine him waiting for her to come down the aisle?

The door to the bride's room opened, and Ava's dad came out looking frustrated. He went to the entrance of the chapel and motioned to Hugo. Nicole swallowed hard. This could get ugly. Her earlier conversation with Hugo replayed in her mind. Hugo loved Ava and was marrying her because she wanted and needed to be married. After nearly walking away because he didn't want to marry anyone, was Ava about to let him off the hook?

Hugo strode down the aisle with an easy, confident gait, nodding to his guests and the bridal party. Their mother and Ben followed close on his heels. Nicole stared at her clueless and controlling mother, certain she was about to mess up another relationship with one of her children. Pamela Zayne opened her mouth to speak as Ben squeezed his brother's shoulder and Hugo opened the door to the bride's room.

In a sudden burst of inspiration, Nicole grasped her mother's wrist. Wide-eyed, her mother turned to see Nicole shaking her head and warning her off.

In the act of closing the door behind him, Hugo saw his mother. "Mother, I need to talk to Ava alone," he said in a harsh tone.

"Of course. I was looking for the ladies' room," she said, managing to fake a look of surprise. Nicole took the opportunity to show her where it was. Drawing her mother into the room, she locked the door behind them.

"Mother, you can't fix or interfere with whatever's going on with Hugo and Ava. You have to let them do it themselves."

Pamela patted her perfect hair in the mirror above the marble sink. "He's putting on a good show out there, but he's afraid of losing her. I just can't believe she's going to dump him after chasing him all these years!"

"Mother, they're going to be just fine. If I were you, I'd go back in and wait for the ceremony to start."

For once in her life, Pamela Zayne listened to her daughter. Nicole was amazed. Maybe her mother was sincere in her efforts to change.

As her mother traipsed back into the church to wait, Nicole prayed that Hugo and Ava would be all right.

The door to the bride's room opened. Hugo stepped out, looking more emotional than Nicole could remember. He sent one of the makeup artists back into the room, instructing her to repair Ava's makeup. Then, straightening his shoulders and lifting his head, he walked back into the chapel. Then he whispered something to the minister and took Hunter from the nanny. The toddler laughed as his father tickled him playfully.

The door to the bride's room opened and Ava stepped out in her beautiful white designer gown. Her twists were threaded with fine gold chains, piled high on her head and crowned with a diamond-studded circlet threaded through a long, opaque veil. Her makeup was flawless, but Nicole knew she'd been crying. Delicate white lace covered her arms and the neckline of her strapless sweetheart gown. The trumpet skirt of the dress emphasized her curvy body with enough room at the bottom to allow her to walk. She held a bouquet of white and purple flowers. A sheer lace skirt clipped over her dress at her waist and secured the two-foot train behind her.

Ava's father signaled someone inside the chapel, and the music cued the start of the wedding. Nicole walked down the aisle with the other bridesmaids, the groomsmen, and Lindsey to Luther Vandross's rendition of "Here and Now." When Ava appeared in the doorway on the arm of her father, everyone stood and the music switched to the traditional "Bridal Chorus" by the German composer Richard Wagner.

A surge of emotion swept over the crowd. Ava's mother wiped away tears. Cameras flashed and the videographer and cameraman jockeyed for the best position. Hugo's gaze was intense as he stood at the altar waiting, as if silently willing Ava to meet him there. She stepped gracefully, holding onto her father's arm, but Nicole noticed the subtle shaking of the bouquet in her hands.

Ava reached the altar and Hugo took her hand. He leaned in and whispered to her. The minister spoke, leading them through their vows and the exchange of rings. Nicole watched her brother's face. He was all in. When the minister pronounced them husband and wife, Hugo lifted Ava's veil, tilted her back, and kissed her passionately. Then he wiped her tears with his fingertips and held her for several moments, ignoring the cheers and applause of the noisy guests.

Nicole patted her face with a tissue. She envied the depth of emotion between Hugo and Ava. She didn't know if she had it in her, didn't know if she could cope with it. One thing was obvious, neither Ava nor Hugo was in control of their love. Nicole thrived on control.

***

Nicole posed for pictures with the bridal party. An hour before the scheduled wedding reception, Nicole hurried to her room with a headache. Still in her bridesmaid dress, she lay on her bed with a cool cloth on her forehead, certain no one would miss her until the reception started. Someone knocked on her door. Reluctantly, she got up to answer.

She opened the door to Jaxson, looking as handsome as ever in his custom tux. He flashed her his million-dollar smile. "I'm glad you texted your room number. You look beautiful. Can I come in?"

"Sure." After glancing at the nearly empty corridor, she widened the opening and drew him in.

Something flickered in his eyes as he watched her check the corridor. It made her want to explain herself. He quickly dragged her into his arms and kissed the hell out of her. A little dizzy and ready for more, she gazed up at his handsome features. *Did he just kiss my headache away?*

He eyed her rumpled bed. "Are you okay?"

"Headache," she mumbled, feeling strangely uncommunicative.

He surprised her by drawing her into another hug. "I can stay and keep you company or let you try to catch a catnap. Which would you prefer?"

Her face against his chest and her arms around his waist felt wonderful. Nicole breathed in his warm, masculine scent. "Please stay, but I need to lie down for a few minutes."

"I'll lie down with you," he said, shrugging out of his jacket and placing it on a chair. He unzipped her dress and helped her out of it. Then he carefully hung it up. "Come here," he said, leading her back to the bed and stretching out on it. She snuggled up to him and fell asleep.

Half an hour later he shook her awake. Her headache was gone. "I hope my table isn't too far away from yours," he said, as he helped her back into her dress and slipped on his jacket. Thankfully, his clothes hadn't wrinkled.

"I'm at the family table close to where the bride and groom will be sitting. I think you'll be a few tables away from there."

He delved into his pocket and pulled out a key card, still in its sleeve. He gave it to her. "Come and see me when you've had enough of the reception. I've missed you."

She pressed her lips to his, letting him deepen the kiss. "I missed you too. If it weren't for my headache..."

He shook his head, dismissing her train of thought. His fingers smoothed her hair. "You're feeling better?"

"Yes."

"Are you going to save me a dance at the reception?"

"Yes." She met his gaze and smiled.

"We've got about fifteen minutes to get there. Do you know the way?"

"I do, so follow me." She opened the door carefully, checked the outside, then stepped out into the corridor with him.

"What are you checking for?" he asked as she closed the door. She thought he sounded a little hurt, but when she glanced at him, she decided she was wrong.

"Friends and family," she said, a little embarrassed. "I'm not ready to answer a lot of questions and explain us yet."

Jaxson's eyes narrowed. "Will you ever be ready for that?"

"I'm working on it. You said you'd give me some time."

"I did, but that time won't last forever," he said in a hard tone.

Refusing to yield to pressure, Nicole nodded, determined

not to let it spoil her evening. "Let's go enjoy the reception!"

***

The food was heavenly, the drinks strong, and the toasts to the newlyweds alternated between the comical and the sweet. Soon after the meal, the band began play, opening with a fast-paced song, and Jaxson came to ask her for a dance. He was very good, but Nicole managed to hold her own. She returned to the table winded and a little hot.

Hugo hovered as Ava came over to whisper in her ear, "Did you and Jaxson finally bury the hatchet and come out friends?"

"Yes," Nicole said, smiling.

Ava squeezed her shoulder. "I'm glad, because he's a good guy and he's so kind and intelligent. Do you know that he has a foundation that supplies millions of dollars' worth of cancer treatments to those who can't afford it?"

Nicole nodded, not ready to say more. She spent most of the evening dancing with groomsmen, the sons of her mother's friends, and a couple of her cousins. None danced as well as Jaxson. She spotted him on the dance floor with Charli and several different female guests, obviously enjoying himself. Suppressing a sharp wave of jealousy every so often, she realized that she was the hypocrite. If she was ready to claim him in front of the world, he would be at her side.

Jaxson came back to ask her for a slow dance, and she glided around the floor in his arms, aware that she hadn't been this relaxed or moved so easily with any of her other partners. When the dance ended, she caught both her mother and Ava watching her curiously as Jaxson melted back into the crowd.

Ava and Hugo were cute and romantic as they fed each other wedding cake and kissed. If Nicole had had any doubts about her brother's transformation, the events of the day would have laid them to rest. Later, Hugo removed Ava's wedding garter and tossed it into the crowd of bachelors. One of the Zayne cousins caught it. Nicole scanned the crowd, her spirits lifting when she saw that Jaxson wasn't vying for the garter.

Nicole purposely avoided the group of women who gathered for the bridal toss. No, she wasn't looking to marry anyone. She eyed the women gathering, wondering if they seriously thought catching the bouquet would help them land a husband. Ava, who had been a pitcher on the girls' high school baseball team, managed to toss her bouquet over the hopefuls and nearly hit Nicole in the head with it. Catching it was a matter of self-preservation.

If I'd wanted to catch the damned thing I would have stood in line! Nicole stared at the bouquet and narrowed a glare at Ava. Her newly minted sister-in-law laughed, and Hugo joined in with several others. When the congratulations and teasing comments got to be a bit much, Nicole tried to give the bouquet to her mother. Refusing to accept it, Pamela Zayne gazed calmly at her daughter and said, "I hope the damned thing works some magic for you. I'm beginning to worry."

Time to go. Family and guests were lining up to wish the newlyweds well as they prepared to leave for their honeymoon. Nicole said her goodbyes to the happy couple and made her escape after assuring Ava she wasn't mad about the bouquet toss.

The hotel corridors were quiet after the raucous celebration. In her room, Nicole put water in her ice bucket and placed the bouquet inside. Outside her window, tiki torches lit the night with the aid of a full moon. She could hear the ocean waves crashing against the shore. Nothing alleviated her feeling of being alone. A long, hot soak eased her taut nerves.

A deep longing filled her. She donned her favorite teddy, covered it with a dress and headed for Jaxson's room.

CHAPTER TWENTY-FOUR

Jaxson sat in the dark watching the tiki torches flickering in the night outside his room. The ocean steadily smashing against the shore should have soothed what was troubling him, but it didn't. He glanced at his smart watch. It was past twelve. After all the sneaking and checking Nicole had done to make sure no one knew she was sleeping with him, why had he been so certain she would be in his bed tonight?

Most of the women he'd dated were proud and eager to let the world know about their involvement with him. Not Nicole. But had he and Nicole had never really dated. It was a sobering thought. He had buddies who had problems getting out of the friend zone. He was the only one he knew with a problem getting out of the *bed* zone. Fuck buddies were a dime a dozen. It wasn't something he usually did, but Nicole was special, and she'd drilled her way into his life. He wanted and needed a lot more from her. Swallowing the last of his favorite cognac, he slid the light robe from his shoulders and tossed it on the chair by the bed.

Abruptly, he heard a key card being fitted into the door lock and the electric hum of the door unlocking. It opened and Nicole stepped into his room on a light cloud of her signature scent. The door closed behind her.

"I had a long, hot soak. I'm glad you waited for me!" she said in a sexy tone that made him want to run up and grab her. "And good things come to those who wait." Her bright hair stood out like a halo in the low light as she bent at the waist and shimmied out of her body-hugging blue dress. The black lace and silk teddy she wore underneath enhanced all her curves. She looked like a sex goddess.

He extended his hand and she took it, her mouth covering his naked chest with warm, open-mouthed kisses. His other hand slid to her lush bottom to squeeze and draw her closer.

"Uh-uh," she murmured, dropping to her knees and fumbling with the waistband of his tented pajama bottoms. She reached into his pants and drew out his stiff member. Briefly, she held him in her soft hands, admiring him. "Hello, beautiful!" she cooed. Her warm tongue and soft lips lovingly licked and kissed him like he was covered in chocolate. Then she used the heaven of her mouth and totally blew his mind.

He was more sexual with Nicole than he'd been with anyone. Their hot, down, and dirty sessions fueled many of his day and night dreams. He didn't think, just lived in the moment as his body took control, fulfilling both their needs. Nicole was naked on the bed, and he was between her spread legs, busy pounding into her when they rolled so that she was riding him. Then he heard a door open. A sliver of light spilled into the room, followed by a muffled shriek and a quick apology.

Nicole quickly dropped onto him. Jaxson turned his head in time to see Charli closing the connecting door between their rooms. He was certain he'd previously closed and locked that door. And what could she want at this time of night, anyway? The interruption killed the moment. He pulled out of Nicole and sat on the side of the bed.

Nicole sat up behind him, hugging her soft breasts against his back, resting her chin on his hunched shoulder, and clasping her arms around his waist. "Was that Charli?" she whispered.

"Yes. I could swear I locked that door. Sorry."

"Do you think she's in trouble? I can't imagine her needing to talk to you in the middle of the night unless something's wrong," Nicole said. "Maybe you should check?"

"I was thinking the same thing." He gently disengaged from her arms, sensing that she was not happy about being walked in on by Charli. "Will you wait?"

Several moments went by before she nodded.

"I won't be long," he said, finding his pajama bottoms and stepping into them. He threw on his robe. Then he went to check on his sister.

Charli was in her room, sitting on her bed, still wearing her evening dress. "I'm so sorry, Jax!" she moaned, bending her head over her hands twisting in her lap. "My pajamas are in your case because I didn't have room in mine. You usually sleep hard or not at all. I thought I'd just sneak into your room and grab the bag with my pajamas. I didn't know you had company."

Relief flooded through him. At least nothing was wrong. "What were you doing out this late?" he asked, feeling some responsibility for his little sister.

"A number of us danced until the band quit, then we went out. I didn't know it was so late."

He patted her shoulder. "I wanted to make sure you were okay. It sounds like your coming into my room like that was an innocent mistake. You're not traumatized, are you?"

"Because I caught you screwing someone? I'm pretty sure that was Nicole Zayne!"

Jaxson wasn't shocked, but he and his little sister didn't discuss those sorts of things. "Don't be crude."

She looked up from her fingers twisting in her lap. "Ha! I didn't say *fucking*. That would really be crude."

From the look on her face, he couldn't help feeling like he'd fallen off his superhero pedestal. "Charli!"

She set her lips stubbornly. "I'm not traumatized. I know what goes on in the world, and I'm not a kid anymore. It looked like you two were having a lot of fun."

"Charli, what I do in my room is private," he reminded her.

"I know. I won't tell anyone, but I thought you two didn't like each other?"

"It's complicated," he said, cutting her off. "I couldn't explain it if I tried." Satisfied that his sister was okay and wouldn't be spreading the news of her discovery, he straightened. "How about I bring you the case with your pajamas?"

Back in his room, Nicole sat in the center of his bed, wrapped in a sheet. "Charli is okay. She got back late and needed some things from my suitcase," he explained. "I'm going to bring it to her."

He located his suitcase and rolled it into Charli's room. "I'll get my suitcase in the morning," he told her. "Good night, Charli." Then he closed and locked the connecting door.

He felt Nicole's burning gaze as he stripped and came back to bed. Drawing her into his arms, he laid a deep, sensual kiss on her lips. Her usual sigh and melting into him was missing. He dropped his arms and threw her a questioning look. "Problem?"

She bit her red-coated bottom lip. "The interruption killed the mood. Do you think she'll tell anyone?"

"She said she wouldn't. I believe her." He trailed a finger down Nicole's neck to the cleavage not covered by the bedsheet. "What's there to tell? We're both adults, and neither of us is married or committed to anyone else."

"I like my privacy. I like doing what I want, when I want, outside of prying eyes."

Jaxson kissed his way down her neck to her bare shoulder. "Who cares if we're sleeping together, hmm?"

Nicole stiffened. "My family, the gossip columns, me... I'd have to explain."

His hand slid down to the curve of her butt beneath the sheets. "What is there to explain?"

Nicole gazed at him, and it was the most vulnerable that he had ever seen her. "Us. I don't do relationships, Jax. Except for one big mistake, I never have."

"What about Idiot, the guy you were at the restaurant with? You've been in the gossip columns with him, you've slept with him."

She shook her head. "Éliott is more of an acquaintance and official escort. He's been trying to get me into bed for years. When I was trying to get you out of my head, I thought I might, but I couldn't."

"Ain't nothing like the real thing," he said, close to the shell of her ear. "You should date me, be with me, and not give a damn about what anyone thinks. I want to show you off to the world. I want you with me and in my bed. I think there's a lot more for us, but we can't get there if I'm the secret guy."

Suddenly her hands were pushing against his chest. "I'm not ready. You said you'd give me time."

He dropped his arms and she moved to sit on the edge of the bed. "You've *had* time, weeks of it. I can't erase the image of you checking to make sure that no one saw me coming out of your room. Are you ashamed of me?"

"No, Jax!" she said quickly. "I-I'm just not used to sharing myself with anyone."

"Then what is this we're doing?" he asked, his tone growing harsh.

"I thought it was just sex, and that we'd eventually get over it," she said defensively. Her blue eyes flashed.

"I want more than sex from you, and you know it." Jaxson's hands tightened into fists at his sides. She frustrated him in that he'd been waiting months for her to realize that she wasn't just scratching an itch. He suspected that he was in love with Nicole, and it was beginning to feel like she didn't return his feelings.

"I don't like being pressured." She stood, wrapped in the sheet, and began gathering her clothes with quick, jerky movements.

He sat naked on the edge of his bed as she dropped the sheet, bent over, and did a reverse strip tease with her black lace teddy. He enjoyed the show. He enjoyed Nicole too, but being secret lovers had lost its appeal. "I don't like feeling like a fuckbuddy to someone I have feelings for. Maybe I should just move on," he said.

She was silent as she shimmied into her dress. "Maybe you should," she said in an even tone. She retrieved her bag from the bedside table. "Do you really want to end things this way?"

He stared at her. He didn't sense any love or affection in her words, expression, or stance. They were fighting about feelings. Most of the women he'd dated were the first to define their feelings. Nicole was fighting hard and backing away from him because he needed to know there was more. You can't force someone to have feelings they don't. "Call me. If we haven't resolved this in a week, I'm done."

"Fine." From her clipped tone, he could tell she was angry. He could almost see her trying to decide whether she should kiss him or not before she left. Finally, she approached him and took his face in her hands. Her eyes looked glassy, and her bottom lip poked out. "In case this is goodbye," she murmured before placing a long, lingering kiss on his lips.

His head swam with the kiss, his hands caressing her soft flesh everywhere he could reach. His questing fingers wandered up her silken thighs and beneath the lace teddy to dip and swirl in her hot, wet core. She moaned, pressing herself against his naked form and riding his fingers. Things were heating up again, getting hot and heavy until she abruptly wrenched herself away from him. Then she quickly walked to the door and opened it. "Good night." She disappeared as the door clicked shut.

Jaxson stared at the door for several moments. Hadn't they gotten the mood back? What just happened?

***

Nicole made it back to her room, too turned on and angry to sleep. She'd wanted to show Jaxson what he would be missing. Too bad she'd been too angry to stay and jump his bones. She took off her heels and paced the room barefoot. The nerve of Jaxson Forest! Would he really walk away? He seemed determined. But she had time to decide, to agree to something other than what they'd been doing.

Nothing in her upbringing or life experiences had prepared her for anything like this. She was a mess. It would be hard, but could she do it in a week?

A hand on her rapidly beating heart, Nicole dropped into the chair by the bed. She wouldn't allow herself to cry. No tears meant that her nose ran instead. She used a wad of tissues. That kiss had been goodbye, and she knew it as well as he did.

CHAPTER TWENTY-FIVE

Back in New York, the next week was rough on Nicole. She spent a lot of time reflecting on her time with Jaxson. Hugo and Ava were still on their honeymoon, and although Ben and Mira spent extra days in Hawaii, they were heavy into their romance when they returned. Was she going to be the only Zayne sibling to strike out?

Physically and emotionally, she wanted and needed Jaxson. Her problem was that commitment scared her. She wanted to be free to do what she wanted, when she wanted in her personal life. She didn't want to explain herself or answer to anyone's expectations. That freedom was something Ben and Hugo seemed to have given up with they realized their love for the women they married.

As fate would have it, she was watching a program on medical breakthroughs when the network advertised an upcoming program featuring Jaxson Forest and his lead scientist, Olivia Henry. Nicole watched the teaser, taking in the other woman's undeniable beauty and brains and the way she looked at Jaxson like he was the most intelligent, handsome, and badass man to grace the planet.

Jaxson was all those things and more, she conceded silently. Too bad she was a mess when it came to relationships. Once Nicole bowed out with Jaxson, Olivia was sure to double down on her efforts to get him. The thought of that happening hurt Nicole more than she wanted to admit.

The week went fast with Nicole mulling over his

ultimatum when she wasn't working. The day came to call Jaxson, and she was an irritable wreck, torn between giving him the answer he wanted and holding out in the hope she could find someone willing to take what she was able to give. She hadn't slept much, and when she did manage to fall asleep, Jaxson's hot body figured prominently in her dreams. She missed him badly, but because of his ultimatum she couldn't call him for a little bedroom delight.

Stubbornness ran in her family, so by evening, she was nearly ready to skip calling Jaxson and force herself to live with the consequences. As she lay on the couch, trying to doze with the Weather Channel on for noise, her concern grew. Jaxson had planned on returning to his island and was probably still there. Now, a major tropical storm was trashing the Caribbean.

"...has hit St. Thomas, St. John, and a string of the surrounding islands..." Hearing that, Nicole sat up, no longer interested in trying to sleep. As the meteorologists updated every ten minutes, she saw a pulsating, rotating angry green and yellow and red blotch on the radar map. There were also pictures of some of the devastation, including uprooted trees, smashed cars and damaged rooftops, and boats that landed in trees. She stared at the map of islands that had been hit, her breath catching when she saw Jaxson's private island, Terris, was included.

She dialed his number, knowing that it probably wasn't working. After two rings, she heard a loud, hissing noise. Her sense of uneasiness grew as she switched off the phone. What if Jaxson was hurt? The prospect chilled her blood. It was the beginning of a long night.

The Weather Channel updates showed the status of rescue efforts and checks on the various islands as the storm ravaged the Caribbean and headed toward Florida. She cared about Jaxson, she really did. Her heart hurt. Viewing the devastation, listening to the interviews, she said a prayer for him.

By the next morning, the media reported that various organizational crews and volunteers were traveling to the islands to help local agencies mount rescues, check on the residents, and provide aid. Several people had been reported missing and more were expected, especially since the storm had gone further than expected.

Tiring of the endless updates and droning on of the Weather Channel anchors, she switched to the local news. Then she saw a spokesperson for Foreststone giving a statement to reporters while a crying Charli and an older woman with her arm around her shoulders were shown entering a compound with a man who was probably his father. "...in contact with the local authorities who are searching for the Foreststone Pharmaceuticals mogul, Jaxson Forest. We know he was not at his home when the storm hit, and his boat is missing."

Nicole's fingers clenched and unclenched the television remote. She could barely breathe. She switched channels and heard all of the story. Jaxson was missing along with his boat after a major tropical storm. Travel would be difficult until the storm ran its course, but various agencies were already organizing search parties to help the injured and locate Jaxson and several other missing people.

The time to go to work came and went. Nicole called in sick. She *was* sick. She had a burning feeling in the pit of her stomach and her chest hurt. She tried to eat but couldn't work up an appetite. What if Jaxson was already dead in the mess the storm had made of the islands?

The next couple of days were pure hell for Nicole. The list of lost, injured, and dead from the tropical storm grew with no news of Jaxson. The need to do something, anything to aid in the search for him, wore at her.

On her third day away from work, Ben dropped by unexpectedly. She tried to ignore the door, but he knew she was inside and threatened to get the emergency key from their mother. When she opened the door, he stared at her in shock.

"I've been worried, and you won't answer the phone. What's happened to you?" he asked, obviously taking in her lank hair, worn pajamas, and face devoid of makeup.

Shaking her head, she held up her hand in the universal gesture signaling him to stop.

Stepping into her condo, Ben closed the door behind him. "If you don't go take care of yourself right now, I'm going to drag you into the bathroom myself and then I'm calling the doctor. Which one is it going to be?"

She cut him with a nasty glare.

Ben's bottom lip jutted stubbornly. "You can hate me later. I'm concerned about you," he huffed.

Without another word, she went into her private bathroom and slammed the door. Inside, the much-needed shower revived her. She washed and towel-dried her hair, surprised at how much better she felt physically. Adding makeup to look like her normal self and slipping into a lounging outfit and sandals completed her efforts.

CHAPTER TWENTY-SIX

The scent of her special blend of coffee hit her nostrils as she exited her bedroom. Ben sat on her couch, sipping a cup, and her mother was in the kitchen, looking uncharacteristically comfortable at the stove.

"Mother?" Nicole said, amazed that she'd gotten unexpected visits from her mother and one of her brothers on the same day.

"Ben said that you didn't look like you'd eaten in the last couple of days, so I'm making those cheesy eggs you used to like." Her mother cracked a couple of eggs into a bowl and began whisking them. She'd already opened a package of extra sharp Cheddar cheese.

Nicole narrowed her gaze at Ben. "Did you. . .?"

"I didn't call Mother. You'd just started the shower when I heard the key in the door. If you give people emergency keys, they'll use them when you cause them to worry."

"You've been out of the office sick for three days and you're not answering your phone. If that's not a reason to be concerned, I don't know what is!" her mother interjected from the kitchen.

Ben's eyes seemed to see right through her. "You don't seem to have a fever," he guessed. "Are you really sick?"

She met his gaze, adding a little pushback. "No, I just needed some time away from the office."

"And you're not answering your phone because...?"

"I didn't feel like talking, Genius."

"Not good enough," Ben said.

"The eggs are ready," her mother announced, placing a plate with the steaming eggs on the counter in front of one of the stools. "And this is my first culinary effort in decades, so you're going to eat them."

It wasn't worth the argument, Nicole decided, making her way to the breakfast bar and mounting the stool. Besides, her stomach rumbled at the delicious aroma wafting off the eggs. She was too hungry to stand on dignity.

Her mother poured her a cup of coffee. She glanced at the television and frowned. "What's wrong, Nicole? You seem depressed."

Nicole chewed and swallowed, savoring the taste of the cheesy eggs. "Why do you say that?"

Her mother gave her a critical look. "Ben may have spurred you into taking a shower, washing your hair, and putting on makeup, but you're still not our usual self. Nicole, you can tell us what's wrong."

Nicole massaged her forehead with her fingers. She was terrified that Jaxson might be seriously hurt or dead, but did that explain everything? And who were these two supportive people who seemed determined to root her out of her depression? Not her messed-up family.

Her mother was known to be the cause of depression in her children and yet she'd come here to check on her. Ben could be a bit flaky, but he'd grown a lot since he and Mira almost divorced. Now he seemed genuinely concerned about her wellbeing.

She chewed and swallowed more of the eggs. In the background, Nicole shut them out and listened to the television. The twenty-four-hour news station was reporting the latest on the storm.

"Maybe I should switch off the TV so we can talk?" Ben

asked, shooting her an astute glance.

"No," she said.

His gaze bounced back and forth between the screen and her face. "Nicole, we did hear that Jaxson Forest has gone missing in that tropical storm. We reached out to his family and let them know that we hope he'll be found safe. Are you worried about him?"

"Yes." Nicole dropped her head on her upraised palm.

Her mother came around the bar and hugged her shoulders. "Oh Nicole, I'm so sorry. You didn't say anything, but I thought you might have bonded over your ordeal."

She wanted her privacy, and she wanted the time and space to figure out what she wanted from Jaxson. Now it might be too late.

"I saw you dancing with him at the wedding and it seemed...intimate. Have you been seeing Jaxson Forest?" Ben asked on a careful note.

Nicole hesitated. This was her moment of truth. "Yes." She forced her head up and straightened her shoulders.

Her mother took the stool next to her. "You've always been good at keeping secrets, but you've been more vulnerable lately."

Nicole knew the vulnerable feeling all too well. She struggled against the need to defend herself. "I was trying to keep our relationship private until I could figure out what it was and what I wanted. But now..."

"Now you might never get the chance," Ben finished for her.

Moisture dripped from her palm and down her arm. Nicole realized that a few tears had slipped down her face. "I feel useless, and I can't stand the waiting. I wish I could do something."

Ben surprised her with his next words. "You can help with

the rescue efforts. They never have enough manpower, food, and funding for the searches and relief of everyone devastated by the storm. You can help in whatever way you feel comfortable."

Nicole nodded, glad at the new prospect for something useful to do. "Thanks, Ben. I'll come up with something."

Her mother studied her face, obviously not happy with what she saw there. "Are you in love with Jaxson Forest?" Her tone was incredulous.

"I-I don't know. Maybe?" Nicole stammered. "I just know that I won't be able to concentrate until I know he's okay and I can talk to him."

"I thought you two looked pretty comfortable with each other when you were dancing at Hugo's reception, too," her mother said. "But you've been fighting him over formulas, processes, and miracle plants for years. I thought you hated him."

Nicole winced. She hadn't hated Jaxson since their escape from the island. Before that, she hadn't known the real Jaxson. "He's the reason things are moving ahead on LZ Formula 237. He gave me a seedling from one of those plants he won in the bid on the island."

Ben's whistle grated on her nerves. "That's an incredibly generous gift! We owe him for that."

Nicole nodded.

"Amazing what passes for a bouquet of flowers these days," Pamela said just under her breath.

Nicole faced her mother. "No one has ever given me anything like it. I can't tell you how much it meant to me."

Ben came and gave her a hug. "It's going to be all right, Nik," he said.

All the Zaynes were usually demanding when it came to Lady Zayne business operations, but her mother and brother urged Nicole to take the next week off. They felt she needed the time to do whatever she was going to do to assist with the search efforts and possibly resolve her uncertainty about her relationship with Jaxson.

CHAPTER TWENTY-SEVEN

Nicole placed a call to Charli at the number on the business card Charli had given her at the taping of the industry association PSA. It took two calls with no message before Charli answered the phone.

"Hello, Nicole. If you're calling about Jax, we're still looking for him," she began.

"Hey, Charli. I'm sorry I haven't called before now. I've been worrying ever since I heard the news, and I want you to know that I've been praying he'll be found safe."

"Thanks. We're all holding our breath and hoping for the best. We've got search and rescue teams helping the authorities with the storm victims, but actively looking for Jax."

An unspoken fear escaped Nicole. "You don't think there's anything besides the storm damage keeping him from being found, do you?"

Charli gasped. "I had the same thought, but the experts assured my parents that it's highly unlikely. The storm was dangerous for everyone."

Nicole hated the choked, wimpy sound of her voice. "I'd like to help. Can I join the search effort? Put together one of my own? I can't stand just waiting and doing nothing."

"We have a lot of people searching for him," Charli said, "but I wanted to go down tomorrow and help. But my parents are against it. They're concerned that I wouldn't be safe. Plus there are issues about where to stay and the food and water supply after the storm." She gave a wistful sigh. "I suppose they're right, but I'd just feel better being there."

Nicole's fingers gripped her phone hard. "I need to be there, too."

"Jaxson hasn't said much to me, but I can tell that he thinks a lot of you," Charli said. After a brief hesitation, she added, "Do you love my brother, or are you just fucking his brains out?"

Flinching, Nicole tried twice to clear her clogged throat. Unchecked tears slid down her cheeks. "I've been trying to figure it out." Gathering herself, she added on a stronger note, "Whatever it is, it's between me and Jaxson."

Charli was silent for several punishing beats. Then she said, "I think he'd want you to be there. Right now, the search and rescue people are in tents and temporary camps. They had to bring in their own food and water in addition to the supplies to aid the locals. I've been trying to find a hotel or Airbnb that wasn't damaged and still has room." She sucked in a breath. "Maybe if you and I went together, my parents would be give their okay."

"I may have a place we could stay, provided it hasn't taken on too much damage from the storm," Nicole said, thinking of Ava's home on St. Thomas. "I'll see if I can arrange it and get back to you."

Nicole called Ava and discovered that she had been communicating with her staff on St. Thomas. The house there had only suffered minor damage from the storm and was available for Nicole and Charli to stay. That, and Nicole's insistence that Liam and one of his team would accompany her and Charli, prompted Charli's parents to not only consent that Charli could go, but to get space for them on the next flight of volunteers and supplies.

They took the flight to the Virgin Islands. Charli would

serve as the eyes and ears for her parents. Nicole packed a bunch of jeans, boots, and T-shirts from her oldest clothes, supplemented with supplies she found at a camping store. After a review of her clothes, she added two nicer casual outfits. The trip back to the islands was a blur. Although Charli didn't seem to know whether to welcome or castigate her, they bonded over their worry about Jaxson.

The plane landed in a field on St. Thomas that had been cleared for rescue and service planes, since the airport remained closed. Due to downed trees, damaged roads and homes, and many wandering homeless people, it took several hours to get to Ava's house on the island. Ava's staff had cleared a path to the gated estate, and a generator was going.

With all the damage Nicole had seen on the way to Ava's house, she almost felt a little guilty that she had a clean, dry, air-conditioned, and relatively luxurious place to stay. The supplies, food, and volunteers they had flown with helped alleviate some of the guilt. The volunteers stayed at a nearby church, while Charli, Nicole, Liam, and his team member, Brock, stayed at Ava's.

The Forest search team used boats and helicopters and focused on the islands closest to Jaxson's Terris. Some of the smaller islands were too barren to support life, but they searched them anyway. Other islands were filled with wildlife, but no housing or developments. When they found survivors, they stopped the search to provide food and medical aid. What concerned Charli and Nicole most was the ticking clock. If Jaxson had no source of food and drinking water, his time was running out.

On the little island where Nicole had lunched with Jaxson, they found a body floating in the water on the beach. From the skin and light-colored hair on the battered body, they immediately knew it wasn't Jaxson. Nevertheless, the sight tied Nicole's stomach in knots. As the men turned it over, both women held their breath.

Nicole fought back tears and fear. If Jaxson were dead, she would feel it, wouldn't she? She recognized one of the guards from her visit with Jaxson. He'd been one who had stayed close and followed her and Jaxson in a small motorboat. A hard search of the island followed with no other bodies or signs of life. By then it was too dark to continue.

CHAPTER TWENTY-EIGHT

The next four little islands they covered had scattered debris, but neither bodies nor signs of life. Nicole trampled through the mud with the others, past downed trees, trash, and remnants of boats and homes, praying for a sign of Jaxson. Still there was none.

It was getting late, and everyone was exhausted from searching. They decided to check one more island for survivors before quitting for the day. Nicole's blood started pumping faster as soon as they spotted the red shirt hanging from a tree branch stuck in the sand on the beach. Rocks on the sand formed the word *Help,* but the debris from the storm may have made it difficult to see from the helicopter.

The team hurried onto the small island. Further in, they found a crude shelter made of branches and palm leaves. Two bodies lay on the ground inside. "Jaxson?" Nicole gasped, her eyes zeroing in on the body that matched his in shape and size. The coloring matched Jaxson's beneath the white substance smeared on the figure's hands and face. It was pure Jaxson to find minerals on the island to use as a sunscreen.

Was he dead? Neither of the bodies moved. *Oh Jax, I never wanted to see you like this!*

"Jax!" Charli screamed, dropping to her knees. Crying, she shook the still figure violently. "Jax, wake up!"

For Nicole, the moment stretched forever. Searing, gut-wrenching pain seized her. *We were too late!* She'd lost that chance at being loved for herself by a man she could never replace. Could she ever be able to forgive herself for dragging her feet and giving in to her fears?

Then she heard a strange wailing sound. Moisture dripped down her face. As she dropped down to the other side of Jaxson's body, she realized that she was crying. The choked, painful sounding sobs were hers. Unable to help herself, she caressed his skin on the arm that would never hold her again. It was warm. She pressed the vein at his wrist and felt a pulse. "He's still alive!" she gasped.

"Ladies, please move out of the way so we can assess his condition and provide the care he needs," Dr. Morgan said, elbowing his way to the front of the group. One of the other doctors and a nurse followed close on his heels.

With a silent prayer, Nicole forced herself to move away, pulling Charli with her. He had a bruise on his forehead and a black eye. A makeshift bandage made from a shirt was tied around his middle and stained with blood. One arm was in a crude sling.

They hugged each other as the medical team got to work on Jaxson and the other figure lying on the ground only inches away from him. The other man was also alive, but unconscious.

The medical team quickly tended to their most serious wounds. Despite their efforts, neither man regained consciousness. Dr. Morgan called for the medical evacuation helicopter. Both Charli and Nicole insisted on accompanying Jaxson to the hospital in the helicopter. There, Nicole was present for Charli's emotional call to her parents. Afterward, Charli lied to the hospital staff, telling them Nicole was Jaxson's cousin so that she would be allowed in to see him. Grateful for a chance to be close to Jaxson, Nicole waited with Charli in the private hospital room while the doctors checked him out.

When the hospital orderly brought Jaxson to his room, he had been cleaned up and his wounds redressed. He was still unconscious when they hooked up the IV. The doctors had ordered an MRI that was performed to rule out bleeding on his brain. The MRI results were negative, but he had a concussion, a couple of broken ribs, and a broken arm. He was also dehydrated.

Charli and Nicole decided to take turns holding the hand that wasn't peeping out of the cast and talking to him. Charli went first, so Nicole left the room to inform her mother that Jaxson had been found battered, but alive. She had no answers about when she would be returning to New York but promised to give an update the next day.

When she returned to Jaxson's room, Charli was talking to an unconscious Jaxson about her childhood and how he had always been there for her. Some of the tales of their exploits brought a smile to Nicole's lips.

When Charli finished, she ducked out of the room to update their parents on Jaxson's condition. Nicole sat beside the bed and studied his face, which looked a lot worse than it had when they'd escaped from Cape Pacifica. She glanced at the door to ensure her privacy with him. She took his hand and held it between both of hers, caressing it. Then she spoke from her heart.

"Jaxson, I suck at relationships. I told you that. I've never had to worry about pleasing anyone but myself, my parents when I was younger, and contributing to the company's profits. I had a rough week trying to push myself to do what you wanted, but the truth is that I...I need you and I don't want to lose you. I was going to call you and tell you that I wasn't ready to be a couple with you, period. Then the storm happened and you went missing. I've been in hell. I thought you were dead. When I saw you on the ground, bloody and bruised..."

Nicole, who had always associated tears with weakness, broke down and cried again. Trying to hold back the tears and blowing her nose instead didn't work this time. Still holding his hand, she mopped at her face with her sleeve. Once again she glanced at the door, not wanting anyone to witness her breakdown. Fortunately, no one was there.

She squeezed his hand and used her other hand to grab tissues from the bedside table to mop her face and blow her nose. "Jaxson, please wake up!" she pleaded, her gaze going back to his face.

Golden brown eyes, glazed with pain, opened and stared back at her. "Nicole. . ."

"You're awake!" she said, more tears falling. "Thank God. How are you feeling?"

"I've been better," he muttered. "I hurt all over."

"I'm sorry that you're hurt, but I'm just so glad to be able to see you, and touch you, and talk to you. Jaxson, I've been through hell!"

"Where do you think I've been?" he shot back in a husky voice. Then he winced, as if the simple act of speaking hurt. "No more tears, Nikki."

Nodding, she grabbed more tissues and mopped at her face. "I thought I'd lost you for good," she said, standing and leaning over to place her lips on his cracked ones in a soft kiss. She'd been afraid that she'd never get to do that again. She gently rubbed her cheek against his battered skin and then kissed his lips again.

"Still can't get enough?" he cracked, flinching.

She shook her head. The tears started again.

His hand tightened on hers. "Nikki, don't cry. I'm right here. I'm not dying, am I?"

She shook her head again. "But you're in a lot of pain." She pressed the call button for the nurse.

"Yes, but I'm glad to be alive," he said, "I got hit by a lot of debris and a tree nearly got me. I thought it was the end. Then I had to try to stay alive until help came."

"You did a magnificent job," she said, "I saw the mineral stuff you used for sunscreen, and the shelter was solid. I even saw something that looked like a crude desalinator in the back of the shelter."

"Marco was with me. Did he make it?"

"He's in the room down the hall."

Charli came into the room with the nurse on her heels. "Jax? Is something wrong?" Seeing her brother's eyes open, she let out a whoop of joy and ran to his bedside.

Jaxson held on to Nicole's hand. Charli went to the side of the bed closest to the door, pressed her cheek against Jaxson's and then kissed his cheek. "I'm so happy you're awake!" She straightened, her hand flying to her heart. "You've got to take better care of yourself, Jax. Mom and Dad are too old to give me another brother."

"I'm irreplaceable!" he choked out in a husky voice that ended with a cough. Nicole grasped the water from the bed tray and held the straw to his dry lips for him to sip. He swallowed. "I wasn't chasing the storm. I got stir crazy and went for a very short run in the boat. I thought I'd have time to get back well before the storm hit. I told the guys they didn't have to come along, but everyone but Pancho did. I think they were as stir crazy as I was. We'd been watching the storm for days."

"We found a body on your island beach," Charli said. "I hope it's not Pancho. The search and rescue teams are still working to identify everyone."

"I've got to account for the rest of my guys," Jaxson said.

The nurse interrupted them. "Mr. Forest, please describe your pain level on a scale from one-to-ten.

His gaze slid to the nurse. "Eight."

"The doctor will order something to help. I'll let him know you're awake, and he'll be in to see you shortly." Then she put fresh ice packs on his ribs. "This should stay on for twenty minutes."

The nurse left, and Charli placed a call to her parents so they could talk to Jaxson. Nicole attempted to leave, but Jaxson's grip on her hand—which he'd never let go of—tightened. "Stay."

***

The doctor came in, examined Jaxson, and confirmed his pain level. I'm going to order pain medication for you through your IV. It'll probably make you drowsy." The doctor grinned. "Welcome back."

"Thanks, doc."

The doctor left the room, and the nurse showed up a few minutes later with an IV bag, which she hung and connected. "There you go." She smiled at Nicole and Charli before leaving.

"You two should probably go back to your hotel and get some rest. There's no need to stay and watch me sleep," Jaxson said, his eyelids already drooping a bit. "I'll look for you in the morning."

"We're staying at Ava's, so don't worry. Her place is pretty much intact. Love you!" Charli kissed his cheek and headed for the door, saying over her shoulder that she'd wait for Nicole outside.

Jaxson held Nicole's hand as she leaned forward and kissed him. Careful not to hurt him, she cupped his cheek with her free hand. "I'm so glad you're going to be okay."

"Me too," he said. "And what did you decide?"

Nicole swallowed hard. "I'm here. I've already told you everything."

Jaxson's brows shot up, but it was plain that he was fighting to stay awake. "I'm drugged and confused. I must have been out of it when you told me everything?"

"You were," she confirmed, smiling. "We'll talk about it in

the morning." She kissed him again and said goodnight. Leaving him like this was hard. At the door she turned back to look at him. He was already asleep.

***

Jaxson awakened to a deep quiet, only broken by the faint sounds of people moving about in the distance. There were no sounds of machines keeping track of his vital signs. He felt groggy. It made it hard to think clearly. Had he dreamed of being rescued and coming to inside the hospital with Nicole and Charli at his bedside? He savored the coolness, not missing the heat he'd endured while he waited for rescue.

His head felt like someone had split it with an axe. His body hurt deep down in his bones. Somehow, it didn't bother him as much as it should have. He suspected that was due to the small bag on the side of a larger bag on the IV going into his wrist. The blinds were drawn, but in the early morning light he saw bandages on his chest and one arm in a cast. He released his breath on a heavy sigh of satisfaction.

He must have fallen asleep again, because when he next opened his eyes, bright sunlight filtered through the sides of the closed blinds. He heard a polite knock. The door to his room opened and Nicole breezed into the room wearing jeans, a T-shirt, and hiking booties. "Good morning!" She lifted a large blue cap off her bright, shining hair and took off her oversized designer sunglasses.

"Are you wearing a disguise?"

Her blue eyes sparkled. "Yes, Liam suggested it, and it seems to be the only way to get the press to leave me alone!" She stowed her hat, sunglasses, and purse on his bedside table. Then she grasped his hand and took the spot in front of the chair closest to his bed. "How are you feeling?"

"My body hurts and my head is killing me, but my mind is fuzzy. It's the drugs they're putting in the IV."

"You could always ask them to give you something different." She bent down to kiss his lips and rub her cheek against his stubbled one. She lingered, nestling her face against his neck.

Jaxson inhaled her familiar scent, wishing he was in better shape. The need to hold her overwhelmed him.

Her normally sweet and sultry voice was low and intimate. "I couldn't stop worrying about you. I thought I'd lost you for good. You don't how glad I am that you're here being taken care of instead of out there somewhere, dead or suffering. That you survived the storm and got rescued for the second time this year is pretty remarkable." She smoothed her fingers across his forehead onto his thick, matted hair. Then she kissed his lips reverently. "I thought about you all night, and I want you to know how important you are to me. I can't see living in a world without you in it."

Her words touched him, but he needed more. "Can you live more of your life with me, by my side?" he asked, holding her gaze.

"I want to," she said, her words ringing with sincerity. "I'm on leave from the company, and I told Ben and Mother about us."

He nodded. That was a big step for Nicole, who had been keeping their relationship in the dark. "And you're ready to stand before the world?"

"Yes." Her blue eyes glistened.

He squeezed her hand. "Ms. Nicole Zayne is officially dating Jaxson Forest."

She smiled. "Yes, I've heard that from a trusted source. I've also heard that they're exclusive."

"I needed to hear that," he said, his emotions cutting through the fog of pain-relieving drugs. His feelings for Nicole were stronger than he wanted to admit. It had taken a lot to get her to his side.

Nicole lay her head against his chest. "I need you, Jax, and for more than anything we could do in the bedroom."

"I need you, too." With his free hand he caressed her neck and back and ran his fingers through her silky hair. A quick knock sounded on the door. Nicole straightened, her hand still in his as she looked at the door. It opened and Charli stood in the opening with three cups of coffee and a paper bag.

"Good morning, Jax! We were in such a hurry to get here this morning that we didn't wait for breakfast. I got an extra breakfast sandwich and coffee, but I see the cart with your breakfast is next door. We can all have breakfast together."

Nicole dropped into the chair at his bedside, and Jaxson instantly missed the soft warmth of her body against his. He hadn't even thought to ask Nicole about Charli's whereabouts.

Charli approached his bed and passed out hot breakfast sandwiches and fragrant cups of coffee. An aide entered the room close on her heels with a tray for Jaxson. It could not compete with the sandwich Charli brought him.

They were nearly done with their meal with the doctor came to check on Jaxson. Charli and Nicole left the room so he could do a thorough examination and send him for a follow-up CT scan.

CHAPTER TWENTY-NINE

Nicole took the elevator to the first floor with Charli. Jaxson's sister was bubbly and lighthearted as they explored the offerings in the hospital gift shop, ordering flowers and balloons to brighten Jaxson's room. Nicole even found a card with a big red broken heart that said, "Mend this broken heart by getting well soon." She bought the card and signed her name before she could change her mind.

Afterward, they found a beautiful flower garden outside the cafeteria and sat in a shaded area for half an hour. Nicole felt Charli's curious gaze on her when she wasn't looking. She sensed that Jaxson's sister had lots of questions.

Although she'd made her stand with Jaxson this morning, Nicole didn't feel she had a lot of answers. Was she in love with him? Hell if she knew, but she cared enough to step out of the comfort of her safe and solitary existence. Would she be willing to move in with him? The prospect scared her, but so did the thought of leaving him, especially right now. Jaxson had gotten a part of her that no one else had been able to claim.

"How long are you staying?" Charli asked, breaking in on Nicole's thoughts.

She turned to look at Jaxson's sister, framed against a backdrop of frangipani, royal poinciana trees, and white spider lilies. "I've arranged to be off until the end of the week, but that depends on Jaxson. I might stay longer."

"I can't imagine him kicking you out," Charli said in a suggestive tone that carried a slight underlying note of *I think it would be great if he did.*

Nicole felt the heat rush to her face. She was blushing? Over something so trivial? "Jaxson is full of surprises," she said, covering all the bases.

Charli tilted her head. "That's true. I'm sorry for intruding on you two at the reception hotel. It was rude and thoughtless. Jax and I are very close, and I just didn't think he would be...be doing what he was doing."

Nicole nodded with a ghost of a smile on her stiff lips. Jaxson had been doing *her.* She still valued her privacy, and Charli had destroyed the mood and the flow of her intimacy with Jaxson.

"Next time, I'll knock," Charli added.

Next time I'll lock the damned door myself! Nicole added silently. "They should be done with him by now," she said, getting to her feet. "Let's go back."

Inside his room, Jaxson, wearing a fresh hospital gown, and with a new ice pack, sat in the high-backed recliner. The IV pole was still there, but the small additional pouch was gone. "They're putting me on ibuprofen," Jaxson explained, "and they expect to discharge me tomorrow. Apparently I had a concussion and I was dehydrated, but there's no reason I can't recover at home."

"Good!" Charli said, bending over to hug him. She ruffled her brother's thick, curly hair. "They combed your hair."

"It needed it," he said, his gaze meeting Charli's and moving past her to Nicole. "I'd kill for a shower, haircut, and shave. They gave me a sponge bath and had me sit here while they changed my bed linens. But at least I'll get a shave."

"From the barber here in the hospital?" Nicole asked, thinking about the one they'd passed on their wanderings.

"No, there's a barber I use when I'm on the island, and he's already set to come and take care of me."

"I know it'll make you feel better," Nicole said. "Will you get a nurse to check on you at home?"

"The arrangements are being made, but I was hoping you'd stay."

His plea touched her, making her heart flutter. "I've scheduled time off until the end of the week, but I'll stay as long as you need me to."

"Are you staying too, Charli?" he asked his sister.

Charli nodded. "I made arrangements with my professors, so I can stay for a few days." She reached into her purse and pulled out a fresh deck of cards. "Look what I've got!"

The rest of the morning was spent playing spades and blackjack. Charli showed an amazing talent for cards and beat Jaxson and Nicole several times. By the time lunchtime rolled around, Jaxson looked tired. He nodded off several times, waking to eat a little of his hospital lunch. Nicole and Charli decided to leave him to rest.

They went back to Ava's, and Charli went out back to call her parents and to alert the staff on Jaxson's island of his imminent return to Terris. Nicole retreated to her room and called Ben. She had to contend with a very noisy and unhappy Ben Jr. in the background. "Do you love the guy?" he bluntly asked.

"I still haven't figured it out," she confessed.

"But you're going to introduce him to the family and bring him around?"

"He's my boyfriend," she said, as if that explained everything.

"He'll be the first man you've thought enough of to introduce to the family," Ben said, "so don't try to make it sound like he's not important."

"He's important to me, and I've realized that I care more about what he thinks and feels than anything the family or the world might have to say." Her airy tone contradicted the pounding of her heart in her chest.

"Hmm, sounds serious. Nik, I think you're already gone. He's got you."

"I've got him," she corrected.

"You could do a lot worse," Ben remarked. "The guy's a genius, a philanthropist, and he's got more money than you. You could get married and have lot of lovable little whiners like little Benito here," he said. The baby's crying stopped abruptly.

"What happened to little Ben?" she asked.

"He fell asleep." Ben's voice rang with satisfaction. Nicole heard Mira's soft voice in the background as Ben apparently handed off the sleeping toddler. "I'm proud of you, Nik, for standing up to claim what you want. I know it isn't easy. I'm just warning you, don't flake out like I did. I almost lost Mira for good."

"I almost lost Jaxson," Nicole reminded him.

"So, you know you don't want to experience that again."

"No."

"So do what you have to do to be you and to keep him," he advised.

Nicole inhaled a shaky breath. "I'm trying, but it's hard."

Ben chuckled. "If Hugo and I can do it, I know you can. You're more lovable than either one of us."

"I hope you're right," she said before signing off.

Nicole had called her mother and brother after Jaxson was found and taken to the hospital. She'd been relieved, but shaky. Her mother had been worrying and was glad to hear from her. Nicole called her again to give her an update. She asked several questions about Nicole's health before asking about Jaxson.

"He has a concussion, is being treated for dehydration, and he's got a broken arm and fractured ribs. He should be discharged tomorrow."

"Oh," her mother said, sounding only faintly sympathetic, "well, if they're releasing him, he can't be in that serious a condition. When are you coming home?"

"I'm coming home when I feel I can leave without worrying about him," Nicole replied honestly. "He's pretty beat up."

"I'm sorry, honey," her mother said, backpedaling a bit. "You know you're my first priority."

"I understand that, Mother, but Jaxson is *my* priority right now. He's my boyfriend, and I care a lot about him."

"He's your boyfriend?" Pamela's voice rang with thinly veiled skepticism.

"Yes."

"Does he consider you to be his girlfriend?"

"Yes, he does, Mother. And I told you I had feelings for him."

"Do you think you're in love with him?"

Nicole's teeth worried her bottom lip. "I-I don't know. I've never felt like this. Does it matter? Being a girlfriend covers a wide range of feelings."

Her mother made a weird, strangled sound in her throat. "It will matter to him, believe me, so you need to start thinking about your answer."

Nicole scrubbed her fingers against her forehead. She thought about the unquestionable love she'd witnessed between both Ben and Mira and Hugo and Ava. She couldn't see herself and Jaxson in that love light, yet she needed him and cared what he thought and felt more than anyone else. "All this is giving me a headache. Mother, I'm not like Hugo or Ben, so Jaxson is going to have to accept whatever I have to give." The truth in the words resonated with her as she hurriedly ended the call.

***

Jaxson woke early from his dream of being injured, hungry, and wondering if he was going to die on the little island after the storm. He was safe and in the hospital for now, but they were releasing him today to complete his recovery at home.

Yesterday, after Charli and Nicole left him to rest, the nurse had him walk the hospital corridor. He'd even managed to shower with a special sleeve covering his casted arm. His body ached with a bone-deep pain that would not go away despite the pain medication. The doctor had informed him that it would take about six weeks to heal. Still, it was a relief to know he wouldn't have this pain forever.

Pulling the cord that connected to the remote control, he switched on the television with his free hand. He saw that his rescue was in the news reports. Someone had filmed his stretcher being removed from the medical evacuation helicopter. Charli and Nicole were in the background, looking traumatized as they ignored the reporter questions directed at them and rushed into the hospital's emergency room.

Jaxson took his cellphone off the charger Charli had thoughtfully provided and made a few calls. He was feeling well enough to worry about Forestone Pharmaceuticals and the status of his projects. He knew he'd feel even better after his barber came to give him a haircut and shave.

As he finished his hospital breakfast, Charli arrived alone.

He was always happy to see his sister, but his spirits dropped when he didn't see Nicole. Maybe it was her turn to pick up breakfast and she'd be along shortly...

Charli kissed his cheek and took the chair where she usually sat, staring at him. "Jax, you look a lot better, even with the bandages and bruising."

He grinned at his sister. "I feel a lot better, even though the rib pain is constant."

Charli assessed him with a smile. "You look almost camera ready."

"I'm not talking to the press. I'll have the community relations department make a statement and thank everyone." He could bear it no longer. "Where's Nicole?"

His sister gave him a sharp glance. "She went to get coffee for us and give us some time alone." Grasping his free hand, she leaned forward and tugged on it. "What's up with you two? Are you serious? Are you in love with her?"

He stared at his sister, aware that her questions were the same ones he'd been asking himself and Nicole. "She's my girlfriend, but she's also a very private person."

Charli glanced at the closed door. "You two seem like you've been carrying on in secret for a while. I've never seen you act like this with anyone else. Are you just friends with benefits, or...?"

Jaxson let his voice deepen in a warning tone. "Charli, I'm glad you and Nicole are getting along, but my love life is my own business."

"Hmph!" Charli narrowed her eyes. "Yes, we've been getting along. I guess she's all right, but there's something a little too detached and perfect about her. If she hurts you, I'm going to rip her a new one!"

Jaxson grinned. "I'm a big boy. I can take care of myself."

"Yeah?" Charli's eyes pointedly went over his battered body in the bed.

"Yeah. I may have taken temporary leave of my senses when I took the boat out with a storm threatening, but it wasn't supposed to come this far. Anyway, we're not talking about that right now."

"If you say so," Charli said. "I just thought that maybe all of Mom and Dad's pressure and talk of marriage and grandkids was starting to get to you."

"It did at first, but I learned to tune them out. But now I'm getting older, and I need more than work and business in my life. I don't know about marriage, but I'm ready to have the right woman at my side." He glanced at the door at the sound of it opening in time to see Nicole enter with a cardboard carrier containing three large cups of coffee and a paper bag.

"Good morning," she said rather flatly. Her tone and her bland expression told Jaxson that she'd heard his last statement.

Returning her greeting, he took in her beautiful features: the bright blue eyes, model cheekbones, perfect straight nose, and wide mouth with pouty lips. He hoped his words wouldn't scare her away. Nicole Zayne was a woman who choked at any thought of forever.

She passed out the coffee and gave him a sandwich like it was something she did every day, then bent and laid those sweet lips on his. His good hand caressed up and down her back, finally settling on her gorgeous butt. *The things he wanted to do to and with her...* His head swam with pleasure, tempered by his pain. He reminded himself that his sister was sitting a foot away.

Nicole's soft skin nestled against his. "Missed you," she whispered close to his ear.

"Missed you too," he said in a low, intimate tone.

She briefly laid her head against his chest. Then she straightened and dropped into her usual chair. "Is your discharge definite?"

Jaxson nodded. "Yes, and I'm ready."

Charli spoke up. "Your driver's coming for us, and we'll go to the marina to catch a boat to your house on Terris. The plane's still being used for searches."

He gave his sister a thumbs up. "I'm ready to be back in my own space, and I don't mind going by boat."

***

Nicole's assistant called to tell her that the company was putting together a planeload of food and clothing for the storm victims and was asking her to do the press conference since she was still in the area. She agreed.

She felt relieved when they finally got Jaxson back to Terris. Having sat up and walked as much as possible in the hospital, and been awake since before she and Charli arrived, he was exhausted. Still, he insisted that she sleep in his room, in his big bed. Nicole hid her smile, certain that her very virile man was still in too much pain to make love to her.

With Jaxson down for the count, Nicole spent time checking her email, performing the job duties she could from a distance, and working out in the gym. Her previous time at the mansion with Jaxson meant she was familiar and comfortable with her surroundings. She and Charli ate dinner on the lanai and sat with Jaxson when he awakened to eat.

CHAPTER THIRTY

Night came quickly. Charli came to say goodnight, but Jaxson was already asleep. Once Charli left, Nicole locked the bedroom door. She was ultra careful as she slipped into bed beside Jaxson in her red silk negligee. Afraid that she might turn over in her sleep and hurt him, she kissed his cheek and lips, then placed one of the pillows between them. She knew she would sleep better tonight because she could reach out and touch him. The need to be with him, whatever it meant, overwhelmed her. She'd never felt this way about anyone.

In the middle of the night, she awakened to Jaxson's warm hand caressing her skin. After all they'd been through, it felt wonderful. The pillow was gone. She turned and carefully pressed her lips to his. Their kiss started softly, filled with affection. It went on for several pleasurable minutes. Then it heated to yearning and urgent demand. "I need you," he said in a husky tone.

She sucked his bottom lip into her mouth and caressed it with her tongue. "I need you too, but I don't want to hurt you."

"I trust you," he ground out.

"*I* don't trust me," she confessed. "I tend to get carried away with you, and Charli will never forgive me if you end up back in the hospital."

"So, you're afraid of my little sister?" His chuckle ended abruptly. "Ow! That hurt. I keep forgetting that laughing is not a good thing right now."

She held his face in her hands and looked into brown eyes.

"You're on hand duty until your ribs and arm are better."

"I'm quite competent with this hand." The sensual edge in his tone sent heat rippling through her body.

"I *know*." She placed his hand where she needed it most.

"There are other uninjured parts of me that you could use for your satisfaction," he teased, his fingers starting to work their magic.

Nicole moaned softly. "One day at a time."

Hours later, Nicole awakened to find Jaxson watching her. "What? Is everything okay?" she asked, trying to speed her awakening process. She yawned and stretched.

"Everything is fine, especially you," he rasped in his morning voice.

"Yeah, right." Her hand touched her wild and tumbled hair. She never slept in makeup, so she knew what she looked like.

He grasped her hand. "You always look beautiful, no matter what you're wearing...or not wearing."

What could she say in the face of such positivity? "I'll take that. I'll take you, too." She kissed his bare shoulder.

He drew a deep breath and let it out. "I thought I wasn't going to make it. I pushed myself to do what I could to survive through all the pain, and then it got to the point where my body refused to move. I thought about all the things I meant to do, the things I wanted to do and say, and everything I was leaving behind."

"But you made it," she said, squeezing his hand.

"By the grace of God, and I'm not a very religious man."

"I thanked God when we found you," she confessed, "and I made a vow to be a better person."

"You're already a good person," he assured her.

"I'm glad you think so." Her eyes stung. What was it about Jaxson that was always moving her to tears? "Maybe you're right, but there's definitely room for improvement."

He raised her hand to his lips and kissed it. His gaze seemed to look clear through her soul. "I don't want to scare you, but you need to know that you mean a lot to me. I don't have all the words right now and my brain is still scrambled, but I know what I want and need."

"I-I don't have the words either." Her body tensed in anticipation of what he might say next.

"I know that discussions of commitments and feelings are hard for you."

She nodded, squeezing his hand hard. It had taken a lot for her to become his girlfriend, to admit her need for him, and own it in front of her family and Charli. She wasn't ready for anything further.

Jaxson broke out a grin. "I'm not ready to get down on one knee, if that's what's got you tensing up."

She *had* been worried about that for a few crazy moments. Releasing a noisy breath, she laughed and rubbed her face against his. She kissed his lips with a loud smack. "Jaxson Forest, you've made me do and say things no one else ever has. What more do you want?"

His fingers combed through her short strands and massaged her scalp. "Right now? I just want your promise that you'll stay and help us figure things out when it gets tough."

"I'm a fighter. You know what I can do." She knew she was no wimp.

"Yes, so I want you to fight for us."

Overcome with a sudden rush of emotion, she nodded and laid her head on his shoulder. She'd never had to fight for anyone but herself and the company, and she'd never wanted to. Right now, she wanted the best of whatever she could get with Jaxson. The scariest thing was that the biggest part of the battle would be with herself.

He let her lay there with her thoughts for another five minutes before he said, "All right, let's go get naked in the shower. I've been dreaming about it."

She widened her eyes. "You're on hand duty and you're still in pain. Jax, you've got to behave."

"*I've* got to behave, but *you* don't," he said, raising an eyebrow suggestively.

She laughed, her gaze covering his battered and bruised, but still gorgeous body. "Come to think of it, you do look like you could use a good washing." She lifted her silk gown and slid it off her head. "See ya in the shower!" Then she leaped from the bed and ran into the bathroom in all her naked glory.

"You're a bad woman!" he said, easing off the bed and following her with slow, careful steps.

"I'm so bad, I'm good!" she called back, turning on the shower.

***

Jaxson, Nicole, and Charli were having a lazy breakfast on the lanai when they heard loud voices coming from the front of the house. They were about to go investigate when a beautiful honey-skinned woman with short, wavy hair and exotic features entered the room. Her eyes and nose resembled Charli's.

"Mom!" Charli jumped up and went to hug her. "I didn't know you were coming!"

"It was supposed to be a surprise," his mother said, returning Charli's kiss. Her gaze strayed to Jaxson, tracing his features, lingering on the sling on his arm and the fading bruises on his face. He started to rise.

"Don't get up, baby." The woman rushed to his side and carefully hugged his shoulders and kissed his face. "Your dad and I have been worrying about you."

"I'm okay, Mom. I'm healing." Jaxson patted his mother's arm. "There's no need to worry about me."

"And nothing you, I, or Charli say can ease her mind!" a deep voice added from the doorway. All eyes turned to the tall, beefy brown man filling the doorway. Jack Forest's handsome features were similar to Jaxson's, but he looked young enough to be his son's brother. Nicole knew that Jaxson's father was a famous doctor and television host.

Feeling a bit outside the warm circle of love, she smiled and took in Jaxson's glamorous parents. Her mother and brothers were trying to mend their family relationships, but the Zayne family gatherings were nothing like this.

"Dad!" Jaxson and Charli cried in unison. The big man came forward and hugged each of his children, his arms shaking with emotion when he embraced Jaxson and held on.

"I'm okay, Dad," Jaxson said, patting his father's back.

Jack Forest stepped back, rapidly brushing a hand over his eyes.

"Mom, Dad, I want you to meet my girlfriend, Nicole Zayne," Jaxson said, changing the mood. His parents looked at her and smiled warmly.

His mother was closest. "Hello, Nicole. Nice to see you again. I didn't get to meet you at the press conference, but we were just so happy to see Jaxson after the two of you escaped your kidnappers we didn't have eyes for anyone else. This time Jaxson's come out on the bad end of a tropical storm." She gave Nicole a brief hug.

"I sincerely hope it'll be under much better circumstances when we meet again, Mrs. Forest," Nicole said.

"I can just about guarantee that," Jaxson said, giving Nicole a significant look. *Was he hinting at love and marriage?* Struggling to keep her breathing even, she felt like a fish out of water. She felt his family's eyes on her. Somehow, she managed to keep her head up and endure the increased scrutiny.

Jack Forest took her hand in both of his. He flashed a wide smile like Jaxson's. "I'm glad to meet you, Nicole. It's good to see Jax worry about something other than cancer treatments, science, and business."

"Good to meet you, Mr. Forest," she said, warmly shaking his hand.

He patted her hand. "Please call me Jack."

She nodded. "Okay, Jack." Nicole's gaze went to Jaxson. "Worry?"

Jaxson shook his head in denial.

His mother's gaze bounced from him to Nicole and back. "He wasn't working, and *something* had him distracted enough to head out on a boat with a major storm threatening the area."

Nicole worked at maintaining her neutral expression. She'd been on the verge of ending things with Jaxson. She knew now that despite her fears, she couldn't have done it. But did he know that? Did he care that much? Surely she couldn't be responsible for Jaxson's loss of judgement.

Jaxson gave his mother an exasperated look. "It was a bonehead move, but the storm wasn't supposed to come this far, remember?"

"You *know* how unpredictable storms can be!" his mother shot back.

"Camilla." Jack Forest said his wife's name in a warm, affectionate tone, but it had an impact.

Swallowing and closing her eyes briefly, Mrs. Forest ended her tirade. She gazed at the breakfast bar set up on the lanai and smiled. "Do you have breakfast for two more?"

***

Nicole's appetite disappeared. She pushed the food around on her plate until Jaxson's housekeeper removed it after serving the senior Forests. Then she stayed on the lanai with Jaxson and his family, drinking her coffee and adding sporadically to the conversation while everyone continued to eat. When she felt confident it wouldn't look like she was escaping, she made a comment about having something to do and went to Jaxson's bedroom.

Alone in his room, she sat on the already made-up bed and gazed out at the water. It usually calmed her. Today she was at odds with herself and didn't know how to feel. She was certain Jaxson's mother did not like her and there was nothing she could do about it. To blame her for Jaxson taking off with a storm threat felt mean and arbitrary. It was actually the type of behavior Nicole would have expected from her own mother.

Nicole clenched and unclenched her fists. A lesser woman might cry. Somehow, just being with Jaxson opened her up for more tears and raw emotion, which she hated. And this being vulnerable? She felt like she could scream in frustration.

Behind her, the bedroom door opened and closed. Suddenly Jaxson was sitting next to her on the bed, his good arm around her. "You okay?"

She stopped herself from leaning back into his chest, but his lips against her temple felt reassuring. She infused her answer with confidence. "Yes."

His hand caressed her face and moved down to massage her neck. "No, you're not."

She turned and met his gaze.

"No way are you responsible for any stupid thing I do, distracted or not, and my mother knows that. She's going to apologize to you."

Nicole's eyes widened. "That's not necessary. It'll just make her dislike me more."

Jaxson's tone softened. His finger traced the curve of her bottom lip, then his lips briefly touched hers. "She doesn't dislike you. She just met you, and she's never met anyone in my space who was staying with me. She knows you mean a lot to me."

On their own volition, her fingers tangled in his thick curly hair, lingering on his nape. "Family dynamics are hard for me. You know that. My family..."

"Is what you were born and blessed with," he finished for her. "But you *chose* me."

"Did I?" She lifted a brow. She'd agreed to be his girlfriend, but she was beginning to realize that there were no boundaries when it came to Jaxson. For every step she took with him there were many more she unconsciously committed to. She was beginning to think she was addicted to him.

"You were with me when I woke up in the hospital." Jaxson chuckled, wincing from the resulting pain in his ribs. "Did you give me up already?"

"It would be very hard to give you up." She kissed him like she wanted forever...and in that moment she did. She only allowed herself to feel. Her lips caught his, her tongue delving into the heaven of his mouth to tangle with his. She tasted coffee and pineapple. Emotion flowed from her heart, and she showered him with it, touching him, caressing him, and moaning into his mouth.

"Nikki," he groaned as the kiss ended. "I wish we could spend the day in bed, but you know the options are limited. My family will be knocking on the door and trying to get in here to make sure I'm okay."

She smiled, knowing he was right. "What do you want to do?"

"I want to be with you. I have a Zoom meeting in about

half an hour, and I have some reports to read and my inbox to go through. After that, I'm free, but it's not like I can ignore my family. I, um, know you left your work at Lady Zayne to be here with me, and that means a lot. I had my staff prepare an office space for you if you want to use it. If not, there's always the pool, the gym, the tennis courts, the boat, and the beach. What do you want to do?"

In truth, she wanted option one, to spend the day in bed with Jaxson. Of course that wasn't a workable option, especially with his family visiting. When she thought about all the tasks she had before she left New York, working to get the pile down seemed the most practical. "I'll take the office, but how about we make an early day of it? Two o'clock?"

"Sounds like a plan." Jaxson smacked her lips with his and carefully got off the bed.

***

CHAPTER THIRTY-ONE

Nicole settled into the office Jaxson had prepared for her. He'd thought of everything, even down to a gold-plated desk sign with her name that he admitted to ordering after her first visit to Terris. She smiled at the sight of it. The man was thoughtful, and he knew how to take care of her.

The amount of mail in her inbox surprised Nicole. She'd been in the islands for five days and she'd been off work a little more than a week in total. She missed a few meetings with the company she'd purchased to develop an alternative to the Poule plant formula. Her master botanist sent a picture of the plant Jaxson gave her, and it had grown enough for him to try splitting the roots. Then there was a new legal snag in the licensing issue she'd been working on in Europe. Thankfully, she was able to talk with her legal team there and get a plan of action started.

Among the latest tasks, the company board had formalized a special request. Since she was still in the islands, they wanted her to do a press conference about the scheduled planeload of Lady Zayne-donated food and supplies for the islands devastated by the tropical storm. She could hardly refuse.

When Nicole finished up, it was close to two-thirty. She found Jaxson floating in a lounger in the pool. He wore an open short-sleeved shirt over his bandaged chest. His parents were swimming, while Charli sat on the edge of the pool, her legs dangling in the water, fiddling with her phone.

"Look who's the workaholic!" Jaxson cracked when he saw

her. "I was done for the day by one-thirty."

"There was a lot to do. Give me a minute to change." Nicole ducked inside to change into her swimsuit. Minutes later, she returned to find Jaxson alone. "Was it something I said?" she asked him, only half joking.

He took a sip of a brightly colored liquid. "They're trying to be more sensitive and give us some alone time."

Nicole eyed his drink, complete with fruit slices and a cherry on top. "What's that you're drinking?"

Jaxson gave her a funny look. "My mom's no-alcohol version of rum punch. Alcohol doesn't mix with my pain meds."

Satisfied with his answer, she dove into the water and swam to his floating lounger. She told him about her scheduled press conference, then added, "You're doing a good job of acting like you're chilling, but you look tired."

He flashed her a look of surprise. "I am tired. If my parents weren't here, I'd be in bed with you."

"And I would be insisting that you sleep." She gazed around pointedly. "Oh snap, your parents aren't around. That means you can go get some sleep."

"After you do a few laps," he said, waving her on. "Never let it be said that I kept you from your exercise."

"You don't need me to go take a nap." She treaded water, waiting for his response.

His tone dipped suggestively. "But I sleep so much better when you're there."

Nicole shook her head. "Flattery may get you what you want."

He flashed a grin as Nicole began her laps. By the time she finished, he was asleep beneath the chair's canopy, his head tipped to one side. Nicole pushed the lounger to the shallow end of the pool. Then she called Liam to help get Jaxson out of the pool.

"How much longer are we going to be here?" Liam asked. He'd been hanging out in the background.

Nicole glanced at Liam, abruptly aware that he was away from his home and girlfriend. "At least through the weekend, maybe longer. I haven't decided, but my work is starting to pile up."

Liam nodded and held on to the chair while she awakened Jaxson. Jaxson tried to get up, but physical strain brought more pain to his body. Finally, Nicole held the chair while Liam all but lifted Jaxson out of the chair and onto his feet. Jaxson insisted he didn't need additional assistance, but Liam helped him all the way to his room. Jaxson moved stiffly, so after dismissing Liam, Nicole insisted that Jaxson take a hot shower. Then she joined him, helping him, and while he sat on the built-in shower bench and watched, she washed the chlorine off her body and out of her hair. After drying off, they climbed into his bed, and she got as close to Jaxson as she dared and fell asleep.

Hours later, Nicole awakened to a gentle but steady knocking on the door. The delicious scent of food she couldn't identify filled her nostrils as she woke Jaxson.

She checked the clock as he called out and learned that his family was waiting to have dinner with them. It was nearly six. Nicole got up and dressed. Then she went through his closet and found the clothes he wanted.

Everyone was already seated when Jaxson and Nicole arrived in the dining room and greeted the family. She was glad she'd worn a dress, because no one wore jeans or shorts. Jaxson drew out her chair with his good arm, then took his seat. "What's for dinner?" Jaxson asked Mrs. Martin as she waltzed into the room followed by a helper with a tray full of soup bowls.

"Conch chowder," she said, placing a small bowl in front of each of them, "pot fish, fungi, and Crucian stuffing."

"Mmm, we're in for a treat," he said. "These dishes are island specialties, and I've got the best cook around."

Everyone had already dipped their spoons into the chowder and pronounced it delicious. Nicole, who had eaten meals prepared by world-famous chefs, was impressed. The food was wonderful. The pot fish consisted of an entire red snapper fish with a spicy coating for each guest. The fungi was a polenta-like dumpling made of okra, cornmeal, and shortening. Most surprising, the Crucian stuffing wasn't stuffing, but a sweet, soufflé-like sweet potato dish with raisins.

Nicole was too full to do more than taste the black cake dessert, another island specialty that was filled with rum. After dinner, the group moved to the screened lanai and played games. Nicole and Jaxson won nearly every game of Pictionary until the group switched to Crazy Eights.

Intent on preparing for her press conference, Nicole bowed out of the next game. Excusing herself, she went to Jaxson's bedroom to try on the nicer outfits she'd packed.

***

Jaxson continued spending time with his family. He knew that although he was recovering nicely, they were still worried about him and hadn't gotten over what could have happened. Once Nicole left, his mother hovered, hugging him and kissing his cheek. When he started to feel smothered, she apologized and said, "I've been so worried. Right now, I just need reassurance that you're all right."

"I'm all right, Mom," he said. But he still tired easily, and when he felt sleepy he headed to bed. His dad walked with him, running interference from his mom.

"Son, I know it's hard to have company when you're not feeling your best. We'll only be here another day or so," his dad said. "I've booked us on a cruise to Tahiti, and Charli needs to get back to school."

Jaxson studied his dad. "Y'all don't have to leave."

His father laughed. "Yes, we do. Unless you just want us hanging around indefinitely, and your mother forgetting that you're no longer her baby. Now that we know you're being well taken care of, we'll come back when you're feeling better."

Jaxson didn't know what else to say. He loved his parents, but having them visit while he was recovering was difficult and tiring, especially with Nicole there.

They arrived at his bedroom door. Jaxson hesitated, not wanting to open the door in case Nicole was in a state of undress.

His dad tapped him on the shoulder playfully and said, "You can thank me later."

Tapping the door lightly in warning, Jaxson entered his bedroom. The sight of Nicole gripped him the way it always did, more now with the knowledge that she'd willingly become his in all the ways that counted. She wore a black and green designer version of a safari suit with buttoned pockets decorating the jacket and pants. It went well with her blond hair, but Nicole was a woman who looked good in everything.

"What do you think?" she asked as he closed the door behind him.

"You look beautiful. You always do."

She showed him the other option , a black pantsuit. "Would this be better?"

"Since you're going to be talking about donations, volunteers, and the relief effort, I'd go with the outfit you have on."

She nodded. "Good."

He was removing his shirt with his good hand when she stripped down to nothing, hung up her clothes, and pulled on a short silk nighty. Captivated, he sat on the bed. "You sure know how to torture a guy."

She came and bent down to kiss him. "I thought you might enjoy the show."

"I did, but I'm not in any shape to do much about it." His gut clenched and he contemplated doing what his body demanded, pain and all. Desire rose, dragging him into a tantalizing feast for his senses as his good hand slid down the silky material to curve around her shapely rear.

She rubbed her face against his. "I can get ready in the bathroom from now on."

"No. My body won't take forever to heal."

She gazed at him silently for several beats, sensing he felt vulnerable, helpless, and irritated. And no wonder...she'd just given him an upfront view of all he couldn't have.

"Let me help you." She unbuttoned his pants and slid down the zipper. He lifted his hips and her hands pushed them down and off. Then she covered his exposed skin with kisses.

"I could get used to this," he groaned, loving the feel of her lips.

She shushed him. "Just relax," she murmured against his skin. He stood to allow her to remove his shorts and briefs, then sat again, this time reclining. She teased him, kissing his stomach and thighs. Her soft hands held and caressed him as she stared in fascination. "I love looking at you. You're a beautiful man, Jax, and incredibly gifted."

Pleasure gripped him when she opened her red-coated mouth and devoured him. The hungry sounds she made told him she took delight in what she was doing. That made it even hotter. Sensual heat armed with need clawed through him, shaking his body, making the arm clutching the edge of the bed tremble with the effort of keeping his body as still as possible. He rode the wave of sensual euphoria until his senses exploded with delight.

The edginess he'd been fighting was gone and his body

was sated. Nicole cleaned them up and found him a pair of pajama bottoms before joining him in his bed. Then they kissed for several delicious moments before they went to sleep.

***

Nicole rose early to prepare for her press conference. The Lady Zayne team was picking her up by helicopter at eight. Dressed, she made her way to the kitchen to get a light breakfast. Camilla Forest was already out on the screened lanai with a cup of coffee.

"Good morning," the older woman greeted.

Nicole returned the greeting, her eyes taking in the rising sun filling the horizon. She poured herself a cup of freshly made coffee, added cream and sugar, and snagged a couple of pastries and some fruit. Then, despite her misgivings, she took a seat at the wicker table on the lanai. She could be super focused when needed, so her mind was on the coming press conference and the things she had to say. "I have to prepare for the press conference this morning," she explained. Her cheat sheet of notes was perched close to her bowl of fruit. She ate and mentally rehearsed her lines.

Minutes later, she glanced up to find Jaxson's mother watching her. "I'm glad to catch you alone this morning," Camilla began. "I want to apologize for my comments the other day. I was upset. I don't really blame you for Jaxson's actions, and I'm sorry for any discomfort my words may have caused."

Taking in the sincere-sounding apology, Nicole smiled. "I appreciate that, Mrs. Forest. I know you love Jaxson and you were worried about him."

"Yes, and there are five more weeks before he's back to normal. My husband is already trying to drag me away."

Jaxson is a big boy. Nicole bit back the comment and said, "Imagine what it's like for Jaxson. I don't know a more vibrant and capable man. It's hard for him to have the use of only one arm."

Camilla Forest nodded, her dark eyes shining with unshed tears. "That's twice within a year that he could have been taken from us for good."

"I've been worried about him, too." Nicole bit down on her tongue to keep herself from saying more.

His mother's gaze narrowed. "Did you two have an argument before he took off with a storm threatening?"

"No." Nicole felt like she was on trial, and the judge was already convinced of her guilt.

"Were you going to dump him?"

The question hit Nicole like an arrow to her heart. She'd let her fear get the best of her. Now she felt guilty for hurting Jaxson, for hurting herself, and for not being better at the games people played in life. The answer wasn't really any of his mother's business, but she knew better than to say that. "I-I don't know."

Enmity and dislike flashed in the other woman's gaze. "You're very pretty, but you're not the sort of woman he usually gets involved with. He likes brainy women, women in medicine and science."

Nicole widened her eyes. This was getting ugly all over again and there was no one in sight to keep things civil. She'd have to take that on herself. "I'm used to being underestimated, Mrs. Forest, but it really stings when it comes from another woman. I have a master's degree in chemistry from Harvard and master's in business from Stanford," she said, gathering her plate and empty fruit bowl and standing. She wanted his mother to know that although she wasn't a doctor, she was no dummy.

Camilla Forest's mouth opened and closed. One hand latched onto Nicole's wrist before she could get away. "Excuse me, I apologize. I don't know what's gotten into me. I'm not usually this rude or confrontational. When we meet again, I hope you'll give me another chance."

Nicole nodded and made her escape without speaking. As she gathered her things, she heard the sound of the helicopter approaching.

CHAPTER THIRTY-TWO

It was after eleven when Jaxson awakened. Nicole was gone and his bedroom door was partially open. Someone had been checking on him. Using the bedside remote, he turned on the local news station. Nicole was in front of the camera, talking about the plane from Lady Zayne that had arrived filled with supplies, food, and volunteers.

She noted the company's connections to the area through its resident, Dr. Ava Grant, who had recently married her brother, Hugo Zayne, and the new wing the company had built at the local hospital. One of the local reporters commented on Nicole being present when pharmaceutical executive Jaxson Forest was rescued from a remote island and asked if there was a personal relationship between them. Nicole smiled again. "I do have a personal relationship with Jaxson Forest, and that's all I have to say about that."

She said it. They were out in the open. Jaxson was proud of her, and it made him feel more secure about their relationship. He knew how much Nicole valued her privacy, and he knew how far she had come to be able to claim him in front of the world. He knew her family was no walk in the park. Hell, the way his mother had jumped her within five minutes of arriving, neither was his.

A tap on his door was followed by Charli sticking her head inside. "Hey there. Are you angling for brunch in bed?"

He drew up the covers. "That's not a bad idea, but I've been instructed not to lie down too much. I had a long day yesterday.

I was tired."

Charli grinned at him. "Okay, then tell me what you want to eat, and I'll go tell Mrs. Martin."

When he finished giving her his order for a ham and cheese omelet, toast, fruit, and coffee, she lingered. "You probably didn't hear Nicole and Mom going at it this morning, but I did. Mom's angry because she thinks Nicole was going to dump you."

He pushed himself up in the bed. "Did Nicole say that?"

"She said she didn't know. For Mom, that equates to a yes."

Jaxson virtually growled. He loved his mother and got along well with her, but lately she'd been hovering and smothering. "When did I fall back to being ten and needing my mother to defend me?"

Charli laughed. "You've scared Mom twice this year, and she's afraid there'll be a third time. She apologized to Nicole, but it didn't stick, especially when she practically called her stupid."

He grit his teeth. "What?"

Charli recanted the conversation she'd overheard while in the kitchen getting breakfast.

"That's ridiculous," Jaxson spat out. "Nicole is *not* stupid."

Charli put a hand on her hip. "I know that, and so does Mom now, especially since Nicole has degrees from Cornell and Harvard."

His brows went up. "Looks like I'm going to have to talk to Mom again."

Charli smirked. "Dad already beat you to it. I told him what I heard."

"I don't understand why she has a problem with Nicole. She's never acted like that toward anyone else I dated."

Charli tilted her head. "You act different with Nicole.

You're always watching her, like she's the center of the world. And you've never openly slept with anyone with us around. I'm still having a hard time unseeing the sight of the two of you together..."

"Charli!" he said in a warning tone.

"I'll go give your order to Mrs. Martin," she said, closing the door.

Jaxson eased himself out of the bed and into the shower. He could take care of himself, but it took extra time without help. The nurse was due to check on him in a few days. He knew he was better.

While Jaxson had his breakfast, Charli and his parents ate an early lunch. His dad announced that they would be leaving in the morning to fly out to catch their cruise ship and Charli was going back to school. Charli was noticeably subdued, and his mother was notably silent.

He drew his mother aside and asked her to go easy on Nicole. She apologized profusely, saying that it didn't excuse her behavior, but she was worried about him, and could see that he was in over his head with Nicole.

Angry and frustrated he said, "Mom, I haven't needed you to fight my battles in longer than I can remember. Let me handle my love life." He loved his mother dearly. He saw the hurt in her eyes but held firm. She apologized again and promised to make sure that Nicole knew how much she regretted her behavior.

He spent time in his office, getting through a third of his inbox. He liked the slower pace of island life, but soon he would need to go back to his office in New York, if for nothing more than to show his employees that he was alive and well.

When he was done working, he found that Nicole had returned and was in his room lying down. She opened her eyes when he came into the room. "I don't want to disturb you," he said.

She turned onto her side. "You're not disturbing me. I want to see you."

He kicked off his sandals and carefully lay down beside her on the bed. "It's been another long day."

"Tell me about it." She took his good hand in hers.

"I saw you on the news, and you did a great job. You came across as beautiful, intelligent, connected, concerned, and caring. The folks at home will be happy."

She thanked him. "What about the folks here?"

"I especially liked the part about your personal relationship with Jaxson Forest."

Nicole's smile was radiant. "I claimed you, and it felt good. No more hiding what you mean to me, even from myself." She pressed his hand to her chest. "What's new on the home front?"

His fingers slid up to caress her slender neck. "They're leaving tomorrow for Hawaii to catch their cruise ship to Tahiti, and Charli's going back to school."

"Wow! That's a long plane ride *and* a boat," she said, leaning into his touch.

"It is, so after tomorrow we'll be alone again."

Nicole inched closer and pressed her soft lips to his. "I'm looking forward to it. You're getting better every day." She grew quiet then spoke hesitantly. "I said I'd be here for as long as you needed me. Do you think you could spare me for a few trips back to New York to take care of the things I can't do here?"

"Absolutely." He knew she had to get back to work, but the thought of her leaving filled him with a deep sense of loss. "Will you come back to me on the weekends, at least until I get the okay to travel?"

She stared straight into his eyes. He knew that traveling for pleasure was one thing, and that she'd had her fill of flying off to Europe and other parts of the world to handle company business. He was asking a lot. If she said no, he wouldn't see her for several weeks. Was she okay with that? Sometimes he didn't know where her head was at. He could only hope that she really cared and that whatever she felt was something like love.

In a few blinks of her eyelids, several expressions flitted across her face. He needed her but knew that she also needed to be free to make her choice. He was almost certain she was about to say no when her features softened. "Yes, because I really need to see you, Jax." She pressed her cheek against his.

He released the breath he'd been holding. He couldn't take anything for granted with Nicole. He pushed a few errant strands away from her forehead. "I need you, too. It's going to get easier; I promise."

**

Back at work the next week, Ben told Nicole that she had that glow of happiness. Back from his honeymoon, Hugo joined in the fun of teasing her. Nicole didn't mind. She was happier than ever and for once, the future looked like it could be filled with all the things she wanted. She was the star of the board meeting that week with good reports on her press conference and the work she'd done with her team resolving the licensing issues in Europe.

Her mother watched her silently, the smile not quite reaching her eyes. At one point after the meeting she privately asked Nicole, "Are you still the person you wanted to be?"

"Yes, I do what I want when I want and I have Jaxson and I'm happy," Nicole answered.

"Good," her mother said, looking notably unconvinced. "Just keep track of your commitments and make sure that it's what you want."

Nicole didn't care to spend the energy needed to convince her mother. There was still a lot unknown about this new version of her mother, and Nicole wasn't going to allow her happiness to be spoiled.

Over the following weeks, Nicole flew to Jaxson's island, Terris, every Friday. She always seemed to be on a plane, but she kept her complaints to herself. Jaxson always made the trip worth her while, and being away during the week meant it was that much easier to see his recovery progress. Sometimes, during the long flight back to New York, she considered staying home the next weekend, but by Thursday she was always eager to see Jaxson.

***

Jaxson's doctor gave him permission to travel when there was only a week of recovery remaining. He returned to New York Wednesday morning, with an abbreviated day of work planned. He and Nicole talked briefly when he was at his laboratory offices, having a quick breakfast.

Nicole floated on a cloud. Jaxson was back in town, almost healed, and she could see him whenever she wanted! All afternoon, she got short texts from him, letting her know what he was doing. They didn't really get a chance to talk and that made her a little anxious. Her phone rang at four in the afternoon and his picture was displayed, but there was no sound. Was it a butt dial? She hung up. When she called back, her call went to voicemail.

Nicole called his office and was told he had gone for the day. Her mind went through all the possibilities for his not returning her call. An urgent phone call? *No accident, please God.* An hour went by. As time ground on and three hours passed, she began to worry.

She called his bodyguard, the one who had been found with him, and was told that he was still in the Virgin Islands because Jaxson had given him two weeks off. He gave her the number of another bodyguard. Nicole's head and chest hurt. She refused to call anyone else. She searched her purse until she found the key Jaxson had given her to his place. She'd never been there, but knew the address by heart.

Thirty-five minutes later, she climbed out of the company limousine with Liam outside Jaxson's loft in Tribeca. The doorman checked Nicole's name on Jaxson's guest list and showed them to his private elevator. Jaxson owned the building and had a penthouse that took up the entire thirty-second floor. Two men were waiting when the elevator doors opened into a large foyer. As Nicole stepped out of the elevator with Liam, the men introduced themselves as the butler, Ross, and Jaxson's bodyguard, Curtis.

"I'm Liam, Ms. Zayne's personal bodyguard," Liam said, shaking hands.

Nicole was too worried to spend a lot of time on the pleasantries. "Is he here?" she asked, cutting to the chase.

"Yes, Ms. Zayne, his private suite is that way." Curtis pointed to a corridor on one end of the foyer.

"I'll inform him that you're here," Ross said, turning toward the direction in which Curtis pointed.

"I can announce myself, thanks." Without another word, she crossed the foyer's natural wood floor.

"His suite is at the end of the corridor," Curtis called after her.

She thanked him and kept walking, but could hear Ross giving Curtis the flux about Jaxson's privacy. "He gave her the key," Curtis said, emphasizing the word *key*. "She's got the run of this place."

The fear she'd had when Jaxson left her hanging was giving way to rage. If he was in his suite working, she planned to give him hell. The closer she got to the end of the corridor, the angrier she became. The thick carpet hid her brisk, angry strides. All three men followed close on her heels.

Her hand hovered over the doorknob. Was he alone? Of

course he was! Grasping the knob, she twisted and pushed the door open to an empty office. The computer monitor on the modern glass and steel desk was still on, displaying the Foreststone Pharmaceuticals logo. The gold framed picture of her on his desk pulled at her heart. *Jaxson!* She'd sent the picture after she'd left Terris.

Nicole trudged past the open door of his gym, a kitchen fit for a chef, a dining area, a couple of bedrooms, and finally, a bedroom with a partially open door. Nicole moved the door out of her way and stepped into the room. Jaxson was sprawled on the massive bed, fully clothed. "Jaxson?" He didn't move. *"Jaxson!"*

Nicole dropped her purse on the bench at the end of the bed and hurried to him. She touched his forehead. It was warm, but not feverish. She tapped his face and pulled on his good arm. Still no response. Finally, she checked his pulse, which was strong and steady. She realized then that he was in a deep, exhausted sleep. "It's all right. He's sleeping," she told the three men hovering in the doorway. "I can take it from here." "Lock the door to the suite behind you. We don't want to be disturbed. How do I reach you if we need anything?"

"Just push three on the house phone," Ross instructed. "I can bring whatever you like for dinner."

Curtis eyed Nicole and the sleeping form of his boss on the bed. "My partner, Finn, is monitoring the cameras and security system. We don't enter this area except under extraordinary circumstances or if Mr. Forest makes a request. If something happens to frighten you or you need our kind of help, there's a panic button in every room. You are safe here." He showed her the panic button and how to use it. Then he left.

CHAPTER THIRTY-THREE

Sitting on the bed, Nicole kicked off her heels. Her feet thanked her. Liam was still hovering outside the bedroom. "I'm not going anywhere until morning, so you're done for the day," she said. With a little wave, he turned and left.

Nicole got up and made sure that Jaxson's staff had followed her instructions. They had. She and Jaxson were alone. Returning to his bedroom, she tried to make him more comfortable by unbuttoning his shirt and undoing his pants. She lifted his hips enough to get his pants off then tripped over his phone, which had obviously fallen off the bed. It was dead, so she placed it on the charger.

He was a big man. She didn't trust herself to fully remove his shirt. What if she accidentally hurt him? It was easier to loosen things. With the stress of her normal workday and the gambit of emotions involved from rejoicing about Jaxson's return, then from worrying about him, Nicole was tired, and it didn't look like he would be waking up anytime soon.

Stripping off her clothes, Nicole climbed into bed with him. She studied her hunk of a man, loving the fact that he was more than everything she'd ever wanted and all hers. She snuggled close to him, needing the comfort of simply touching him. He mumbled something in his sleep. She caught her name. "Jaxson?"

He turned to his side and drew her into the circle of his arms. He groaned. The bandages were gone, and his cast was scheduled to come off at the end of the week. She studied him for more signs of discomfort, not relaxing until she heard the steady sound of his breathing once more. Jaxson was still asleep. Soon, she was too.

Nicole awakened to Jaxson's lips on her temple and his hand gently caressing her breasts. "I missed you. Sorry I overdid everything," he murmured close to her ear, "I couldn't seem to stop myself."

She turned and her lips fused to his in an emotional kiss that went on until they were both out of breath. "I was worried. You can't disappear from me again. My imagination is too active." Her hands framed his face, then slid along his neck to finger the tight curls at his nape.

He drew her closer to his chest, but she was careful not to lean into him. "I was exhausted, but I remember calling you. My phone died. I don't remember much after that."

She playfully tugged a lock of his hair. "I found it on the floor by the bed and put it on the charger for you. What are you trying to do, kill yourself?"

"I did what I could from Terris, but I've been gone a long time. I have several important projects going, and some of them can't be addressed outside of the office. I did a lot of catching up today, and it barely dented the pile."

Nicole let her breath out in a huff. She knew from experience that you never got to the bottom of the inbox and to-do lists. "Did you save a little something for me?"

His tone turned husky. "I have a week left before I'm cleared for everything, but I've always got something for you, Nikki."

"Really? All this from the man who was virtually out cold when I got here?" She gazed up at him in the semi darkness lit only by the night lights along the woodwork, catching the heat in his eyes. "Show me what you've got!"

He leaned into her once more, kissing her until she

was dizzy with desire. His mouth and lips wreaked havoc on her sensitive skin while his hands quickly dispensed with her underwear. Then he made slow, sensual love to her until she lay limp and sated in his arms with her body tingling and throbbing. Her senses were overloaded. "Okay, you've proved your point," she said as he started another round.

Jaxson chuckled, and this time there was no grimace of pain. "Are you sure?"

"Yes, it was wonderful. You are wonderful."

"Everything you want and need?"

"Yes."

"Everything you'll ever need?"

Jaxson was a man who was confident of his skills and his worth. Nicole chuckled at his question, her hand caressing his damp shoulder. "Probably. No one else has ever come this close."

"Then marry me, Nikki. I've been trying not to say it because I didn't want to scare you, but I love you."

His words shocked her. He'd said he loved her, and he wanted to marry her. She was one of the unlovable Zaynes, apparently the most unlovable one. No one, except for the man now rotting in a prison upstate, had even claimed to love her, and he'd lied.

Her body shook as she struggled to breathe. Jaxson loved her. Her mouth moved, but she found she couldn't string a sentence together. When moisture slid down her cheeks, she realized she was crying.

"Nikki? Talk to me." He pulled her into his damp body. His fingertips wiped her tears.

"How can you love me? I'm a mess."

"You're a great partner, you understand me and the things I want and need, you're beautiful, intelligent, loyal, sexy, you have my back, you're great in bed, I can count on you, and you're *my* mess."

Something seemed a little off in the way he listed her supposed attributes. "In that order?" she asked, calling him on his list.

His hand slid up and down her arm, the warmth of his body enveloping her. "In any order you want. It's the way I feel. I love you." He grabbed a tissue from the nightstand, mopped her face, blew her nose, and discarded the tissue. His lips brushed hers. "What's wrong?" He lowered his tone. "You don't feel the same?"

"Jaxson, I don't know about love." She didn't even know if she believed in it. Months ago, she would have said she did not. He gave her hope and made her question her feelings.

His arm tightened around her shoulder. "I think you do. When I'm with you I can feel your love. It's more about what you do and how you do it than it is the word."

"And that's enough for you?"

"Yes. You're everything I want. Being away from you while I recovered and almost losing you were the hardest things I've ever had to deal with." His soft lips captured hers. He kissed her like he was addicted to her taste, her lips, her touch.

When he finally ended the kiss, she said breathlessly, "I wouldn't have gotten on that plane every weekend for anyone but you. You've made me face my fears and challenge the things I've always thought about myself. You make me a better person. I need you and I don't want to be without you, Jax."

He paused a few seconds. "Is that a yes?"

"Yes, I just need you to know what you're getting."

"I'm getting you, right? Forever and ever?"

"Yes, Jax. I don't ever want to be without you."

He made a whooping sound that was part laugh, part joyous sigh of relief and pulled her into his body. Face against his bare chest, she could feel his heart beating as his hands caressed her. She, Nicole Zayne, was no longer one of the unlovable Zaynes. Happiness that she never thought she would experience filled her at the prospect of a future filled with Jaxson Forest and the life they would make together.

She pressed her lips to his chest. "Where's my ring?" She said, teasing him, because he usually thought of everything. "I can't believe you proposed without a ring."

His hands froze in the act of sliding down her back. "You want a ring?"

"What do you think? What man proposes to the woman he loves without a ring?"

"Not me." Releasing her, he eased away and sat up in bed. She blinked in the sudden light from the lamp on his nightstand as he went through the pocket of his suit that was hanging on the bedpost. Her mouth jaw dropped when his hand reappeared holding a small black box. "I've been carrying this around for a while."

He opened the box. Nicole stared at the emerald-cut diamond mounted on a platinum double infinity band. It had to be at least twenty-five carats. It sparkled and shimmered in the light as if it were powered by magic as he removed it from the box and reached for her hand.

"It's beautiful! I love it!" she breathed, mesmerized as he slipped it on her finger. It fit perfectly. "It just keeps on getting better!" she exclaimed, locking her arms around his neck and drawing his head down for her kiss.

"I hoped you'd like it. You can get something else if you don't," he said between kisses.

"I love it!" she repeated.

"I love you," Jaxson said, feathering kisses from her lips to her neck and down to her cleavage. He turned and switched off the light. Then Nicole lost herself into the pleasure of making love with her future husband.

The End

ACKNOWLEDGEMENT

Special thanks to my husband, Chet, who is always supportive and to my longtime critque partner, Karen White Owens. Thanks also to Red Pen Edits by BLU: It was was a slog, but I like the results.

BOOKS BY THIS AUTHOR

The Billionaire's Proposal

On a mission to support her supermodel friend who is in danger of losing her husband, financial Wiz, Aubrey Merrill is offered the opportunity of a lifetime. Real estate Billionaire, Carson McDonald wants her to run the company he's purchased as his partner. Soon his admiration for her skills grows to much more and they embark on an intense relationship. When things get too deep, commitment phobic Carson pulls back like he always does. Can true love come through?

The Billionaire's Ex

Latina supermodel, Mira, grew up on the road with her ballerina mother, but has managed to land a lucrative modeling contract and four glorious years with sultry, sexy, and demanding billionaire playboy, Bennet Zayne of the Lady Zayne Cosmetics empire. The interruption of their honeymoon-like vacation in Fiji sounds the death knell for her happy life as she discovers that although Ben still desires her, he does not love her and is determined to end their marriage. Devastated, Mira accepts a role in a sexy movie with a hot Italian actor. But as the end of their marriage approaches and circumstances prompt Ben to reconsider, will Mira continue building her exciting new life or give in to Ben's demands for another chance?

The Billionaire's Baby

What would you do for love or money? Do you think having infinite resources makes it easier? This is book three in the Love and Money series. What happens when you find yourself pregnant by the man you have loved since you were old enough to know the difference between men and women, and he's vowed to never have children? Adopted as a baby by wealthy New Yorkers, African American cardiologist, Ava Grant has got a secret and when Lady Zayne Cosmetics billionaire Hugo Zayne finds out, both their lives are forever changed.

Best Of Friends

Do best friends make the most enduring lovers? Modeling agency owner, Mariah McCleary, has been best friends with lawyer, Ramón Richards since her sophomore year at the University of Michigan. She's leaned heavily on Ramón through the pain and heartbreak of being left at the alter by prominent Detroit area surgeon, Cotter Eastwood. Ramón and Mariah have become closer than ever. Now that Cotter is determined to mount a comeback, Ramón realizes that his feelings for Mariah go way beyond friendship.

www.ingramcontent.com/pod-product-compliance
Lightning Source LLC
Chambersburg PA
CBHW060313260626
47160CB00007B/2594